THE WORLD ENDS IN APRIL

Also by Stacy McAnulty

The Miscalculations of Lightning Girl

STACY McANULTY

THE WORLD ENDS IN APRIL

Random House New York

Text copyright © 2019 by Stacy McAnulty
Jacket art and design by Michelle Cunningham

All rights reserved. Published in the United States by Random House Children's Books, a division of Penguin Random House LLC, New York.

Random House and the colophon are registered trademarks of Penguin Random House LLC.

Visit us on the Web! rhcbooks.com

Educators and librarians, for a variety of teaching tools, visit us at RHTeachersLibrarians.com

Library of Congress Cataloging-in-Publication Data
Name: McAnulty, Stacy, author.
Title: The world ends in April / Stacy McAnulty.
Description: First edition. | New York: Random House Children's Books, [2019]
Summary: "When seventh-grader Eleanor reads an article online claiming that an asteroid will hit Earth in April, she starts an underground school club to prepare kids for the end of the world as we know it." —Provided by publisher.
Identifiers: LCCN 2018052249 | ISBN 978-1-5247-6761-7 (trade) |
ISBN 978-0-593-12390-4 (intl.) | ISBN 978-1-5247-6762-4 (lib. bdg.) |
ISBN 978-1-5247-6763-1 (ebook)
Subjects: | CYAC: Friendship—Fiction. | Family life—North Carolina—Fiction. |
End of the world—Fiction. | Clubs—Fiction. | Emergency management—Fiction. |
Blind—Fiction. | People with disabilities—Fiction.
Classification: LCC PZ7.M47825255 Wor 2019 | DDC [Fic]—dc23

Printed in the United States of America
10 9 8 7 6 5 4 3 2 1
First Edition

For Lily (Margery and Geoff 4ever!)

Chapter 1

Mack Jefferson, my best—and only—friend, reads to me from his Braille edition of *The Outsiders*. I'm spread out on the floor of my bedroom with my dog, Bubbles, running my hand through her soft belly fur and wondering if we have any pudding cups in the pantry. Also wondering if Mack will notice if I slip out for a few minutes. Probably. I've tried in the past.

"Elle, are you even listening?" he asks.

"Of course. Always. I love this book."

"Lies. All lies." Mack uses a ridiculous accent like he's a vampire from Transylvania, when actually he's a black, blind twelve-year-old kid from North Carolina.

"Just keep reading." I pull Bubbles into my lap.

"Dude, I finished the chapter."

"Oh, good." That means our language arts homework is done. Mack's a good student. I'm *a* student. "Do you want to—"

A loud knock interrupts me. Bubbles jumps up, barks once, and then hides under my bed.

"Go away! No one is here!" I'm expecting one of my brothers.

But the door opens, and it's Grandpa Joe in his camouflage pants, an army-green T-shirt, and a matching cap. His cheeks are red and his eyes flash with excitement.

"Hey, what're you doing here?" I ask. Even though he lives only ten minutes away, he rarely just stops by.

"Private Eleanor Dross, it's time. We have to bug out. Now!" He smiles but quickly covers his grin with his hand.

"What?" I say, as if I don't know what he's talking about. But I totally do. Grandpa Joe is here for one of his *drills*. He spends his days getting ready for catastrophes. And whenever he can, he drags me and my brothers along for practice.

"We can't," I tell him. "I have a friend over." I motion to Mack in case Grandpa Joe missed him.

"We'll take Private Mack with us. But we gotta roll now. Giddyup!"

"What's happening?" Mack rocks in his seat.

"Get moving, soldiers. I'll explain in the truck." He claps his hands three times.

"Grandpa Joe, stop. You're scaring Mack."

"I'm not scared," Mack says, smiling.

Bubbles wriggles out from under the bed and jumps back into my lap. She must sense that this is not an emergency.

I look at the time on my phone. "It's almost six. Dad's going to be home any minute." And he has no patience for these drills.

"Your daddy is gone," Grandpa Joe says, and for a second I feel sick, as if he just told me Dad was *gone* gone.

"Stuck in Columbus on business. Called to ask if I could look after y'all tonight."

I understand now. Grandpa Joe has decided to seize the moment.

"I don't have time for a drill," I whine. "I have homework to do." *And Netflix to watch.*

"Who says this is a drill?" Grandpa Joe puts his fists on his hips and puffs out his chest. "Grab your bug-out bag. Be in the truck in two minutes. I'll round up the boys." He backs out of my room.

"Cool," Mack says as he stands and unfolds his cane. "Drill or not, I've always wanted to bug out." Mack's one of those people who like everything. If he were an emoji, he'd be the smiley face. Me, I'd be the eye-roll emoji.

Some grandfathers bowl, play golf, or build model airplanes. At least in movies. Mine is a prepper—someone who spends their time and money *preparing* for the apocalypse.

"Trust me. This is just a stupid drill." Then I get an idea. "And you're my ticket out. Tell him you can't go with us. Tell him to take you home, and I'll escape with you. Please."

"No, Elle. I want to do this. I've heard you complain about these drills forever. I want to experience the torture."

"Thanks for nothing." I pull myself to my feet and set Bubbles on my bed. "You're the only one who understands me, girl."

My bug-out bag—or BOB—is packed. Mostly. Grandpa Joe gave me all the supplies years ago. I dig it out from the bottom of my closet, under clothes and stuffed animals that I can't seem to throw away. The bag flips over. Everything spills out.

"Shoot!" I grab handfuls of whatever and shove them into the bag.

"One minute, Team Dross!" Grandpa Joe hollers.

My brothers crash through the hallway like a herd of acrobatic elephants. They're in elementary school and still think this is fun.

I yank on sneakers. I wore sandals once for a bug-out drill, and the lecture lasted longer than the exercise.

"Darn. I can't find my flak jacket." It's army green and

has about a thousand pockets. Instead, I slip on a purple cotton hoodie and pull my blond hair into a ponytail. This isn't going to end well.

"What do I need?" Mack asks. He wears the same thing every day: jeans, sneakers, either a black or gray T-shirt, and dark glasses.

"Nothing. You're fine." There's no chance Mack will disappoint Grandpa Joe. Me, on the other hand—it's pretty much guaranteed.

The lights go dark for a few seconds and then come back on. I assume Grandpa Joe has hit the main power breaker to the house. He's done it before.

Mack grabs his own backpack. It's filled with normal stuff like schoolwork, his iPad, and a lunch bag.

"Come on, Mack." I lead him to the stairs and place his hand on the railing. Mack knows my house well. He ought to; we've been friends since kindergarten.

Bubbles tries to follow us out the garage door. I have to stop her from escaping. She's small (only fifteen pounds) and sweet, and she'd be totally useless in an emergency situation. Real or imaginary.

"Stay here, Bubbles. Trust me, I'd rather be home with you." I kiss the top of her head. She's essentially the only girl in my life.

My brothers are already in the back seat of the truck. Grandpa Joe lays on the horn.

"Coming." I stumble across the driveway, trying not to step on my untied laces. Mack is next to me with one hand on his cane and the other on my elbow.

I collapse into the front seat and slide to the middle. Mack takes the passenger seat.

"Good work, soldiers. We're buggin' out." Grandpa Joe puts the truck in reverse and eases down the driveway.

"Dad doesn't like it when you turn off the electricity," I say to Grandpa Joe.

"Who says I turned off the power?" Then he leans toward me and whispers, "Don't worry about your daddy. He doesn't scare me. At least not while he's out of town." He elbows me playfully.

I don't share Grandpa Joe's enthusiasm for catastrophes any more than my dad does, but somehow Dad gets to opt out of these adventures. Maybe feeling guilty is something I will outgrow, and I'll finally be able to say, "No thanks. I'm staying put."

"What are we running from?" Phillip sticks his head between me and Grandpa Joe.

"Is it an alien invasion?" Edward kicks the back of my seat, unable to sit still. He's excited, not terrified.

"Something worse," Grandpa Joe says, looking at them through the rearview mirror. "It's the black plague. People are dropping like flies, and we need to get away from the general population before we all get sick and keel over."

"You'd better not give them nightmares," I warn.

Grandpa Joe chuckles but quickly puts on his serious face.

I turn around and point at the boys. They're all smiles. "Seat belts. Now."

Both my brothers have curly blond hair and freckly pale skin, and everything they do is loud. People mistake them for twins, especially when Phillip isn't wearing his glasses. But Edward is in third grade and has more energy than a nuclear bomb. His teacher makes him run the track before he's allowed into the classroom. Phillip is slightly taller and a fourth grader who smells like an old man because he insists on wearing cologne that he bought at the dollar store. He has a lot of energy too. But if you give him a book—any book—you can deactivate him. He also thinks he's the smartest in the family and probably is. He's been labeled *advanced gifted,* and we're basically learning the same things in math class. He reminds me of this all the time. It's hard to say which brother I find more annoying.

"Are we going to your secret bunker? Is that how we avoid the plague?" Mack asks.

"Not exactly a bunker," Grandpa Joe replies.

Ten minutes later, we pull in front of his house. At least we're not in the woods, pretending to be on the run. I'm not in the mood to search for a suitable cave or hang a tarp. Grandpa Joe and I have been doing drills and preparing for the end of days since I was in preschool. I remember bringing a snap light and Mylar rescue blanket to show-and-tell. As the boys got older (Grandpa Joe insisted they be potty-trained before being prepper-trained), they joined us on the adventures.

I don't know the exact moment it all stopped being fun. Maybe about the same time I stopped playing with dolls and believing monsters live under my bed.

Inside, Grandpa Joe turns on a battery-powered lantern that sits by the door. His house has electricity, running water, and Wi-Fi, but I guess we're not using any of that today.

"To the shelter," Grandpa Joe says. He holds the lantern over his head and leads us to the basement stairs.

We follow quietly. The only sound is Mack's cane tapping on the wooden floors. The boys tiptoe down the steps while Mack and I bring up the rear. Grandpa Joe unlocks a door at the bottom with a key he keeps chained to his belt. He's very cautious about his safe space and the supplies he's collected.

The basement is lined with rows of cabinets, each labeled and some locked. It's basically a small Walmart down here, but with fewer fluorescent lights. He's got food, clothes, bedding, tools, weapons, toiletries, first-aid supplies, and even dog food for Bubbles.

"Gather around, soldiers." Grandpa Joe motions to a

wooden table that's surrounded by five chairs—one for each of my brothers, Grandpa Joe, me, and Dad. But I can't remember the last time Dad was down here.

"Pack inspection," Grandpa Joe announces.

"Aww," Edward whines. "Does that mean this is just a drill?"

"You thought aliens were actually attacking us? Or the plague had struck in the three hours since you got home from school?" I shake my head.

"I was hoping it was real too," Mack says, smiling.

Edward opens his bag and dumps the contents onto the table. Grandpa Joe sorts through the items, nodding his approval.

"What's in the pack?" Mack asks.

"Everything you need to survive for a few days after the world ends." I hand him each item to check out: flashlight, wool socks, tarp, packaged food, first-aid kit, canteen, envelope with some cash, aspirin, fire starters, and a dozen other things. He turns each in his hands and then holds the item an inch away from his face to see it. Like most visually impaired people, Mack has some vision.

"So cool. I need all this stuff." Mack holds out an empty palm, and I place my hand in his. "You can help hook me up, right?" He squeezes.

"Sure." I squeeze back.

I'll admit, this bug-out drill is less awful with Mack here.

9

His excitement and interest make the evening bearable. I could say the same about a typical school day.

"Where's your rope?" Grandpa Joe asks Edward.

Edward looks at his feet. "Um . . ."

Phillip rats out his brother. "He used it to tie up Aidan Wheeler in the backyard."

"You can't play with the equipment in your bag. And if you take something out, it needs to be replaced ASAP." Grandpa Joe lines up Edward's three MREs—meals, ready-to-eat. Vacuum-sealed pouches filled with high-calorie, gross-tasting food that's already cooked and can last decades on a basement shelf.

"Overall, good job. Pick your dinner, Private Edward."

"Ooh, what's for dinner?" Mack asks, rocking on his feet.

"Ten-year-old toxic food product," I answer. "And I don't really mean food."

"Don't listen to her," Grandpa Joe says. "We're having MREs. They're plenty tasty and packed with nutrients."

"I've always wanted to try them. Elle has talked about them a lot." Mack obviously wasn't listening carefully, or he wouldn't be asking to try one.

"I'll take the chili and macaroni!" Edward grabs a foil pack that's meant for soldiers in the field, not kids in the suburbs.

"Isn't it wasteful to eat it now? Especially when there's

a McDonald's right down the street." I'm desperately trying to avoid a dinner from a pouch. "Shouldn't we save them for a war or something?"

"We're not wasting anything if we actually eat it," Grandpa Joe answers. "Private Eleanor, it's important to set expectations. Being prepared is not just about having supplies. We eat the food. We use the tools. We know what to expect."

I expect my gag reflex to kick in. I've tried at least twenty MRE flavors. Given a choice, I'd rather eat a bowl of twigs.

"Who's next?" Grandpa Joe asks.

Phillip jumps in when I should have. I need to get this over with. My bag is a mess. Half the necessary things are at the bottom of my closet.

Of course, Phillip's pack is perfect. He has everything, and even some extra stuff like books.

"Excellent," Grandpa Joe says. "But be careful of the weight. If you can't bug out with a vehicle, you'll be walking. And you could be walking for days."

"Got it." Phillip salutes. Then he selects his dinner.

"You're up, Private Eleanor." Grandpa Joe turns to me.

"Go, Elle! Go, Elle! You got this." Mack cheers like this is a game.

"My bag is a disaster," I admit, just to get the lecture over with. "Do you want me to drop and give you twenty?"

There's no way I could do twenty push-ups. I want to make Grandpa Joe laugh. I love him. I just don't love bug-out drills and prepping and MREs.

Grandpa Joe removes his hat and runs a hand over his head. He has some hair, but it's so short and so white that it can only be seen in certain light. "I don't want to lecture you. I want to keep you safe and give you skills you will one day need to survive."

He gently takes my bag and opens the top. He pulls out one dress shoe that doesn't even fit, a couple of headbands, some old school papers, and a tangle of rope.

"At least I have my rope," I say. "Together, as a family, I think we would survive." I smile wide, trying to outshine Grandpa Joe's disappointment.

He sucks in a big breath. "This bag is unacceptable, soldier. I want it repacked when you get home. Understood?"

I nod.

He fishes around in my backpack until he finds a foil pouch. "And it looks like you're eating chicken chunks. It's the only food you've got."

"I'm not hungry." Chicken chunks are the worst MRE option. They look like canned dog food. I don't even know how they got in my bag. Then Edward giggles, and I know. He switched it out. The chili and macaroni should be mine.

"I'll eat it." Mack rocks in his seat.

"This is Eleanor's," Grandpa Joe says with a stern face.

"I got extras here for you, Mack. You in the mood for chili with beans, buffalo chicken, or maple pork sausage patty?"

"What do you recommend, sir?" Mack asks.

Grandpa Joe gives him the chili.

"Wanna trade?" I whisper to Mack.

"Don't do it!" Edward says. "Chunks are the worstest."

Bug-out drills are the worstest. I tear open my MRE, certain that training for the end of days has to be worse than the actual end of days.

Chapter 2

We all survive the survival drill. When we drop Mack off, he thanks Grandpa Joe for an experience of a lifetime and even suggests we do it again. I butt in and tell him you can't have an experience of a lifetime twice.

As soon as I get home, I brush my teeth three times and gargle with mouthwash. The chicken chunks don't seem to want to move through my digestive tract.

"You okay?" Grandpa Joe asks through the closed bathroom door.

"Yes."

"Can I help you repack your bug-out bag?"

"Nope, I got it." I head to my room and plunge into my closet. Everything I need is on the floor. Bubbles and

I sort through the mess. She has a knack for finding dirty socks.

I pull out two MREs, both chicken chunks.

"Edward!" I shout. "Give me back my MREs!"

He doesn't hear me, or he ignores me. I take the chunks downstairs to the basement and trade them out for slightly tastier options: spaghetti with beef and sauce, hash brown potatoes with bacon, and chicken pesto pasta. Grandpa Joe gave us a case of MREs a few years ago. We keep the box on a shelf near our holiday decorations and a broken toaster that Dad thinks he can fix.

After I finish repacking my BOB, I let Grandpa Joe inspect it.

"Perfect," he says. "You make this old man feel better when I know you're prepared for anything."

"That's me. Always prepared." *Not that I've done my math homework for tomorrow.*

He raises an eyebrow. "It wasn't that long ago you actually liked bugging out and growing crops and eating freeze-dried ice cream."

"There's a big difference between chicken chunks and freeze-dried ice cream."

He laughs. "True, true. I try to make survival training fun for you and the boys because it's important."

I take a deep breath and concentrate on *not* rolling my eyes.

"Eleanor. I've seen war firsthand. Hurricanes. Torna-does. My granddad told me stories about the Spanish flu. Terrorist attacks are on the news all the time. Bad stuff happens, and it's my job to protect my family." He slaps his palm to his chest.

"I know," I say, then add, "Dad says you take it too far."

"That boy has known better than me for forty years." He laughs again. "I look forward to the day he thanks me for getting y'all ready for the inevitable."

Now I raise *my* eyebrows. "You look forward to it?"

"Not the disaster part. But the thank-you part won't be so bad."

"Can I just thank you now on behalf of all of us? And then we can avoid the apocalypse." *And preparing for the apocalypse. And eating for the apocalypse.*

"You're welcome, soldier. Now put your BOB somewhere safe."

"You mean where Edward can't get to it."

I stand on my chair and place my bag on the top shelf of the closet. I know Edward and Phillip could still reach it if they wanted to. Those boys could break into FBI head-quarters or out of a maximum-security jail. They can't be stopped.

"Good night, soldier." Grandpa Joe wraps me in a bear hug that makes me feel safe and guilty. I shouldn't give him a hard time. He thinks he's helping. Like when Edward washes the dishes and Dad or I have to rewash them because he does a crummy job and leaves food stuck to the plates.

After Grandpa Joe lets go, I kiss his cheek. He tells me not to stay up too late and then goes downstairs.

I should finish my math or actually read *The Outsiders,* but instead, I turn on my laptop. Bubbles and I crawl onto my bed.

"Ten minutes and then I must do homework," I say to Bubbles.

I search the internet for end-of-the-world memes. Maybe I can find something funny to print out and share with Grandpa Joe. After a few minutes—probably more than ten, if I'm honest—I come across a website that is meme-free. The page is pretty crappy. It looks like someone threw it together on a slow school computer.

But the headline's interesting.

WORLD TO END NEXT YEAR

There's only one picture. It's of a white guy with gray hair, a beard, and thin glasses. He's wearing a blue shirt and a red tie and looks like a normal, boring adult. Under the picture is his name. Martin Cologne, PhD. Astrophysicist.

I start reading because even though it's not a meme, I want to know what this nerdy-looking man is talking about.

Urgent! Asteroid 2010PL7 will strike Earth next spring. 2010PL7 is an Apollo Class NEA and is more than 5 km across. Because of the size, this asteroid will not burn up in the atmosphere. This impact will have significant consequences for life on Earth regardless of where it strikes. This is a 10 on the Torino Impact Hazard Scale. Code red. Certain collision. Expect global catastrophe.

And that's it. There are no links for more information. But there's certainly stuff to Google.

I start by researching the author. Dr. Martin Cologne isn't some wacko. He teaches at Harvard, and he's written three complicated-looking books on space and physics. He's won awards that I've never heard of, and he's published in about a million science journals.

Next, I look up 2010PL7. According to NASA, it *is* an asteroid, and NEA stands for *near-Earth asteroid.* The agency also lists values for things abbreviated as *e, a, q, I, peri, M,* and *Q.* I don't understand any of it. Nowhere does NASA say 2010PL7 is headed toward Earth. It's actually listed as a "removed object" on the Sentry: Earth Impact Monitoring system. That's good, assuming the NASA scientists know what they're talking about.

Why do you want to scare people, Dr. Cologne?

I know the internet is filled mostly with lies. My dad's

profile on social media says he's married, and Mom died seven years ago. Maybe an impostor used Dr. Smarty's name and picture. There are typos on the website. Someone who teaches at Harvard should be a better speller.

Before closing the site, I bookmark it. Then I go back to searching for memes. If Dr. Cologne had listed his email, I would send him a cartoon of dinosaurs taking selfies while an asteroid flashes across the sky behind them. The professor could probably use a laugh.

Chapter 3

The next morning, I manage to get through breakfast without one word from Grandpa Joe about the end of the world. Then I go to school and experience the three ways a gym class can be made even worse than it already is: having an overexcited substitute teacher who played some college sport, being partners with anyone other than Mack, and playing basketball.

Our sub insists on being called Coach Holmes, not Mr. Holmes. He's at least ten feet tall, and he twirls a basketball on his finger the whole time he talks.

"Line up by height," he yells. "Make eight teams."

Usually, I'd join Mack, the other special-needs students, and their teacher on the far side of the gym. Ms. Stuckley, our PE teacher, lets me partner with Mack. Sometimes we run together. He holds a sliding handle on a rope or my elbow. Sometimes we play soccer outside with a beep ball.

But I'm not about to ask this man, who's probably closer to fifteen feet tall, for special consideration. Plus, Mack isn't even in class today. I hope the MRE isn't seeking revenge on his digestive tract.

I slide into place near kids who are about my height. We count off, and then we're ordered to different locations across the gym. Each team is given an orange ball that'll be used for today's torture.

Coach Horrible blows his whistle, then yells, "Warm up with some passing."

My team includes Graham Engle, Terrell Rodgers, and Londyn Diggs. They chuck the ball at each other and ignore me. I'm not complaining. Every few passes, Londyn glares in my direction. Her eyes are circled in dark makeup, which enhances her I-want-to-punch-you-in-the-throat look.

"We don't have enough for a team," Graham says.

"The three of us are enough," Londyn says. She bounces the ball between her legs and then passes it from behind her back. It's only impressive if you care about basketball.

Londyn is skinny and tan, and everyone always compliments her long, curly dark hair with its purple streaks. Most people would describe her as pretty and popular. I'd say she's pretty evil.

"Eleanor is on our team too," Terrell says, a bit clueless.

Londyn sighs. "She's not going to play. She never does."

"Give her a chance," Terrell says as he throws to Graham.

Then Graham turns suddenly and bounces the ball to me.

I jump out of the way just in time.

"It's not dodgeball. You're supposed to catch it," Londyn says.

We all watch the ball roll across the gym.

"Should I go get—"

"No, balls usually come back on their own, like boomerangs." Londyn gives me a tense look like she's trying to shoot lasers at me from her eyeballs.

I jog across the gym to get the ball. I carry it back to the group and gently hand it to Terrell.

"Nice pass, LeBron," Londyn murmurs.

The ball goes around their triangle a few more times before Coach Holmes blows his whistle.

Please make us run laps. Please make us run laps. I'm certain I'm the only kid in class reciting this little prayer in my head. Then I think of a better idea.

Please have a fire drill or an intruder drill or any drill that doesn't require a stupid ball.

"Team one versus team two." He points to a basket. "Three versus four. Five versus six. Seven versus eight."

I follow my team to our court. My plan is to stay out of the way and not draw attention to myself. This is always my plan when it comes to sports or any class participation. I'm basically an armadillo during school hours. If you don't move, you become invisible.

"Guard him," Londyn orders me. She nods toward a big kid. I have no idea what she expects. But I move closer. He smells like breakfast sausage.

The other team starts with the ball. A boy I'm not guarding dribbles. He takes about two steps, and then Londyn steals the ball from him. She dribbles to the basket and scores.

Terrell and Graham give her high fives.

This time my guy starts with it. He dribbles. I watch.

"Defense!" Londyn yells. But I don't know what she wants me to do. I shuffle my feet and wave my arms like a baby bird flapping its wings uselessly after it's fallen out of the nest. The boy shoots, and I duck. I assume he misses, but my eyes are closed. I can't confirm.

When I refocus, Londyn has the ball again. And she scores again. She pumps her fist in the air but doesn't smile. She actually looks angrier than before. I wonder what her reaction is when she misses.

"Four to nothing!" Graham yells.

I step to the far corner of the court. My team doesn't need me. It doesn't need Graham or Terrell either. Londyn is some kind of basketball wizard. I focus on the clock, not the game. We still have ten minutes left.

Coach Horrific wanders from court to court. As he nears ours, I slide back into the mix, hoping he doesn't notice that I'm as helpful as one of the orange cones that we have to sprint between.

Londyn scores again.

"Pass the ball around. Use your team."

Now Londyn glares at the coach.

The next time she gets the ball, instead of dribbling toward the basket, she hurls it. She hurls it at me!

I've heard the expression *my life flashed before my eyes.* This isn't quite like that. It's more like I see the future. I imagine the impact, being escorted to the nurse's office, the pain, the ice pack. I also imagine an asteroid hitting Earth.

And that's what it feels like.

I fall back on my butt. My eyes water so hard that I can't see. This is what happens—I play with the sighted kids one time, and I go blind. At least I don't have to endure any more of Londyn's nasty glares. My time in gym class ends about five minutes early. I'm not complaining.

• • •

I sit in the office with a half-melted ice pack on my face. My nose has finally stopped bleeding. My dad was called, but the nurse assured him my injury didn't require X-rays, a ticket home, or any sympathy at all, really.

"Ready to go back to class, Eleanor?"

"No."

She ignores my answer and hands me a hall pass. As I leave, I see Mack standing outside the guidance office. His parents are with him and some white guy in a suit. The adults shake hands and seem to be saying goodbye.

I round the corner toward the seventh-grade hall and wait for Mack. A minute later, I hear the tapping of his cane. He calls it Candy, which seemed clever in first grade. This one isn't the original Candy, because he outgrows canes—like shoes, his mom says. He's had Candy Two and Candy Three, but around Candy Five or Six, he lost track and just went back to plain Candy.

"Hey, Mack."

"Elle, what are you doing out here?" he asks. "Shouldn't you be in science, young lady?" He does an awful accent that I think is supposed to be our teacher Mrs. Walsh.

"I've been in the nurse's office with a broken nose. Londyn Diggs tried to knock my head off with a basketball. I'm lucky to be alive."

He laughs.

"What were you doing in the guidance office?"

"You spying on me, Elle?" He holds out his hand, and I give him my elbow. "They had a dude come in from the Conrad School to talk with blind students and our parents."

"What's the Conrad School?"

25

"I've told you. The Conrad School for the Blind and Visually Impaired."

"The high school?" Mack has mentioned it before—a boarding school for the blind, somewhere near Raleigh. He went there once for a week in the summer and hated it. Well, as much as Mack can hate anything. I think he said it was "all right."

"No. It starts in sixth grade and goes *through* high school."

"Sounds like a waste of time," I say.

"It wasn't a waste. They had hot Krispy Kreme donuts and orange juice. I ate like six." He pretends to burp. "And it was cool. The Conrad School has a lot more activities than I thought. It has a band *and* an orchestra."

"You don't play any instruments."

"And lots of sports," he continues. "I could be on the swim team."

"You could be on the swim team at Hamilton."

"And there's every class you can think of. I could live in a dorm with a roommate."

I stop walking and turn to face him. The more excited he gets, the harder it is for me to breathe.

"Wait. Are you thinking about going?"

"Not today or anything."

"When?" In that one word my voice breaks.

"Maybe next year, or the year after. I don't know. The

future is full of possibilities." He mockingly sings the last part. It's like he doesn't even realize I can't go with him.

It's only October, but I imagine next year without Mack. I could go days—weeks, maybe—without talking to anyone. Except for teachers, and they don't count. No one would be my lab partner or save me a seat at lunch or invite me over for taco night. I'd basically disappear.

"Dude, come on. We're already late for science." Mack says. "I don't want to stay after school."

But all I hear is *I don't want to stay.*

Chapter 4

For over a week, all Mack talks about is the Conrad School—at lunch, on the phone, when we run the track. If I'd been paying attention, I'd know the number of students, the address, the name of the dean, and the school's mascot. But I tried to block it all out. (The mascot is a train engine named Steamy. That's hard to forget.)

So on Saturday, when he invites me over to play video games, I make him promise not to bring it up.

"I swear on your life," he says in a fake British accent.

We play in his family room. Mack's vision is something like 20/300 with his glasses, which is blind but not 100 percent sightless. If he stands super close to the screen or uses a CCTV, he can see enough to beat me every time. Except when I cheat.

"Dude, you should practice more," Mack says as he kicks my butt. "It's not fun to win all the time."

I have to stand close to the TV too because he blocks most of the screen if I sit on the couch.

"Maybe you should practice less. Seriously, I'm going to talk to your mom. She needs to limit your screen time." I'm joking, but it's the truth.

He laughs. "She's the one who plays with me when you're not here. And she's the only one who can actually beat me."

"Mrs. Jefferson. Mrs. Jefferson." I pretend to call her into the room. "Haven't you heard? Video games rot your brain. Mack's brain is ninety percent moldy oatmeal at this point." I pull hard on the controller, willing my car to take the lead. It doesn't work.

"Video games may rot your brain, but they won't give you a massive head injury."

I touch the bridge of my nose. The black-and-blue is mostly gone.

"They should have kicked her out of school," I say, and not for the first time.

"You should learn how to catch. Think of the blind population. I would do anything to play catch with my dad even once without using the beep ball." He fake cries.

When our game ends, I refuse to go again.

"Whatever. That girl has problems. She knocked over a cart of Chromebooks last year." I'm not exactly scared of Londyn—except on the basketball court—but I'd be happy if our paths never crossed again.

"That wasn't Londyn Diggs. It was Lauren Duggins. And she didn't knock over a cart. She dropped one Chromebook, and they made her parents replace it. This is how rumors start."

"Is it?" I retreat to the couch.

Mack keeps playing.

"You gotta admit," I continue, "Londyn's trouble. She's a bully, and people are afraid of her."

"She's never bothered me."

"You'd feel differently if she threw a ball at your head with the force of an asteroid."

"Probably," he says, still focused on the video game. "We'll discuss when it happens."

"Speaking of asteroids, let me see your iPad."

He pauses his game. "Why?"

"I read something about an asteroid hitting Earth. It was kind of weird and vague. I want to see if there are any updates."

"Really?" He rifles through his backpack, finds the iPad, and gives it to me. He does most of his schoolwork on it. If he magnifies the screen and holds it a few inches from his face, he can see it. His para-assistant has a Braille machine in her office. He knows how to use that too. An iPad is much smaller and faster, has games on it, and makes our classmates jealous, since we're not allowed phones or tablets in class.

"Yeah, the scientist guy—a doctor—says it's going to happen soon, like in the spring."

"That's not soon. It's October." Mack sits on the other side of the couch. At home he doesn't need Candy to get around.

"It's not soon if you're talking about a due date for a book report, but we're talking about the end of Earth." I type in Mack's passcode.

"Is this a prepper thing? Your grandfather promised me my own bug-out bag. Then we need to go on another drill. I want to be ready!" After our little exercise, Mack might have become brainwashed.

"I don't think Dr. Cologne is a survivalist. He's not like one of those YouTube preppers, anyway." I find the website. It's changed since I logged on last week. There are pictures, several new posts, a guestbook, and a visitor count. Over three thousand people have clicked on this site.

"Read it to me," Mack insists.

I share the first article, the one I'd already read. Then I go to the newer posts.

"'No one wants to listen to me,'" I read. "'The government, banks, and big business are concerned my prediction will cause mass panic. It *should* cause mass panic. Here's a satellite image of the asteroid.'"

The picture is black and white and looks like a cluster of stars. Dr. Cologne has circled one and labeled it 2010PL7. I give the iPad to Mack. He holds it an inch from his face and moves the screen left to right to take it all in.

"I hope he has more evidence than this." Mack hands back the device.

I continue reading. "'Those who do know are preparing. You should prepare too. Before it's too late.'"

Mack clicks his tongue. "The dude used the word *prepare* twice. He's definitely a prepper."

"I guess. Sort of. Not really. Have you ever watched a real prepper or survivalist video? They don't tell you when the world is ending exactly. It's about being ready to the max."

"Nope. Never seen any, but now I'm gonna check them out." Mack leans back on the couch. "Keep reading."

"'You still have time. I calculate that 2010PL7 will enter Earth's orbit in April or May. The location of impact is unknown, and we won't know until days before. We must all be ready. Think of your families and friends. If you love them, you will take heed.'"

"This is awesome," Mack says.

"Awesome?"

Mack gets excited about anything and everything. Three things Mack has gotten excited about today: a new Marvel movie trailer, a pack of Mentos he found in his backpack, and "the smell of fall." (He literally said that.) It's my job to remind him how awful things can be.

"The planet isn't going to explode and disappear," he says. "Some people will survive. The smart ones. Like us."

"We would totally survive." I nod. "I've got a grandfather with a basement full of supplies."

"What do we need to survive the apocalypse?"

"Not apocalypse. That sounds too much like a cheesy movie. This is TEOTWAWKI—the end of the world as we know it."

"That's a thing?" he asks. "A real acronym?"

"I've said too much already." I fake a gasp as I slip his iPad back in his bag.

"No, no, no. Elle, tell me about this secret society where people think the world is going to end. I want to know. I want to learn. Teach me." He holds out his empty palms for my hand. He's not being romantic, and it annoys me when people think that's the reason. This is his way of knowing he's got my attention and I've got his.

"It wouldn't be a *secret* society if I went around talking about it. Geez. I'm going to lose my membership card."

"Who should we warn? Who should we save? Who would we invite into the bunker?" Mack's smile is enormous. I can see every tooth in his mouth.

"Family. And maybe a doctor and a decent cook."

"Good call, Elle. And how should we spend our last few months on Earth?"

"I don't know."

"We're playing pretend here," he says. "Like we did when we used to build forts in your basement, and I was the Lord Ace of Dragonton and you were the evil sorcerer Flintina. Use a little imagination, Elle."

I sigh loud enough that his parents in the other room could probably hear me.

"Um. Drop out of school and go to Paris."

"You want to go to Paris?" He laughs.

"Not really. It's the first city that came to mind that was far away and exotic. What would you do with your last months on Earth, Lord Ace?"

"Glad you asked." He clears his throat and sits up straighter. "I'd climb a mountain. A tall one. I'd swim with dolphins. I'd ride a camel or an elephant or a zebra. I'd jump out of a plane."

"With a parachute, I hope."

He ignores me. "I'd sing the national anthem at a baseball game. I'd set some kind of world record. I'd kiss someone nice."

"Aren't you the romantic?" I make smoochie noises.

"Dude, I'm going to get married someday. And that person is going to be super lucky to have me as a husband."

"If you say so. But remember, we're talking about stuff

you can do before the asteroid. As your best friend, I can't allow you to get married when you're twelve."

"Right, right. I'd like to win a chess tournament. Be captain of the swim team. Meet a celebrity. Audition for *Jeopardy!* Maybe run a marathon. Try all the flavors at Dave's Donuts."

"Gee, is that all? You should really aim higher." I pat his shoulder.

"For now. If the world was really ending in the spring, I'd just want to spend as much time with you and my family as I can. Before it's too late."

"You're such a dork." I make a gagging noise. Even though I totally agree with him.

Chapter **5**

My three favorite days of the week are Saturday, Sunday, and Friday after 2 p.m. My least favorite is Monday (unless it's a three-day weekend, obviously).

Today is Monday, and I'm prepared for a new level of awful.

Recently, a lot of girls and a few of the boys started dyeing their hair bright colors. Some did streaks, and some had color just on the ends. I've never worn makeup or owned cool clothes. But this was different. I liked it, and the internet made it sound so easy to do. An article I read recommended using a powdered-drink mix. So I combined a packet of purple passion punch with a little water and brushed the liquid onto the ends of my blond hair. Disaster. The dye was uneven. And it came out old-lady gray-blue. I didn't end up with streaks. I had uneven clumps. I tried to fix it by mixing a dark-blue concoction made from berry-berry drink mix and some food dye I found in the pantry. I soaked all of my hair and put plastic wrap over it. An hour later, my hair was the color of the shared water cup in art class that everyone dips their brushes in. Then I tried to cut it myself, just a few inches.

No one in the history of the world has ever given herself a good haircut.

My brothers laughed, and Dad tried not to. I begged him to take me to get it fixed. We went to the walk-in salon next to the frozen yogurt place. A girl with a nose ring used a special rinse to get rid of most of the muddy color, and then she started cutting. And cutting and cutting! I should have stopped her. It's like I was paralyzed. In shock maybe. When she finished, I had a blond (slightly bluish) bowl that barely covered my ears. Dad didn't laugh when he saw me. He gave me the saddest smile and said, "You're still beautiful to me." Which means, to everyone else I resemble a troll.

In homeroom, Jeremy Donahue, who has sat in front of me since the first day of school almost two months ago, turns around and flashes me his crooked grin. I've heard some of the girls say he's the cutest guy in all of seventh grade. I'm not disagreeing.

"Hey, new boy," he says. "You can't sit there. That's

Ellerie's seat." He looks over at his friend. They high-five and laugh.

I immediately lean over, pretend to pick up something off the floor, and stay down there long enough that I could complete a one-hundred-piece puzzle. It's the closest I can get to disappearing under the desk. I don't know what's worse, that he's making fun of my hair—which is awful—or that he doesn't know my name? (We were partners in art class last year. We drew each other's portrait!)

All morning, kids make jokes about my hair. Then I fall in the hall on the way to gym. I slip on nothing. Nothing! Like the universe stuck out its foot and tripped me. No, not tripped. The universe kicked me in the back. I also get a seventy on a math test, and sixty on a social studies project. Dad will have to sign both of them.

Even science class—the only class I usually like—is terrible. I forgot to do the assignment, but it's not my fault. We rarely have science homework, and I was distracted by my hair-tastrophe.

Mrs. Walsh corners me at the end of class. She's a white lady who wears a lab coat and a messy bun every day. She takes her job of educating seventh graders very seriously.

"Eleanor, no homework? Want to tell me what's going on?" She drums her fingers on the pile of papers that does not contain my assignment.

I shrug.

"Eleanor, it wasn't that challenging. You only had to come up with three science questions that interest you."

"Sorry. I'll do better next time." This is my go-to statement to get out of a lecture from my dad, a teacher, or any other adult.

"Let's brainstorm together. So, what do you want to know the answer to?"

How can you get hair to grow back overnight? Why do school days last twice as long as weekend days? Am I going to be late to Spanish?

"I don't know." I cross my arms. What I *want* is to go home.

She falls back dramatically in her chair and throws her arm over her forehead. "Well, I guess *my* experiment failed. I was trying to discover what interests my students."

"Sorry. You shouldn't expect too much from your students. That's my advice. Rookie mistake, Mrs. Walsh."

She smiles and shakes her head. "Ha ha. I'm not a rookie. It's my second year. And I'm not ready to give up yet. There's got to be some question that has intrigued you in your twelve years. Something you want to know more about."

The asteroid and Dr. Cologne pop into my head. I've checked his site a few times since Saturday, but he hasn't posted anything new.

"Um . . . I guess there's one thing I want to know." I try to think of a way to bring it up.

"Yes?" She leans forward again.

"How's the world going to end?"

"Wow!" She holds up her hands like she's about to catch a giant ball. "That's a big question."

"I don't mean the planet blowing up, but how's it going to end for humans?" I ask. "What's going to make us go extinct? Like your dinosaur friends." She used to be a real-life paleontologist. The first week of school she showed us pictures of her working at a fossil site.

"I can certainly tell you how the dinosaurs went extinct," she says. "An asteroid struck Earth in what's now Mexico. The localized destruction was massive, and it set off a series of events that altered the planet for years."

"An asteroid? Really? Are you sure?"

"An asteroid or maybe a comet, but yes, I'm sure!" She pumps her fist and then points to my face. "There! There! I saw it. A spark in your eye. Oh, thank you, Eleanor. You've restored my faith in seventh graders."

I shake my head and try not to laugh. "Okay. I guess asteroids and extinctions are a little interesting."

"Just a little?" She leans back and locks her fingers behind her head. "Dinosaurs were around for more than one hundred and fifty million years. Modern humans have been walking around for less than three hundred *thousand* years."

"Do you think it could happen again? Could an asteroid wipe out a whole species?"

"Anything is possible. Earth has experienced five major extinction events."

"Were they all because of asteroids crashing into Earth?" My nerves tingle. I should tell her about Dr. Cologne and the website. I wonder if Dr. Cologne knows this has happened before. He must.

"No." She swivels in her chair to face the bookshelf behind her desk. She runs a finger across the spines and finally pulls out a book that looks more like a novel than a textbook. *The History of Earth's 4.5 Billion Years.*

"Here. You might enjoy this." She holds it out for me, and when I don't take it, she lays it on the corner of her desk.

"No thanks." I know she's trying to trap me into doing extra work. Or worse, she's going to suggest I do a science fair project.

"Take the book and we'll forget about the missing homework assignment and watershed map I know you didn't finish in class." She taps the cover. "Maybe you'll find it useful. Maybe you'll want to do a science fair project."

I knew it! All science teachers—even the cool ones—are obsessed with the science fair. They must get bonuses or something.

"Gee, thanks." I sigh heavily before grabbing the book.

"Oh, you wait and see, Eleanor Dross. Science can change your life." She clasps her hands in excitement.

Chapter 6

The book from Mrs. Walsh might be the most interesting thing a teacher has ever given me. I sit in the family room with Bubbles on my lap and reread the chapter on the K-T extinction (which stands for *Cretaceous-Tertiary* and should be C-T, in my opinion).

Sixty-five million years ago, an asteroid at least six miles wide crashed into the Yucatán Peninsula in Mexico. It was traveling at 67,000 miles per hour, and the crater it created was over a hundred miles wide. Any animal within six hundred miles was obliterated immediately. It was like millions of nuclear bombs going off at once. The impact caused tsunamis with walls of water over two thousand feet high and earthquakes that would have made the ground in western

North America act like a trampoline. (The book says T. rexes flew several feet into the air.) Bits of asteroid and rock and dirt were thrown into the atmosphere. When this debris fell back to Earth, it was on fire. It rained fire! Volcanoes across the globe went into overdrive. The biggest animals—like dinosaurs—died off quickly. The animals that survived were the smallest, and most lived underground.

My heart pounds in my chest like I just watched a horror movie, and I hate horror movies.

"Eleanor!"

I jump. And so does Bubbles.

Dad stands in the doorway. "What's this?" He's holding the math test and social studies project that require his signature. I'd left them and a pen on the counter. Teachers don't trust us to hang our poor grades on the refrigerator for all to admire.

"It's *your* homework," I joke. "But don't worry, it's an easy assignment. Just sign."

"Eleanor, you can do better than this."

"I'm not an A-student. Phillip is your brainiac. You should be happy that you were blessed with one smart kid. The results aren't in for Edward yet, but I wouldn't get my hopes up. I've seen him stick Legos up his nose."

"Eleanor," Dad sighs. "You don't have to be an A-student. I want your best, and this is not your best. Look. You didn't even finish." He points to the report. I hadn't bothered to add a bibliography. That was worth five points, but probably would have taken me hours, maybe days.

"I'll make it up."

"Yes, you will, and no going anywhere, including Mack's house, until it's done." He hands me the papers. "And if you need help with math, I'm your guy."

"Yeah, I know." Dad's a mechanical engineer and an all-around numbers geek. He actually likes doing math stuff, including checking his kids' homework. But he doesn't just check if our answers are right. He makes up additional problems to make sure we "get it."

You learn math by doing, he's told us a billion times.

Bubbles and I go to my room. I consider doing my homework. The bibliography will probably only take twenty minutes—not hours—if I actually get started. But I can't stop thinking about asteroids—both the dinosaur one and the new one. Scientists say the K-T extinction asteroid was about six miles across. I can't remember the estimated size of Dr. Cologne's. I get online.

The asteroid 2010PL7 is a bit smaller. It's about three and a half miles wide and potato-shaped, not round. None of this information makes me feel any better.

I click around the website hoping to find a "ha ha, just kidding" GIF. I don't want to be crushed by an asteroid or caught in a fiery rainstorm. Instead, I find a video.

On the screen, Dr. Cologne is sitting in a messy office. He clears his throat.

"I'm Dr. Martin Cologne. Professor of astronomy and physics. I'm recording this in my office at Harvard University. Today is my last day and not of my own choosing. While I'm a tenured professor with multiple publications and awards and the director of the Origins of Planets Initiative, I'm being forced out for telling the truth and attempting to save lives."

He runs a hand through his wild gray hair and scratches his white beard. He looks left at something off the screen. He seems worried, but not crazy.

"I could fight this," he says, looking back at the camera. "Legally fight this out in court. But some things are more important than career and prestige."

A loud knock in the video causes Dr. Cologne to pause. Then he leans closer to the camera.

"Please spread the word. I am not wrong. I haven't been wrong in my entire twenty-year career. Read my research. I promise I'm right, and I'm sorry that I'm right!" He's screaming now. Spit flies from his mouth. Okay, he does seem a bit crazy.

He lets out a loud breath. "Your life depends on this information."

There's mumbling out of view. Dr. Cologne pushes back

his chair. It crashes into a stack of books. The screen turns sideways and then goes black.

That's the only new post. I go back and reread what I already know. The world is ending in the spring when 2010PL7 crashes into our planet.

Links have been added to his picture. It's like his résumé. I click a few and see the papers he's written on subjects like black hole evolution, space-time theories, and the Kevlar mission. I don't even understand the abstracts written at the tops. But anyone who can use that many ten-letter words in one paragraph must be übersmart. He doesn't make any spelling or grammar mistakes in his official work—that I can tell. Unlike the website, which has lots of errors.

Still, he's someone who deserves to be listened to. He's earned it. Who am I to question him? Not that I ever really doubted the Harvard astrophysicist. I just thought maybe he was exaggerating. From experience, I know most adults exaggerate at least once in a while.

I text Mack.

ME: check out Cologne's website NOW

He uses VoiceOver to read his messages, and he does speech-to-text to send. Using punctuation and words in all caps is a waste. I do it anyway. And I always have to consider that he might listen to my messages in front of his parents.

ME: Let me know what you think

Mack texts back ten minutes later, which feels more like ten years when you're waiting for important advice.

MACK: OMG we're all going to die

I assume he's being sarcastic, and this isn't the time. I call him.

He answers the phone, laughing.

"You're not being serious!" I accuse him.

"No, no, no. I am. Sorry." He clears his throat and uses his deepest voice. "We should all be concerned and heed this warning."

"Honestly, he seems smart," I say. "But in the video, he was getting upset. Like freaking out."

"He is talking about the end of the world. TEO . . . what is it called again?"

"TEOTWAWKI." I flop back on my bed, and Bubbles is forced to find a new spot. "What should we do?"

"I don't know. I mean, Grandpa Joe is already prepared for this," he says. "You don't have anything to worry about."

"I haven't told him yet," I admit.

"Seriously? This is Grandpa Joe's jam. Why haven't you told him?"

"I don't know."

"Okay," Mack says. "I would tell him and your dad. This dude seems pretty sure."

"Are you going to tell your parents?"

"Definitely. Soon as I have time." He answers like I've

asked if he's going to watch a new YouTube video I've recommended.

"Mack, I'm totally serious here. I think this is real. Don't you?" I hold my breath as I wait for his reply.

"Yeah, I do." His voice softens, and I can tell he's not just saying what I want to hear.

We hang up, and I immediately call my grandfather, the only prepper I know.

"This is Joe. Leave a message, unless you're a telemarketer; then go eat a sock." He laughs at the end, which makes it much less threatening.

"Hey, it's Eleanor. Can you call me, please? When you have the time. Nothing important. Everything is okay. I love you. But call me." Then I disconnect. I'm sure I didn't sound like everything was okay.

Dad, Phillip, and Edward are playing a game downstairs. My interruption won't be appreciated. Plus, they'll invite me to play, and I'm not a fan of Risk. Or worse, Dad will ask if I've finished my work. My standard answer is always "I've got it under control." This is neither a lie nor the truth. I'm the only one who can do the work, so it is under *my* control.

I decide to tell Dad later, after the boys are asleep.

So many questions fill my head. Like, is Dr. Cologne for real? Everyone warns students that you can't trust the internet. Our media specialist spent three classes on reliable sources. I'm pretty sure you could end up in a juvenile detention center if you ever use Wikipedia on any project. And Dad has warned us too. He's put parental controls on the computer that the boys use. When I started middle school and got my own laptop, he told me he wouldn't install monitoring software if I promised to be responsible. And if I had any questions about what was okay, I was supposed to ask him. I haven't gotten in trouble yet.

I scan the site again, and I notice there's now an email button.

Click.

I type my message as fast as my two fingers can go.

Dear Dr. Cologne,

Are you sure about this asteroid? Like, 1,000 percent sure? I want to tell my family, but I'm afraid they'll think I'm crazy. They might think you are crazy even though it's obvious that you are smart from all your awards. I don't know what to do. Please help.

Sincerely,
E.J.D.

I don't put my full name because I'm not supposed to give my name on the internet. Maybe Dr. Cologne will even think I'm an adult, since I didn't say my age.

My hand shakes a little bit when I hit send. I really

should do my makeup work and tonight's homework. Instead, I take a shower, which doesn't take long now that I have no hair. Then I go to the kitchen for a snack. I wear my headphones to avoid Dad's questions about the progress of my work. When I go back to my room, I promise myself it's time to get my bibliography done. Right after I check my email. There's no way Dr. Cologne could have written me back yet, so it's not really stalling.

But there *is* an email.

And it is from Dr. Cologne. For a second, I forget to breathe.

Dear E.J.D.,

You must tell your family. It is up to each of us to protect the ones we love. If you don't do it, who will? They may not accept it at first. I've run into resistance from numerous colleagues. They do not want to see what's plainly in front of them. There's too much pride among scientists. Most of our career is spent competing for discoveries and for glory. This is not the time. We need to get ready. I've attached some images of the asteroid. Maybe these will help your family realize the threat.

I understand if you are having doubts. People have predicted the end of the world before. None have been right. But our world has been struck by objects from space countless times. Some impacts have caused major extinctions. Mathematically speaking, we are overdue for a severe, life-altering collision. We've been forturnate. But our luck runs out this spring.

Be brave and take care of yours.

Sincerely,
Dr. Martin Cologne

I read the email one more time, and I have no doubt what I need to do.

"Dad, come here!"

Chapter 7

"What is it?" Dad shouts as he runs up the stairs. "What's wrong?"

Maybe I shouldn't have screamed. This is important and life-threatening but not a right-this-minute emergency.

He stops in my doorway and looks around. He's still wearing his work clothes—navy pants and a baby-blue button-down shirt that's now untucked.

Bubbles jumps off my bed and runs to Dad, then me, and then Dad again. She barks, probably confused by the excitement.

"What?" Dad asks again.

Edward pushes in under Dad's arm. "Is it a spider? Is it a big spider?"

"No. Go away. I want to talk to Dad alone." Of course, that's like a magnet to my brothers' curious little brains. Now both Edward and Phillip are standing in my room.

"Boys, let me speak to your sister." Dad sounds calmer. He realizes I'm not on fire or anything. He shoos them out and closes my door. Judging by the shadows, they haven't gone far. I wonder if life would be easier if I had sisters.

"What's going on?" Dad asks.

"Here." I point to the computer. I've got the website up, but my email is closed. I know Dad wouldn't want me contacting this guy or any stranger.

He leans over and reads, but not for long. His eyebrows pull together.

"What's this?"

"Dr. Cologne is tracking an asteroid that's going to crash into Earth in the spring." I was nervous about telling my dad, but now I'm excited.

He starts reading again. I chew on my lip as I watch him scroll through the posts. I never noticed he's such a slow reader. When I can't take it anymore, I reach over and click the video from Dr. Cologne's office. My eyes jump from the screen to my dad to the screen to my dad.

"What do you think?" I ask when it's over.

"That was . . . that was interesting." He taps his fingers on the side of the laptop.

"What should we do?" My head is buzzing with ideas.

Do we need a bunker? How much water should we have? As much as I hate MREs, I think we need more. Should we call my aunts and uncles? Maybe it's better to tell them in person. We need to help Mack's family get ready too.

Dad chuckles. "What do you mean, what should we do? This is one of those satire videos."

"No, it's not." My face grows hot.

"Eleanor, you believe this nonsense?" He tilts his head and stares like we're speaking different languages.

"Dad, this doctor knows when it'll be TEOTWAWKI."

Dad groans and pulls out my desk chair to take a seat. "I'm going to strangle your grandfather."

"This has nothing to do with Grandpa Joe. I found the website. Me." I clench my fists. My fingernails dig into my palms. Bubbles tries to make her way into my lap, but I push her aside.

"Most kids don't know what TEOTWAWKI stands for. He's always talking about it and getting ready for the end of the world. He put the ideas in your—"

"No! I hate bug-out drills and lessons on water purifying. Edward and Phillip love that stuff. Not me." I shake my head. Dad should know this.

"Okay." He holds up his hands in surrender.

"Please. Just take a closer look." I get up and hand him my laptop. "Make sure you read everything. I'm going to get ready for bed."

I take my time brushing my teeth and getting a glass of water. I need Dad to study the evidence.

When I get back to my room, he's already closed my laptop and is scratching Bubbles behind her ears.

He looks up at me. "Thank you for showing me the website."

"And?"

"This asteroid is not a legitimate concern."

"The asteroid is real!"

"Perhaps. But it is not a threat to Earth. This is not how the world will end."

"Then how will it end?"

"No one knows, Eleanor. Not this guy. And not your grandfather."

"Dr. Cologne does know. He has a PhD from Harvard. He's one of the top astrophysicists in the world. He's written—"

"Calm down." Dad stops me. "Sometimes experts are wrong, or they abuse their position for notoriety."

"No."

"Everything about this feels wrong, Eleanor. This is not legitimate science. His website only has grainy satellite pictures and dire warnings."

I don't want to cry but can't help it. "But what if he is right?"

"It's my job to take care of you, and I promise, you are

safe from asteroids." Dad gives me his pity look—sucking in his lips, raising his eyebrows, and tilting his head.

I nod because I want to believe him. My dad is smart and knows stuff. But he's a mechanical engineer who designs air-conditioning systems for cars. He's not an astrophysicist.

"You need to promise me, if you're worried about this or if you have more questions, talk to me, please. I know you get worked up about things."

"Okay." And this is an absolute lie. I won't talk to Dad again until I have more proof. Until I can convince him this is real. As the asteroid gets closer to Earth, there's no way other scientists will stay quiet. There will be better pictures and more data. I have to be patient. Even though the world is ending in the spring, that's still two quarters of a school year away. And school years last forever.

• • •

My phone rings before my alarm goes off in the morning. The caller ID says Grandpa Joe.

"What's wrong?" he yells as I try to say hello.

"Nothing."

"Both you and your daddy called me last night. That never happens. Everyone all right?" He sounds like he's out of breath.

56

"When did Dad call?" I sit up and rub gunk from my eyes.

"Sometime after you. Are you going to tell me what's going on or should I ring him?"

"Don't call him unless you want to be yelled at."

"Wouldn't be the first time," he says.

For a second, I consider not telling him about Dr. Cologne, the asteroid, and the website. Adults have a funny way of looking at things. They make up their minds quickly. Sometimes before you've even finished explaining.

"Hello? Eleanor? You there?"

"Yeah." But Grandpa Joe is different than most adults. "Turn on your computer. I want to show you a website." I tell him the web address. Then I put my phone down on the bed and run to use the bathroom and let Bubbles into the backyard.

"Did you find it?" I ask when I get back to my room. My hands are still wet. I wipe them on my pajama pants.

"Holy Toledo," he says. "How'd you find this?"

"Kind of by accident," I admit.

"This . . . this . . . this is incredible." He whistles loudly, and I have to pull the phone away from my ear.

"So you believe it?" I ask.

"What's not to believe? This is a gosh-blang scientist telling us the world is ending. "Man, oh man, oh man, oh man."

Suddenly I worry that I might give Grandpa Joe a heart

attack with this news. I should have warned him, told him to sit down or something.

"Are you okay?" I ask.

"Sorry. Just trying to read it all. There's so much to take in."

"I know." I perch on the edge of my bed.

"Spring, huh? We've got five or six months to be ready."

These words take a weight off my shoulders. I'm not alone.

"Dad doesn't believe it."

"That boy. He always knows better. Is that why he called me late at night? It was after eight. Almost nine, actually."

"Yes, and nine o'clock is not late, Grandpa Joe."

"It will be after this asteroid strikes. We'll be going to bed when the sun goes to bed and gettin' up when the sun gets up."

"If we survive," I add.

"Oh, we will survive. Drosses are survivors." I can imagine him puffing out his chest.

"What are you going to tell Dad?" I ask. "He doesn't—"

"Don't you worry your pretty little head. I'll take care of your daddy."

"That's kind of sexist. Don't tell girls not to worry their pretty little heads."

"My apologies, soldier." He lowers his voice. "But I was serious about the other part. Don't worry about your daddy."

My phone vibrates in my hand. It's my alarm going off. Time to start the day.

"Thanks, Grandpa Joe. I gotta get ready for school. I'll talk to you later."

"Love you, Eleanor. And thanks for sharing this with me. We're going to be okay."

"Love you too."

I stare at myself in the mirror over my dresser. I still have an awful bluish haircut. I didn't finish my homework and need to do it over breakfast (without Dad seeing). I have gym class today, which always has a risk of embarrassment and injury. Yet somehow, everything feels like it's going to be okay. Not that an asteroid crashing into our planet is a good thing, but it does put everything else into perspective.

Chapter 8

Having a private conversation at lunch is impossible. I sit at the end of a table with Mack to my right. But because space is limited, there are kids across from us and on the other side of Mack. They talk to him sometimes, never to me.

We don't have assigned seats, but we always sit in the same spots. By the end of the first week of school, you know where you'll be parking your lunch bag for the rest of the year.

"Why don't our parents believe it?" Mack says. "This internet dude is a genuine scientist. Why would he make it up?"

"He's not making it up," I whisper as I tear my peanut butter and Fluff sandwich into bite-size pieces.

"At least your grandfather's on board." Mack holds his juice box inches from his dark glasses to see the flavor—cran-grape.

"Yeah, and that's probably more important than my dad or your parents buying it. Grandpa Joe knows stuff, and he can teach us. And our parents will have to come around eventually. It'll be all over the news."

Mack dips an apple in a caramel sauce. His lunches are always organic and healthy and still yummy.

"I just hope it's not too late. How long does it take to fully stock a bunker?" he asks.

"I don't know. If the weather forecaster predicts two inches of snow, all the stores run out of milk and bread. What's going to happen when they put the asteroid on their satellite maps?"

"Prepare for impact." Mack whistles and makes a sound like a bomb dropping. Half the table looks in our direction.

"Shh," I warn him.

"What are y'all talking about?" Spencer Davidson asks. Usually, he chats with Dominic Miller or Ajay Finley, but they're still in the lunch line.

"Nothing," I say quickly.

Spencer is white, with wild, curly red-brown hair that

flops over his eyes. He also has huge teeth that aren't exactly straight. And right now he's got chocolate stuck between all of them.

I can't help but run my tongue over my teeth.

"You said something about a bomb," Spencer insists. Then he imitates Mack's sound effects.

I shake my head.

"You can't talk about bombs at school. Not unless you're in social studies class." He crosses his arms, and he might be threatening to tell a teacher that we were talking about explosives.

"We were not talking about bombs!" I say this too loudly as Dominic and Ajay join the table.

"What bombs?" Ajay asks as he sets down a tray.

I elbow Mack in the side. "Tell them!" People always believe Mack. He's the most trustworthy kid in seventh grade.

"Okay." Mack swats at me. "Eleanor found this website that says—"

"No! Not that. Tell them we're not talking about bombs."

But it's too late.

"What website?" Spencer asks.

"What did you find?" Ajay asks.

"Was it about Mr. Furman? I heard he's been to jail," Dominic says.

Everyone is asking questions. My face grows hot and

sweaty. I want to run to the girls' room, but then I won't be here to keep Mack from telling them everything.

"Yes. We were talking about bombs," I say, trying to cover our tracks. "Did you know that they still find unexploded bombs and land mines in Germany from World War Two? I saw it on TV."

For a second, I think my plan has worked. I just need Mack to back up my story. I wrap my hand around his wrist and squeeze. We've been best friends for years; he should know what I'm trying to say without saying it.

"*That's* what you were talking about?" Spencer asks.

"Yes," I say, and squeeze Mack's wrist tighter.

"No," Mack says. He puts his other hand over mine and squeezes back. I know he's trying to calm me down, but my heart starts racing.

Spencer, Ajay, and Dominic lean closer.

"Tell us, Mack," Spencer says.

"So," Mack whispers. "We found a website that's predicted the end of the world. There's this Harvard professor who's tracking a meteor that's going to crash into Earth in March."

Ajay, Spencer, and Dominic look at each other, like they're trying to decide if they should believe it.

"A meteor? Really?" Spencer asks, speaking for the group.

"It's not a meteor. It's an asteroid. And not March. It's

April or May," I correct. If we're sharing information, we might as well be correct.

"It's going to be huge. Like the asteroid that killed the dinosaurs." Mack takes a drink of his organic cran-grape juice.

"No way," Dominic says. He's the shortest of the three boys. He's black, with light-brown skin and dark-brown hair, and wears plaid shirts all the time.

"No one knows if an asteroid killed the dinosaurs. Maybe cavemen overhunted them," Ajay says.

I stare at him hard. He takes off his glasses and cleans them on a napkin. He's Indian and has dark eyes, thick black hair that's neatly combed, and bushy eyebrows. I look to see if he's joking. He has to be. He's one of the *gifted* kids.

"No," Dominic says. "The dinosaurs went extinct because they didn't get on Noah's ark. Bon voyage, suckers!"

The three boys bust out laughing.

"That's totally what happened." I close my sandwich box and try to change the conversation. "Mack, did you finish your science homework?"

"We didn't have science homework." He's absolutely no help.

"So you're not fooling?" Spencer asks. "The world is going to blow up in April?" He's looking at me, not Mack.

"Or May. And the asteroid isn't big enough to destroy the

whole planet. Earth will still be around, but everything will be messed up. It's the end of the world as we know it."

"Unless we're in the direct path," Mack adds in his deepest voice. "It could totally evaporate us."

"Are we in the direct path? What's the trajectory?" Ajay asks. He sounds worried.

"Um . . . I don't know. If it is headed here, there's nothing we can do about it." I clear my throat. "What we need to worry about is the aftermath."

All eyes are on me. It's a weird feeling to be part of the lunch conversation for the first time ever.

"No electricity or clean water. We'll run out of gas within days. You'll only have what's left in your car. You won't be able to pump more because no electricity," I explain. "And it's not going to be like a tornado. They won't be able to clean it up in a week." I'm winging it. I don't know exactly what it'll be like, but Grandpa Joe and I have watched our share of prepper shows on cable over the years.

"How long until things are cleaned up and back to normal?" Spencer asks.

"Never!" Mack answers excitedly. I slap his arm.

"No. Years, probably. Because we will experience an ice age. At least that's what happened after the K-T extinction." They all stare blankly at me. I clarify. "The dinosaur extinction."

"What about global warming?" Ajay asks.

"Global warming won't help."

"So if the world is going to end, we don't need to worry about end-of-year testing?" Dominic asks.

I just shrug.

"Awesome! We shouldn't even bother with homework. Who's going to care about grades when there's no electricity or water or food?" Dominic smiles, and his brown eyes get squinty.

"If it lands in the ocean?" Spencer asks. "We'll be okay?"

"Hardly," I say. "Ever heard of a tsunami?"

He shakes his head.

"Look it up on the internet," I say. "There was a tsunami in 2004 that created a wall of water over one hundred fifty feet high. It took down buildings and drowned whole villages." After I read in Mrs. Walsh's book that the K-T asteroid created a tsunami, I had to look it up myself.

"No way." Spencer wrinkles his upper lip.

"An asteroid impact in the Atlantic could cause an even bigger tsunami."

"Asteroids, tsunamis, and bears. Oh my!" Londyn Diggs leans in from behind me. I jump, hitting my head on her lunch tray. How long has she been eavesdropping?

"Go away, Londyn," Spencer says.

"Losers will believe anything." She seems to be talking to the entire table, but she's staring at me.

"Whatever," Dominic says.

"I don't believe in fairies or trolls or leprechauns," Mack says in what I think is supposed to be an Irish accent.

She snarls and then walks away, proving that it only takes five seconds to ruin someone's day.

"What happens if the asteroid hits the Antarctic? If it hits ice?" Spencer asks.

"I'm not talking about this anymore."

The cafeteria lights dim and come back on, warning us we've got five minutes left to finish eating. I open my pudding cup and take a spoonful.

"This can't be real. I don't believe you," Ajay says. I know he's talking to me, even though my head's down. "I watch NASA TV all the time. They've said nothing about this."

I should have said nothing about this. More importantly, Mack should have said nothing.

"So it's not real?" Dominic asks. "It's a joke. Eleanor, I need to know. I have a book project due on Friday. 'Cause if it's real, and even if it's not coming till spring, grades from this whole school year aren't gonna matter. I don't want to waste my time. So is it real or not?"

"Dudes, calm down. Eleanor has told you all she knows." Mack packs up his lunch trash and unfolds Candy. "It's your life. Good luck in the apocalypse."

Our end of the table is quiet for a few seconds. Then Ajay asks a question.

"What's the website again?"

Chapter 9

Thursday after school, Grandpa Joe stops by our house unannounced. I worry it's another bug-out drill, but maybe that's not a bad thing.

"What's going on?" I pick up Bubbles as I hold open the front door. She's got a bad habit of bolting given the opportunity.

"Just dropping off a few things. Thought it would be best to do it while your daddy wasn't home." He winks at me.

"Have you talked to him?" It's been a few days, and Dad hasn't mentioned the asteroid or Grandpa Joe.

"We've exchanged some messages. He's worried about you when he should be worried about this dang asteroid.

Here." He hands me a tattered book he's been holding. "This is a good one. It'll get ya going."

"Really? I can have this?"

He nods.

I know this book. It's like a prepper's bible, and it's been in his living room as long as I can remember. I open the cover, and on the inside is a picture I drew of me and Grandpa Joe—stick figures. I think I was five or six when I created this masterpiece.

"Hang on one sec." He runs back to his truck and returns with a large blue plastic bin.

"What's in here?"

"Supplies. We're going to need more than bug-out bags." He steps inside the house.

On top of the pile are new water filters, a huge first-aid kit, and a small ax.

"We already have water filters in our packs."

"Oh, these are the best money can buy. The army uses these. We're not taking any chances, soldier. At least not with water. Got one for Mack too." He looks around the house. "Now, where should we put this so it won't be in your daddy's way?"

We find a spot in the basement behind my old Barbie Dream House. I throw a ratty blanket over the top, and it looks like another bin of toys and clothes we've outgrown. Bubbles tugs at the fringe, and I have to shoo her away.

"Thanks, Grandpa Joe. I'm glad you're on my side."

"Private Eleanor, there are no sides here. This is about survival. We are all in this together. Understood?"

I nod.

I invite him to stay for dinner, but he makes an excuse about running errands. I think he doesn't want to see Dad yet. It's easy to say there are "no sides" when the opponent isn't around.

In my room, I thumb through the book Grandpa Joe gave me. The first chapters cover water and food. We need to stockpile, but we also need ways to grow and raise more food. We can't live on MREs and canned goods forever. We'll be hunting, fishing, and farming. I've grown tomatoes, watermelons, and cucumbers at Grandpa Joe's house. Never been fishing or hunting. Maybe I'll become a vegetarian after the impact.

I grab an old notebook that's mostly empty, except for a few pages Edward or Phillip scribbled on with a red crayon. The cover has a drawing of dinosaurs grazing peacefully. *If you only knew what was coming!* I start a list of what we need and what we need to do.

Grandpa Joe's book also has a big section on personal protection. There are pages and pages on guns and ammunition. I know he has this stuff and keeps it locked in a huge safe in the basement. Adults can be in charge of all the firearms and ammo. Fine by me. But there's more to safety than weapons. Thankfully! This book says we should have dogs for perimeter protection. Not dog. Dogs! Two work better because they act as a team, and we will all form a pack like wolves.

"What do you think, Bubbles? Want a brother or sister?" I scratch under her head. She stretches her neck and closes her eyes. "We need something bigger and more vicious. No offense, but I've seen butterflies scarier than you."

On my computer, I search for "protective dogs." The internet suggests bullmastiffs, Doberman pinschers, Rottweilers, and other big breeds including German shepherds. That's the dog I really want. They're beautiful, loyal, and smart. Bubbles is beautiful too—long white fur, with a few dark spots and big brown eyes.

I find a website that sells fully trained shepherds for seven thousand dollars. Since we paid about one hundred dollars at the shelter for Bubbles, I don't think Dad is going to agree to the online attack dog.

"Maybe I can train you," I whisper in Bubbles' ear. "You don't have to attack. That's not your style. But you could bark and alert us to danger. What do you think? We'll all need to earn our keep. Okay?"

She licks my chin, which I interpret as her saying, *Not going to happen.*

• • •

Mack closes his locker and grabs my right elbow. Candy is in his other hand. He can get around the school as well as anyone, but we still like to walk this way. It's faster. At the start of sixth grade, people joked that we were girlfriend and boyfriend. Then they got used to it.

"Hey, Eleanor." Spencer runs up to us. "I checked out your website."

"Not *my* website," I mumble.

"You weren't lying. The asteroid is coming. What are we going to do?"

I blink hard. "What?"

"The world ends in April. Or May. Are we going to let it happen?" His voice grows louder, and other kids look over.

"What do you want us to do?" Mack asks. "Send up a missile to blow the asteroid to smithereens? We don't have that kind of equipment in our science class."

"Eleanor! Eleanor!" Ajay calls from behind us.

I debate abandoning Mack and ducking into the girls' bathroom. But he has a tight grip on my arm, like he can sense my desire to run away.

Ajay shoves a piece of paper at me. "Do you know about the Chelyabinsk asteroid? It was smaller than your asteroid."

I shake my head and groan. "Not *my* asteroid."

"What's Chelyabinsk?" Spencer asks. He stares at me, and I shrug because I have no idea.

Ajay waves us closer and whispers, "In February of 2013, an asteroid flew over Chelyabinsk in Russia and then crashed in Siberia. It was probably sixty feet wide, and none of the satellites or technology detected it. It was a surprise. If it had hit a city like New York or Tokyo, millions would have died. We got lucky."

"Was anyone hurt?" Mack asks, rocking on his feet.

"No one was killed," Ajay says. "But the sonic boom blew out glass in hundreds of buildings, and lots of people got cut up."

"Whoa!" Spencer said.

"There's video of it too." Ajay starts to pull out his cell phone, then stops. Phones aren't allowed in school, and the Wi-Fi is lousy.

"We need to warn people," Spencer says.

"The website's out there for anyone to see," I say as I try to walk past him. "It's everyone for themselves."

"My parents don't believe it." Spencer follows us.

"Mine neither," Ajay says.

What's with parents not believing Dr. Cologne?

Londyn Diggs passes us. She glares at me; her eyes are red and swollen. I try to step out of her path, almost knocking Mack into an open locker door.

"There's gotta be something we can do to be ready."

Spencer won't give up. He blocks us from going into home-room.

"Elle, you could teach us how to be prepared," Mack offers. "You're practically a prepper."

"What's a prepper?" Spencer asks. He pushes his floppy hair off his forehead.

"A *prepper*"—Mack emphasizes the word—"is someone preparing for the end of the world."

"Prepper," Spencer repeats. Then he pulls out a blue pen and writes it on his arm.

"Can I be a prepper?" Ajay asks.

"I'm not a prepper," I say. "I can't help. Look it up on the internet."

"Dude, you could totally do this," Mack says.

"Shut up." I elbow him hard.

"Ooof!"

"We're going to be late." I drag Mack into the classroom. "I can't help anyone. You should never have told them about the website. I wish I'd never found it." I say the words but don't mean them.

"Why? This is your chance to save the world, Eleanor Dross." He uses his deepest voice.

"No, I can't. And I don't want to."

"You're going to let our classmates die in a fiery asteroid crash?" Mack squeezes my arm. "That's not very nice."

"Nice is overrated. Besides, if it hits Hamilton or any-where in the Carolinas, there's no surviving."

We take our seats. Dominic walks by and drops a note on my desk. I slowly open the paper while the announcements begin.

When EXACTLY is the world ending?

Ugh. This is all Mack's fault.

I crumple the paper and turn my attention to the an-nouncements to avoid more questions. Every classroom has a TV in the corner. During the day, it looks like an analog clock with messages that occasionally scroll across the bot-tom. Like: *Bus 78 will be substituted for Bus 101* or *Volleyball tryouts are on Friday.* But in the morning, the TV actually works as a TV, and our daily announcements are brought to us live by a group of wannabe newscasters. The anchors sit behind the desk and read all our need-to-know news. It's usually dull, and the broadcasts are mostly ignored, but every once in a while something funny happens. Once Hope threw up while giving us the lunch menu, and Zariah ac-cidentally swore when he knocked over his mic. (It was the f-word.)

"The stuff about your asteroid should be on the an-nouncements," Spencer whispers loud enough for half the class to hear.

"Stop," I hiss through gritted teeth.

He nods rapidly. "Okay. We'll talk about it later."

Thanks to his warning, I avoid Spencer the rest of the day, even eating my lunch in the media center. Telling them about the asteroid and the website was more than generous of me—or generous of Mack; he's the one who yapped. My focus needs to be on saving my family, my dog, our house, and my one friend. That's enough to keep me busy until spring.

Chapter 10

No one at our end of the lunch table can keep quiet about the end of the world. Every day, Spencer, Ajay, and Dominic bug me for prepper information. (I'd eat in the media center, but Ms. Richmond has gotten strict about the no-food policy, claiming crumbs from my Rice Krispies Treats will attract the mice.) They ask questions about supplies and strategies, and Mack is no help. He makes it sound like I'm an expert. I know more than they do, but I'm still an amateur.

"We need to start a MAG," Mack suggests.

"What's a MAG?" Spencer asks.

"Stands for *mutual aid group*," Mack explains. He only knows this because last night on the phone I read him the MAG section from my book. "We should start one at school."

"Yes!" Spencer agrees.

"No," I say. "You weren't listening to me, Mack. That's not how it works. A MAG is for *mutual aid.* Like, you want someone in your group who can stitch up a cut and someone who can cook over fire. You need hunters and farmers and doctors. It's not an after-school club."

"It can be."

"According to most of our teachers, middle schoolers are useless. Ms. Regan doesn't even trust us to do our homework. We have to get our agenda signed nightly." I usually forget every third day or so. Maybe Ms. Regan is right about us.

"This is more important than homework."

Dominic shrugs. "Is homework ever important?"

"Let's do it," Spencer says. "Please."

"I think it's a good idea," Ajay adds, nodding.

"Like the school will let us start an end-of-the-world club. No way. Won't happen." I roll my eyes.

"We'd have to call it something else." Mack literally scratches his head.

"Scouts!" Spencer says, knocking over Dominic's milk in his excitement.

"Duh, that name is taken." I was a Brownie for half a minute. I liked the field trip to the science museum and hated selling cookies and singing songs.

"Elle, we need to do this." Mack pats my arm. "Start a club. Save lives."

"Not something that's on the top of my to-do list." Though I've never been a fan of to-do lists.

"How about this," Mack says, rocking in his seat. "A club will give us a time and a place to talk about prepping, and the asteroid, and the end of the world. We won't bring it up at lunch or in homeroom anymore. You don't talk about our MAG club outside of MAG club."

I like the idea of limiting when kids at school can discuss TEOTWAWKI. Maybe lunch will return to normal. I'll get to eat my sandwich in little torn-off pieces without everyone asking me questions.

"And you'll do this with me? You're not running off to that Conrad School tomorrow or something?"

"I will," Spencer says, even though I was talking to Mack.

"Dude, I'll totally do it with you." Mack doesn't say he's not running off.

"And you'll be the president, because I don't want to be president."

"Why do we need a president?" he asks.

"We don't. No titles." This might work. "You *all* have to promise not to talk about any of this outside the club."

I point at Spencer, then Ajay, and then Dominic and get them each to agree.

"Okay," I say, and squeeze Mack's hand.

"We're going to need a teacher. Someone to be our faculty advisor. And a place to meet." Mack has been part of clubs before. He even started a short-lived book club last year, so he probably knows what he's talking about. I've never joined anything that wasn't required.

"It's got to be Mrs. Walsh," I say.

"We'll ask her tomorrow."

For the last five minutes of lunch, no one talks about the end of the world. And it's wonderful.

• • •

The next morning, my dad drops off Mack and me early. Mack grabs my elbow, and we walk through the mostly empty school. Candy taps as we make our way to Mrs. Walsh's room.

My favorite school subjects are science, lunch (as long as no one talks about TEOTWAWKI), and homeroom (ditto about TEOTWAWKI).

Mrs. Walsh is nice to me even though I'll never be the top student and I rarely have the right answer. Teachers have favorites—the kids that get A's. You can't blame them. It's their job to educate. The kids with A's know stuff. Every profession must have favorites. A dentist probably likes the patients that brush and floss their teeth three times a day. A salesperson likes customers who buy lots of things.

Teachers like the smart kids. Case closed.

"Hey, y'all," Mrs. Walsh says when I knock on her open door. "Come in."

I lead Mack to seats in the back of the room near her desk.

"You caught me eating my breakfast." She holds up a cup of instant oatmeal. "What can I do for you?"

"Eleanor and I want to start a club, and we need a faculty advisor," Mack says.

"What kind of club?" she asks. "I ran a science club last year. There wasn't a lot of interest, to tell you the truth."

"It's a nature club," Mack says. We'd debated the name all night. We considered Genderless Scouts, Explorers, Adventurers, and Researchers. We hated them all, including Nature Club, but we didn't think End of the World Club would be acceptable.

"Nature Club? Do you think that's something your fellow students will want to join?"

"Hopefully not," I mumble under my breath.

"What was that?" she asks.

"Hmm, nothing." I look around to avoid her gaze.

"So what will this club do?" she asks, taking a scoop of oatmeal.

"Ya know, nature stuff." Mack folds his hands in his lap. "Eleanor is the brains behind this."

"Oh." She turns to me, and I guess I have to talk.

"It's kind of like . . . it's like learning to . . ." I'm trying desperately not to use the word *survive*. I thought about this all night in bed. And I even wrote notes to myself with tips but left those on my nightstand.

Mrs. Walsh tilts her head and raises her eyebrows like she's trying to decipher my mysterious language.

"It's about loving nature!" I spit out the words quickly. They're not the right words, but they'll do.

"And about what plants are edible and which ones will give you diarrhea." Mack is smiling, but he's not joking.

Mrs. Walsh turns to look at him. "Well, I don't like the idea of students eating plants that might make them sick."

"Or worse," Mack adds.

"No, no," I assure her. "We won't be eating any deadly berries." Why did I say *deadly*? You can't say *deadly* at school. It makes people nervous. When I'm not supposed to say something, why is that all I can think about? I wipe sweat off my forehead.

"Eleanor, are you okay?"

"Yeah. The club would be about appreciating and learning about nature. Specifically our local environment."

"Did you know some cultures eat bugs?" Mack asks.

"We've got a lot of bugs around here. Especially in the cafeteria. Kids who buy their lunch are probably eating them already. And I'm disadvantaged because I can't see if I'm about to bite into a cockroach."

Mack is not afraid of saying anything.

"We're not going to eat bugs either," I promise.

"So what do you need from me?" Mrs. Walsh throws away the empty oatmeal container and takes a sip from her water bottle.

"We want to use your room for meetings. You don't even need to be here." I can't tell if I'm asking for too much or not enough. Maybe she feels left out.

She holds up her index finger to make a point. "Technically, I do need to be here after school. Job requirement. My day doesn't end at two."

"Oh."

"But I like the idea of a student-led club. It shows initiative." She nods as she stares at me. If it were any other adult, I'd be suspicious—like she was trying to trick me into doing more work.

"Totally student led," Mack pipes up. "You don't need to do a thing. We got this!"

She clasps her hands. "Sounds good to me. I can do Wednesdays or Thursdays after school. And you have to promise you will not eat anything."

"No snacks?" Mack asks.

"Only the store-bought kind. Parents aren't going to be happy if someone gets sick from eating dandelions."

"They are edible," I say.

"Not on my watch." She points two fingers at her eyes and then at me.

We decide we will meet every other Wednesday starting next week. Mrs. Walsh recommends putting up signs in the hallway to advertise and adding it to the morning-announcements broadcast. I'd rather keep the whole operation classified.

We stand up, and Mack holds out his hand for me.

"Y'all make a great team," Mrs. Walsh says. "I hope your club is a tremendous success."

"Thanks. I hope so too." Even though I don't know what would make an end-of-the-world club a *tremendous success*.

Chapter 11

In the days leading up to the first Nature Club meeting, I have nightmares. I dream that the whole school shows up and demands all the supplies that Grandpa Joe has given me. As I'm handing out stuff, Mack turns on me. He tells everyone I'm a fake, and they lock me out of the school right as the asteroid is about to hit. It doesn't make much sense, except it's obvious that I'm dreading the meeting.

I write another email to Dr. Cologne to get his advice.

Dear Dr. Cologne,

I've found a group of colleagues who want to know more about this event. They want to be prepared. I've agreed to share what I've learned with them, but I'm afraid I'll stink at this. Do you have any suggestions?

Sincerely,
E.J.D.

He writes back the next day. It's a short, simple message.

E.J.D.,

If we are to survive as a species, we need more people like you.

I print out his email and tape it to a page in my dinosaur notebook. Maybe it'll give me the courage to survive the Nature Club. Then I make a list of things to talk about at the first meeting. I wouldn't be much of a prepper if I wasn't prepared for this (probably) catastrophic meeting.

• • •

On Wednesday, I feel like I have the flu or rabies or the plague. My body aches. I have chills. I want to throw up. But I know it's not a virus. It's the meeting.

When Mack and I arrive at Mrs. Walsh's room, two girls are already there. I don't know them—maybe they're sixth graders.

"Mack," I whisper. "We might have a problem."

"Stop stressing," he says.

"I'm not stressing. Not much." This is a useless lie because both of us know it's a lie. "What do we do about people who show up for a real Nature Club?"

"What do you mean?"

"What if people are actually here to learn about nature? They don't know about TEOTWAWKI. They think this is a legit club." I knew this was a bad idea.

"Oh, like in a movie when a customer goes into an Italian place, and they don't realize that it's not a normal restaurant, that it's a front for the mob," Mack says.

"What are you even talking about?"

"Those dudes who send back their spaghetti don't know that there's a hit man in the kitchen."

"You're no help." I put my backpack on a chair near the front of the room. I smile at the girls but look away before I see if they smile back.

Mrs. Walsh waves me to her desk.

"This is exciting. The first meeting." She grins. "Are you okay?"

I swallow. "I'm fine."

"Do you need me to do anything?"

"Maybe call the meeting off," I say without thinking.

"Is that what you want?" she asks.

I shake my head.

"Are you nervous?" She puts a hand to her chest. "Am I making you nervous?"

I shrug. "I don't know." She's not the reason I'm freaking out. I hate talking in front of people—especially my *peers,* who I'm certain are making fun of me in their heads. And sometimes they don't even bother to keep it in their heads.

"How about I stay in my office?" She gestures to a small room behind her that has a large window. I wouldn't have called it an office. It's more of a closet where she keeps the dangerous and fun science equipment like chemicals and Bunsen burners. "It might be easier to be yourself without a teacher hovering over you."

"It might be easier without *anyone* hovering around. I've been having nightmares about this meeting." I let out a breath that blows the hair off my forehead.

She clasps her hands suddenly. "Let's try an experiment. Instead of thinking about this as a nightmare, let's imagine it's going to go well. Fantastic, even."

I raise my eyebrows. "That's not much of an experiment."

"True." She laughs. "But I hypothesize that this meeting will be great if you expect it to be great. Can you give it a try?"

I want to roll my eyes, but she's being nice, so I nod.

"Wonderful."

Other kids, including Spencer, Ajay, and Dominic, file

in. The meeting doesn't start for three more minutes, and we've already got eight people. If we reach ten, my chest might explode.

"Once you start, I'll be in my cave, if you need me." She points with her thumb. "But I know you can handle this."

"Okay." Every part of me is sweating. I should go home. Nature Club is a threat to my health.

Mack, meanwhile, makes his way to the front of the class. Candy taps across the floor. He positions himself in Mrs. Walsh's usual spot. He can't see that all eyes are on him, but he knows it—and loves it.

It makes no sense that my best friend adores the spotlight, while I'd rather hide in a dark hole. Or maybe it makes perfect sense.

When his watch beeps, he loudly claps his hands twice.

"Let's get this meeting started," he says in his center-of-attention voice. "I'm Mack Jefferson, co-founder of Hamilton Middle School's one-and-only Nature Club." He rocks back and forth as he talks.

"Let me speak to your members this once," Mrs. Walsh whispers to me. "Then I promise to get out of the way."

I slide into a seat near the windows as Mrs. Walsh joins Mack at the front of the room.

"Listen up, y'all." She reminds everyone to keep the room clean, to be respectful of the school and each other, and that all science-class rules apply after 2 p.m. like they do before 2 p.m. Then she goes to her office. She closes the door part of the way.

"My co-founder is Eleanor Dross," Mack picks back up, and I do a little wave. "Who else is here? Introduce yourselves."

"I'm Spencer."

"Hey, Spencer," Mack replies.

"Dominic Miller."

"Hi, Dominic," Mack says.

"Ajay Finley. Seventh grade. I'm in Mr. Furman's homeroom."

"Thanks, Ajay, for all the information," Mack jokes.

"Wyatt McClure," another boy says. I don't know him. He's tall, white, and dresses like my dad in khaki pants and a blue collared shirt.

"Oh hey, Wyatt. Thanks for coming." I can't tell if Mack knows Wyatt or if he's just being friendly Mack. He probably knows him. Mack knows everyone.

The white girl with long blond-and-pink hair speaks. "I'm Jade Gilchrist, and she's Izabell Medina-Flores."

Izabell is Hispanic, with shoulder-length black hair, and she's tiny. She could pass for a fourth grader easily. Both girls wear well-worn matching friendship bracelets. I can imagine they've had them on for years.

"Hey, Izabell. Hey, Jade. I'm glad you came," Mack says to the girls.

There's a pause.

"Is that everyone?" Mack asks.

"Yep," Spencer answers.

"Okay. Nature Club is a very special club," Mack says. "It could literally save your life."

The girls exchange looks. I can't tell if they're confused or scared or maybe even amused.

"We will talk about ways nature can hurt us and harm us," Mack continues. "These might be the most important lessons you've ever learned in a school."

I pull out my dinosaur notebook with my ideas. It's not going to be easy to teach a class on survival without explaining that's what I'm doing.

"Can we get to the good stuff?" Dominic asks.

"Yeah," Spencer agrees. "Like how do we build a bunker?"

I glance back at Mrs. Walsh. She's staring at her computer.

"That's for my co-founder to address." Mack adjusts his dark glasses. "Take it away, Elle."

I can't move. I might pee myself if I try to stand.

"Um . . ." I look at my notebook. Everything is blurry.

"Come on. Tell us how to build a bunker," Spencer whines. "I haven't bothered you at lunch all week."

"We're not building bunkers," I mumble. "That's not the purpose of Nature Club."

Izabell raises her hand, which is weird because I'm not a teacher. "Isn't this the secret club to get ready for the end of the world?" she asks, her voice even softer than mine.

"Um . . . where did you hear that?" I ask.

She points at Mack. *Of course.*

I turn to Wyatt. "Is that why you're here?"

"I guess," he says. "My goal is to join every club at Hamilton Middle. I'm building my résumé."

"How can you join every club?" Ajay asks. "Some meet at the same time. Chess Club meets on Wednesdays too."

"I was in Chess Club in seventh grade," Wyatt explains. "I don't need to be in everything at once. I need to join each for a school year. I even joined the Girls in STEM Club."

"You did?" Jade asks.

"Yeah, my father threatened to sue the school if they didn't let me in. I was the treasurer. Do y'all need a treasurer?"

"No," I answer.

Mrs. Walsh still isn't paying us any attention. I wave for everyone to come closer. Spencer leads Mack over. We form a tight circle.

Expect it to be great, and it will be great. I take a deep breath.

"Okay, officially, this is Nature Club. Don't call it anything else." I look around for nods of agreement. "We won't be building bunkers. That's not realistic. We've got to keep it real."

"I always do," Mack says.

"And don't invite anyone else. This is enough." Maybe I should get these *rules* in writing. "Everyone knows about the asteroid, right?"

The boys from lunch nod. Wyatt, Jade, and Izabell look lost.

"I guess we need to start there." I review everything I know about 2010PL7, which is still very little. But it's kind of amusing to watch everyone's reaction. Spencer has a big, goofy grin. Wyatt's eyes are enormous. Izabell nods her head like it all makes complete sense.

"I don't believe this," Jade says, throwing up her hands.

"Then why are you here?" I ask.

"Two words." She holds up her fingers. "Global warming."

"Oh."

"Oceans are rising. Extreme weather events are happening all the time. Greenhouse gases are choking our environment. By 2080, half the plants are going to be gone, and one-third of the animals!"

"All true, I think." I'm not going to argue with her. "But this asteroid will be here well before 2080. It'll be here next year."

"Are we all going to die?" Dominic clutches his heart dramatically, like we're acting out Shakespeare scenes in language arts class.

"No, assuming it doesn't hit close to North Carolina. We will live, and we will be prepared. This is natural selection. The prepared survive."

"I don't think that's what Darwin meant," Mack says.

"Who's Darwin?" I ask.

"Dude, he came up with natural selection." Mack laughs.

"That's right." I feel stupid for a second, but then I make a joke. "I thought he was that new kid from Portland in our homeroom."

"Get to the point, please," Spencer says. "I know about the asteroid. What do I need to do to survive?" He takes out a composition notebook that I know is meant for journaling in language arts class, because I have one just like it.

"Okay, okay. Let's start with basic needs. We all know what those are, right?"

"Food, water, and shelter," Ajay says, giving the standard social studies answer.

"Yes, sort of. But we need clean air first. Oxygen," I explain.

"You can't breathe, game over." Mack slumps in his chair like he's a goner.

"Our air already has too much carbon," Jade says.

"This will be worse. Depending on where it strikes. I've been reading a lot about the asteroid that killed the dinosaurs. The K-T extinction. If this hits land, like the dino asteroid did, it will throw rock and dirt and dust into the air. But it's not only rock. The pressure and speed will make them flaming rocks—flaming glass, really. As they rain down, forest, fields, buildings will catch on fire. Then we will have dust, dirt, *and* smoke. So, yeah, clean air might be a problem." I don't bother to tell them that, over time, oxygen levels could decrease if plants are deprived of light and can't photosynthesize. That's down the line, not a problem to discuss at our first meeting.

"Did you know that every year an asteroid bigger than a car strikes Earth somewhere?" Ajay adds.

"Is that true?" Izabell asks, staring at me.

I shrug. "I don't know. Ajay is smart, so I assume he's right."

"I am right! I love astronomy. Ask me anything about our universe. I can name all the planets and most of their moons." Ajay takes a breath like he's about to drown us in space talk.

"Don't get him going!" Dominic puts a palm in Ajay's face.

"I don't care about other planets," Spencer says. "I care about surviving on this one. I'm going to buy a gas mask off Amazon or eBay, just in case."

"Do what you want. Back to the other needs. Clean water is at the top of the list. You can go for days without food, but water is super important. The sinks in our homes might not work, and if they do, the purification plants won't be running. So the water in your house could be contaminated. Drink it, and you'll get sick."

"Our oceans are already contaminated! They're more acidic than they've ever been in human history." Jade's wearing an aqua-blue shirt that says ONE EARTH, ONE OCEAN. I wonder if she wore it specifically for today's meeting. Or maybe she cares about the environment all the time.

"You can't drink ocean water, anyway." Spencer turns his back on Jade. "How can we tell if the sink water is clean, Eleanor?"

"Assume it's not," I say.

"Get a water purifier," Mack says. "Do it like today. I got one."

"After water, we need food and shelter. The food should include ready-to-eat meals and stuff to cook, and even seeds to grow. As for shelter, it's not just your house."

"Yeah, it should be a bunker," Spencer says.

I ignore him. "Your house needs to be protected, and you have to remember there won't be any electricity. You'll have to cook without a stove or microwave. You'll need to heat the house without the thermostat. Shelter isn't only the building. It's all this stuff."

Izabell raises her hand again. "How do you know all this?"

"I've read a few books."

"And her grandfather is a major prepper. He does have a bunker, sort of," Mack says. I should elbow him in the ribs, but he's too excited. Nothing short of a gag is going to keep him quiet.

"He doesn't have a bunker, but yeah, he's really into this stuff." I was worried my prepper grandfather would be an embarrassment, but in Nature Club, he's kinda cool.

"I think Eleanor should be president," Spencer says.

"I'll be treasurer," Wyatt offers again.

"She doesn't want a title," Mack answers. "No titles!"

"I don't know." I shrug. I've never been president, captain, or boss of anything. No one has ever suggested that I could be. "Maybe being president wouldn't be so bad."

We hold a quick election by raising our hands. I'm unanimously selected as president. Mack is vice president. Wyatt takes the treasurer spot (I don't know what funds he'll be tracking), and I'm also assigned secretary because of my neat handwriting.

The rest of the meeting flies by as we randomly talk about first aid, gardening, building fishing nets, bartering, and dogs. It probably would have been better if we went in some kind of order, even alphabetical, because most of the group looks overwhelmed.

"That's a lot to think about," Ajay says.

"I know." I close my notebook. "We've got some time to figure this all out."

"When's the next meeting?" Jade asks.

"In two weeks," Mack answers. "Same time. Same place."

"No," she whines.

"That's too long to wait," Spencer adds. "Can't we meet every Wednesday?"

I smile and say, "I'll think about it."

Starting this club might be one of the smartest decisions I've ever made. Right behind adopting Bubbles (I picked her out) and agreeing to be Mack's special helper in kindergarten. Or maybe I should wait for the next meeting before declaring myself a genius.

Chapter 12

On Saturday, Mack and I go to Grandpa Joe's house for a class on tying knots and starting fires. This lesson was my idea, but I didn't realize we'd be doing it outside in the freezing cold. We sit on his back deck in our warmest coats and the wind still cuts through.

"These are skills everyone in my generation learned when they were knee high," Grandpa Joe says as he untangles various ropes.

I tilt my head and stare at him. "I thought your generation invented fire. Ya know, when you were living in the caves and hunting mammoths."

Mack laughs and then blows on his hands to keep them warm.

"Soldier, this is serious. No more jokes." But Grandpa Joe isn't being serious either. He smiles and winks at me.

"Yes, sir." I salute him.

He holds up two bundles, one white and one blue. "This is rope." He gestures to the white one. "And this is cordage."

"What's the difference?" I know it's not the color.

"This isn't an English class, but here's how I think of it. Rope is made of natural fibers and it's thicker, at least a quarter-inch diameter." He hands me the white bundle and I share it with Mack.

"And cordage is synthetic, smaller, and usually has an outer layer called a mantle. This is military five-fifty cord, or parachute cord."

"We going skydiving?" Mack asks.

"We're trying to survive, not die." I give him the parachute cord to check out.

"And I got you these." Grandpa Joe reaches into a plain plastic shopping bag and pulls out a handful of braided rope. He gives me a brown-and-green version and a gray one.

"A paracord bracelet. Thanks!" I've had these before but always seem to lose them. "In case of emergency, you can unravel it and have about two yards of strong cordage. To pitch a tent or tie a bear," I explain for Mack's sake. I place the gray bracelet in his hand and put his finger on the plastic-dipped end that you pull to unravel.

"You can also use them to tie up your britches."

Grandpa Joe yanks his pants up under his giant belly. "Got one for each of the boys too. Don't want 'em feeling left out."

I fasten Mack's around his left wrist before clasping my own. In a way, they're friendship bracelets, like the ones Jade and Izabell have. But these have an even bigger purpose.

"Now let's get movin' on knots, soldiers. We'll use the rope, not cordage, 'cause it's easier to work with. We'll start with a slipknot."

"Can we build a fire first? It's so cold out here." I hold up my gloved hands. My fingers don't feel like they're able to cooperate.

"Private Eleanor, we've got to toughen you up." Grandpa Joe shakes his head but can't hide his grin.

He launches into a lesson on fire that starts with the reasons we need it—cooking, protection, warmth. The easiest way to start a fire is with matches or a lighter. Of course, he's not going to let us go that route. He takes out a flint-and-steel set from a nylon bag.

"To start a fire we need a starter, oxygen, and fuel." We have the starter and oxygen, and he teaches us how to build a "bird's nest" for fuel. I'm relieved when we don't have to snatch one from a tree. We build our own with twigs and grass and bits of rope.

"Good job, soldiers," Grandpa Joe says when we have our nests ready. He demonstrates how to use the flint and steel.

He holds the C-shaped piece of steel in his right hand and quickly runs the piece of flint over it. Sparks fly with each strike. Then he moves his tools over his bird's nest and ignites it.

I give Mack a play-by-play of the demonstration.

"I smell the smoke," Mack says. "We should have s'mores."

Grandpa Joe makes fire-starting appear easy, and I'm excited to try. I hit the flint against the steel. Nothing. I do it again and again, turning the rock in my hand, trying to find the sharpest edge. I might as well be hitting my head against a tree. It would have the same outcome.

"Ugh." I throw down the tools after I hit my knuckles for the tenth time.

"This is why we practice," Grandpa Joe says.

Mack is anxious to try too. Grandpa Joe guides his hands so he gets the motion down, and I'm jealous when I see a spark. But it's not enough to light the bird's nest. Mack gives it several more attempts on his own. No fire.

"I think we need to stockpile matches," I say.

"Dude, that's a good idea."

Grandpa Joe takes pity on us and lights my bird's nest. He uses it to start a bigger fire in his outdoor pit. Now I really am in the mood for s'mores. We're about to turn our attention back to tying knots when Mack's phone joins the conversation.

"Text message from Mom. Do you want me to read it?" Siri asks.

"Yes."

Siri speaks again. "I need to pick you up early. Gavin Smithfield is coming over this afternoon."

Mack tells Siri to text his mom "Okay." And he gets a reply that Mrs. Jefferson will be here in fifteen minutes.

Grandpa Joe shakes his head. "I'll be glad when cell towers go down. I'm tired of these blasted phones." He chuckles.

"Who's Gavin Smithfield?" I ask Mack. I usually like cell phones, but now I kind of agree with Grandpa Joe.

"He's a student from the Conrad School. He's in town for the weekend, and my mom wants me to meet him."

My heart sinks. "Why?"

"Obviously, Mom is trying to find me a new best friend," Mack says. "Better watch out, Elle—you're being replaced."

"Ha ha. Like anyone else could put up with you." I try to make it sound like I'm joking around and don't care.

"You're not replaceable," Grandpa Joe butts in. "You'll always be Mack's number one girl."

"Ew, Grandpa. That sounds gross."

Mack laughs. "Mom thinks talking to this kid will help me make a decision about Conrad. It's my chance to ask questions that I wouldn't ask a teacher or counselor. *What are the parties like? How much homework do you get?* That kind of stuff."

Decision?

"Mack, you're wasting your time. The world is ending."

"I know, right? This asteroid is messing with all our plans. We won't be going to *any* schools next year, or the year after that, or the year after that." He rocks in the lawn chair.

"Then why talk to Gavin?" I ask, trying to keep my voice from sounding jealous or annoyed.

"Makes Mom happy."

"Smart man," Grandpa Joe says. "Now we'd better wrap up this exercise, soldiers. We have enough time for a slip-knot and a bowline." He hands us each about three feet of white rope. I'm not as interested as I was two minutes ago. Still, I watch and repeat.

Then Grandpa Joe tries to demonstrate for Mack.

"I always say I could tie twenty different types of knot with my eyes closed. But this is the first time I'm going to actually try." Grandpa Joe and Mack both laugh. I'm not in the mood. We practice our knots until Mrs. Jefferson's Volvo pulls into the driveway.

"Guess that's it for today, Private Mack." Grandpa Joe gathers up his rope.

"Thank you, sir," Mack says, and they shake hands.

Then I guide Mack to the car. He thinks he needs to make a decision about his future. But 2010PL7 has already decided the future for him, for me, for all of us.

Chapter 13

Mack doesn't mention his meeting with the kid from Conrad, and I don't ask about it. I'm too busy preparing for the next Nature Club meeting, which requires sacrifices like skipping math homework and ignoring my brothers. After the asteroid crashes, I'll be spending all my time with Edward and Phillip—not by choice—and I already know enough math to survive an apocalypse.

At lunch on Wednesday, I scribble a few last thoughts in my dinosaur notebook.

"Why so quiet?" Mack asks.

"I'm just thinking about the meeting."

"Shh. We aren't supposed to talk about *you know what*," he whispers.

"I didn't say what meeting. You did." I close my note-book. Today we're going to focus on the first seventy-two hours after impact.

"Does this mean I'm banned for life?"

"Consider it a warning." I open my chocolate pudding and lick the lid.

"You can ban me just for today, because I'm not going to be there anyway."

"What?" I shout, and half the table looks at me.

"Dude, calm down. I have swim tryouts."

"That's Thursday," I say.

"Got switched."

"You have to go to Nature Club. I can't—"

"Ah! You said Nature Club! You're banned." He laughs.

"Stop messing around, Mack." I grab his arm and squeeze so he knows I'm serious. "Skip the tryouts. Have your parents write a note. There's no way they won't let you on the team. That would be discrimination or something."

"*You* stop messing around, Elle. I'm going to the try-outs." He pushes my hand off his arm.

The lights dim, giving us the five-minute warning. Mack doesn't say anything else for the rest of lunch, and neither do I. There's nothing left to say.

After school, I walk into Mrs. Walsh's room alone. Twelve kids are there, and none of them is my best friend. All afternoon, I was hoping he'd have a change of heart. Lately, his priorities seem out of whack. Swim team and Conrad aren't important. Not now and not in the spring.

Still, I'm ready. I have over ten pages of notes, and we only have an hour. Explaining the difference between a water filter and a water purifier could take half that time. I practiced my lesson last night in the mirror and timed myself. (I wonder if teachers do the same thing.) I think I can do this.

Then I notice Londyn Diggs in the second row. Londyn I-Want-to-Ruin-Eleanor's-Life Diggs! Maybe she has detention, because I can't imagine why she's here. Maybe to torture me. It's not enough to do it in gym class. I'd run out right now if I could still catch my bus.

Everyone is chatting in small groups. I take a seat by myself. I don't know what to do. I pretend to play on my phone for about five minutes.

"Eleanor?" Mrs. Walsh stands in front of me. "Are you ready to start the meeting?"

"Mack's not here," I blurt out as an explanation.

"I can see that." She smiles. "You're here. You're in charge."

My stomach rolls over.

"Do you want me to do something? I could call the meeting to order," she offers.

"No, I'll do it." This is too important to let Londyn ruin my meeting. I suck in a big breath. It does nothing to stop my legs from shaking.

Mrs. Walsh retreats to the back office and leaves us alone. I walk to the front of the room where Mack stood at the last meeting.

"Hey, um . . . I call this meeting of Nature Club to order."

"What's this stupid club about?" Londyn asks, and one second after a call to order, I'm ready to adjourn.

"You don't know?" Spencer looks at Londyn and then at me.

"I'm new. I want to hear it from her." She points her black-painted fingernail at me.

I freeze under her stare.

"I could give the financial report," Wyatt offers after a few agonizing silent seconds. "So far, we've taken in zero dollars and we've spent zero dollars."

"Gee, thanks," Dominic says, rolling his eyes.

"What's this club about?" Londyn asks again, pausing between every word.

"We want to learn about and celebrate nature." I hold up my notebook. I wrote our fake motto on the cover in the sky above the dinosaurs. I thought it would keep prying eyes out if I had a boring description. "If that doesn't interest you, feel free to go."

"Oh no, I'm very interested. And that's not what this is

about." She smiles, and I expect to see fangs, but she has normal teeth.

"Isn't it a survivalist club?" one of the other new guys asks.

There's no point in denying it.

"Shh." I hold my finger to my mouth. "No, it's not. Not officially."

"Who told you?" Dominic asks the kid.

"Mack Jefferson," the boy says.

"And who told you?" I ask Londyn.

She raises one eyebrow. "Mack Jefferson." I don't believe her.

"No one can tell anyone else about this club, okay?" I stare at my hands. "And I'll talk to Mack and make sure he keeps his trap shut. Let's get started. The first seventy-two hours are critical. Obviously, you can't survive a year if you don't make it through the first three days. Let's go over what we—"

"Excuse me, Eleanor," Spencer interrupts. "Shouldn't we be telling everyone?"

Izabell raises her hand. I point to her, and she speaks. "I told my cousin." She shrugs.

"They'll find out soon enough," I say. "At some point, the asteroid will be so close that NASA and other government agencies will have to say something. All the planetariums across the world will see it in their big telescopes. There will be a panic." I twist my new paracord bracelet. It's stiff and uncomfortable, like this meeting.

"Won't it be too late?" Spencer asks.

"It might be," Ajay answers. "Just last week, ATLAS spotted an asteroid over a thousand feet wide, and it will pass between Earth and the moon on Friday. That's less than a ten-day warning. And no one spotted the Chelyabinsk asteroid that crashed in Siberia. It was—"

"You've told us!" I cut Ajay off.

"What is ATLAS?" Spencer asks.

"It stands for *Asteroid Terrestrial-impact Last Alert System*. It's in Hawaii." Ajay pushes up his glasses and looks ready to give a longer lecture on terrestrial-impact systems.

"Guys, stop. We're not here for an astronomy lesson. That club can meet on Mondays. I agreed to show you some basic survival techniques. So you won't be zombies."

"Zombies?" Dominic asks. His eyes are wide, and I can't tell if he's surprised or scared or excited.

"There's going to be zombies?" Spencer smiles like this is the best news he's heard yet.

Londyn laughs. "This is more messed up than I'd hoped."

"Not the undead kind of zombie. Not brain-eaters. A zombie is someone who isn't prepared. It's a silly nickname." I guess these people aren't spending hours watching prepper YouTube videos and training with their grandfather on weekends.

Jade groans and takes out her phone. I wonder if she's bored or double-checking my information.

I continue. "Ya know how in movies zombies walk around lost and basically are brainless idiots. That's how we imagine the unprepared after TEOTWAWKI."

Most everyone looks confused, like I'm teaching algebra, except Spencer.

"I know that one." He practically jumps out of his chair. "The end of the world as we know it." Maybe Spencer has a YouTube addiction too.

"Yes." This gives me an idea. "Maybe we should have a vocabulary lesson." I decide to delay the seventy-two-hour discussion.

Spencer pulls out his composition notebook. "Great!"

"Okay. You know zombies are the unprepared who will be the lost souls after TEOTWAWKI. Then there's SHTF."

I look around to see if anyone wants to guess what it means. Nope.

"The PG version is *stuff hits the fan.*"

Londyn announces to everyone what the R-rated version is.

"Thanks, I think we could've figured that out," I say without looking at her.

"What else?" Spencer asks. If this were a class, he'd be the annoying student who asks for more homework and interrupts the teacher with *interesting facts* every two seconds.

I open my dinosaur notebook. I've been jotting down acronyms as I learn them, but I don't have an official list.

"WROL. That stands for *without rule of law*. It's basically a world without laws."

"I like the sound of that," Dominic says. He leans back in his chair and clasps his hands behind his head.

"Don't be stupid!" I snap.

Dominic flinches.

"Sorry. I'm not talking about rules like no bedtime or homework. There won't be police to arrest thieves or even murderers. No one will be running the jails. It'll be chaos. It'll be scary."

"What's going to happen to the police?" Ajay asks.

"It's going to be every family for themselves," I say.

"Or everyone for herself," Londyn adds. She chews on one of her blackened nails.

"The police will be home taking care of their own families. No one will go to their jobs because no one will be getting paid." I don't know why they can't imagine the world after the asteroid.

Everyone looks serious. Maybe I'm finally getting through to them.

"Next," I say. "BOB is for *bug-out bag*. You should have three days' worth of supplies packed and ready to go. BOL is *bug-out location*. If your primary shelter is destroyed, where are you going to go? MAG is *mutual aid group*."

"Slow down," Spencer says as he scribbles in his composition notebook.

"We don't need to know all this," Londyn says. "Definitions aren't going to save anyone."

"No . . . but, um, it's helpful, I think." I hate that I sound like a little kid.

She throws her head back and gives an evil, cartoon-villain laugh.

I twist my bracelet again and again until my wrist burns. She notices.

"What's that for?"

"It's a paracord bracelet," I mumble.

"I know that! Why do you need it at school? Are you going to pitch a tent? Make a tourniquet? Totally useless. I can't believe anyone would listen to you." Londyn puts her feet on the desk. Her black combat boots land with a thud.

My face burns and my throat dries up. I should kick her out or tell her off or maybe even smack her. Instead, I look down and blink a lot to keep my eyes from filling with tears.

"I want to know this stuff," Izabell says. "Even if the asteroid misses us, it seems like important stuff."

"It won't," I mumble.

"But *if* it does miss us," Jade says, "we'll still have to deal with global warming."

"I want to know this stuff too," Ajay chimes in. "Knowledge is power." He pumps his fist in the air.

Londyn drops her feet from the desk and leans forward.

"Waste. Of. Time." Her stare dares me to say something. I can't.

I close my notebook, shove it in my backpack, almost tearing the cover, and then leave the meeting. If Mack doesn't need to be here, neither do I. My leadership days are over. Let them all—especially Londyn Diggs—turn into zombies.

Chapter 14

That evening, Mack calls my cell three times before I finally answer. I figure he's not giving up, and my only options are to talk or turn off my phone.

"What?" I say.

"Hello to you too. How was the meeting?"

"Just because I answered the phone doesn't mean I'm talking to you." I grab Bubbles, and we curl up on my bed. She's the only one who can make me feel better.

"That makes a lot of sense. Well, if you're not talking to me, I guess I'll talk to you. Hmm. You probably want to know how swim tryouts went."

He pauses. I stay quiet.

"I made the team." He imitates the sound of a crowd cheering. "Yay, Mack! You da man!"

His celebration feels like it lasts for ten minutes. I ignore him and pick bits of grass out of Bubbles' white fur.

"Well, I assume I did," he continues, "because there are twenty spots and only twelve guys showed up."

I groan.

"And I won every heat, including backstroke, which is my worst."

"So you didn't even need to be there." I break my short-lived silent treatment.

"Yeah, I needed to be there. Doofus. If you want to be on the team, you try out for the team."

"You committed to the Nature Club first."

"I've been swimming since I was a fetus." The usual cheerful sounds in Mack's voice are gone. He doesn't get upset often, hardly ever. But he's well on his way, and I keep pushing.

"I didn't want to do the Nature Club. You made me, and then you abandoned me." I could cry, the angry kind of cry where my tears sting my eyes. Bubbles nudges me with her paw.

"It's not abandoning you if I have something else to do. Come on. You know that."

I huff. "I needed you."

"What happened?" His voice softens.

"Londyn Diggs showed up." I pause to keep myself from yelling. "Did you tell her about the club?"

Silence. For a second, I think he's hung up, but I look at the phone and see we're still connected.

"Mack?"

"Yeah."

"You told her?" I ask again.

"Yes. I told her."

"Why?"

"We were both waiting in the guidance office yesterday. And she was crying."

I imagine her bawling and feel no sympathy.

"I asked her what was wrong. She wouldn't say. I told her whatever it was wouldn't matter after spring because the world is ending."

I hit my head against my pillow. Why does he have to talk to everyone?

"I didn't think she was even listening, but she texted me last night. I gave her the website and told her to come to the meeting."

"She hates me."

"No, she doesn't."

I think about her pushing me around at the meeting, bothering me at lunch, and trying to take my head off with a basketball.

"She's evil," I say.

"Sounds like *you* don't like *her,*" Mack says.

Londyn Diggs used to be nice in elementary school—well, at least not mean. We were in the same dance class that I quit after two months. She used to draw cool comics and would win all the art awards at the end-of-year school celebrations. She even invited me to her birthday party—I didn't go, of course, because Mack wasn't asked. (It was girls only.)

Then in sixth grade she got new friends. I guess they were the popular kids—they're the ones with colorful hair now. Londyn and her group hung out all the time and went to Skate World every Friday night. She was going out with Jeremy Donahue, the unofficial cutest guy at Hamilton. By the end of the year, she had a new boyfriend, Cole somebody, who had gone to a different elementary school than us. Sometimes it's hard to keep track.

"I *don't* like her. Not after the meeting. The only thing she did was interrupt me and insult me."

"She interrupted?" Mack shrieks, mocking me. "How awful. We should hand out demerits."

"If she shows up again, I'm out. I'm not doing it."

"Don't be like that, Elle," he says softly.

"We basically hate each other. Why should I be around that? The world is ending soon. We should be spending our last precious months with people we like."

118

"Or . . . maybe we should spend our last few months being more kind and tolerant."

I wrinkle my lip in disgust. "You sound like a teacher."

"I also think we should make a bucket list for these final months," he says.

"What? Being kind and tolerant isn't enough?"

"Nope. We need to get tattoos and body piercings and gauges." He laughs, but I worry he's at least partially serious.

"I'm going to hang up now," I warn, trying not to encourage him. I can only imagine Mrs. Jefferson's outrage if Mack put gauges in his ears. "Congrats on making the swim team that accepts everyone. I'll talk to you later."

"Dude, I'm not kidding. We're getting matching tattoos. We'll go—"

I don't hear the rest because I've hung up. Tattoos are not part of my survival strategy.

• • •

The next day, I creep through the morning like I'm waiting for an attack. Londyn and I only have PE and lunch together. Classrooms are safe. The halls, cafeteria, and gym are not.

"You seem nervous," Mack says as we enter the lunchroom. Maybe he can feel my elbow shaking or smell me sweating.

"I'm fine."

"Liar."

"I don't want to deal with Londyn Diggs anymore. Okay?" Three things I hope to avoid between now and the end of the world: Londyn Diggs, head lice, and broken bones. I plan to avoid them all after too. "Just please tell her not to come to the next meeting."

"Not doing it."

We take our regular seats. Seventh graders dominate the cafeteria. I look around to see where Londyn's sitting. She's not at the popular kids' table. She's not squished at ours or the next one over. Then I spot her alone in a booth, a place usually reserved for teachers or adults visiting the school.

Londyn isn't with an adult. She's alone, pushed into the corner like the booth made for four is crowded with seven. I've always thought of Londyn as someone with dozens of friends, and another twenty kids wanting to be her friend. This doesn't make sense. Maybe she's been assigned that seat by a teacher for swearing in class. That I could believe.

I take out my peanut butter and Fluff sandwich. While I tear it into little pieces, I watch Londyn. No one joins her. A girl named Hannah says something to Londyn as she walks past. By the way Londyn sinks deeper into her seat, I assume it wasn't "hello."

"Why so quiet?" Mack asks.

"Fine," I say through clenched teeth. "I'll go to the next

meeting. But if Londyn is there and says anything nasty, I quit."

"Um, okay?"

The chances are pretty good that I'll be resigning from Nature Club. No way Londyn Diggs can be civil for sixty whole minutes.

Chapter 15

Thanksgiving is so uncomfortable with Dad and Grandpa Joe fighting that I almost look forward to going back to school.

They argue when Grandpa Joe calls us soldiers as we set the table. "It sounds like you're starting a cult or a militia," Dad says.

They argue when Grandpa Joe says he's ordered us a rainwater collection barrel. "We get our water from the tap, thank you," Dad says.

And Dad *accidentally* breaks his wineglass when Grandpa Joe says grace. "Lord, thank you for this meal. Thank you for my fine family—my son, my grandsons, and my amazing granddaughter. Thank you for this great nation. Thank you for everything. We realize this may be our last true Thanksgiving. We pray to continue to provide. Now and when the world ends."

Grandpa Joe leaves before we have pie, and Dad spends the rest of the holiday watching football with his eyes closed. I sneak off to my room to get organized for the next Nature Club meeting. I create a vocabulary sheet and write up some of the most important information from Dr. Cologne.

The site has gotten much bigger. Dr. Cologne posts almost every day. There are complicated math calculations and satellite images. They all kind of look the same, but what do I know? He's also added a message board, where people post comments and questions. Sometimes, they're not nice, but someone takes those down quickly. The messages come from all over the world. I read things from Iceland and Australia. Luckily, they're all written in English. This information is going global. I don't want to post on the boards; instead, I send another email.

Dear Dr. Cologne,

Happy Thanksgiving. I'm thankful for all the information you give on your website. You're saving lives. I think you're a hero.

Sincerely,
E.J.D.

• • •

It's the first Wednesday of December. Mack and I arrive at the Nature Club meeting before the others. (I followed him from his locker to make sure he didn't skip out again.) Mrs. Walsh was absent today, and I worried that the substitute would cancel. But Mrs. Walsh left instructions that we are allowed to meet in her room after school. The sub doesn't ask any questions except "What time is the meeting over?" Then she goes back to playing with her iPhone.

Spencer, Ajay, and Dominic come in next. Spencer shows me a survivalist magazine he bought over the weekend. It's curled and wrinkled like he's read it cover to cover a bunch of times. And Ajay has brought a metal suitcase.

"What's in there?" I ask.

"A Celestron NexStar Six-SE." He pats the side of the case.

I shrug.

"It's my portable telescope. I have a bigger one at home, but that's mounted in our family room. I couldn't bring that one to school."

"Do you think we could see the asteroid with that?" It doesn't seem possible, but I get excited anyway.

"Don't be ridiculous. The asteroid is too far away, and it's daytime." He motions to the window in case I didn't realize it's the middle of the afternoon.

"Then why did you bring it?"

"Because it's cool." He opens the case and gazes lovingly at his toy.

Another new kid joins us. "Is this the End of the World Club?" he asks.

"This is Nature Club," I say.

"We're here to learn about and celebrate nature," Mack adds.

We need to have a better motto. Next thing you know, we'll be touring the botanical gardens.

"I thought—" The new kid looks confused.

"I give up," I cut him off. "You're right. It is the End of the World Club."

Jade and Izabell walk in, followed by Wyatt. Originally, I wanted the club to be me and Mack—and maybe the boys from lunch. But now I feel responsible for the others.

"Hey, Eleanor," Jade says. "I brought you this." She gives me a packet of papers stapled together. It's a printout from a science website. Across the top it reads *What You Need to Know About Climate Change.*

"Thanks."

I sit next to Spencer and flip through his magazine. There are two useful articles and about a thousand pages of ads for weapons and equipment. I glance at the doorway every few seconds. I'm waiting for Londyn, hoping she's somewhere else—torturing someone else.

"What's your name, new kid?" I ask.

"Brent." He pushes his long dirty-blond hair out of his face and flashes a ridiculously big smile, showing off his braces. He's white, pimply, and thin.

"Okay. I guess this is it for today."

"So what are we doing, Madame President?" Mack asks.

"Water-filtration systems." I hold up my personal one that Grandpa Joe got me. The same one he gave Mack. It costs over a hundred dollars. "You can only survive a day without water. Bottled water is good to have around, but when the situation is ongoing, you need long-term solutions."

I place the filter on the desk. "After SHTF—"

"That means when the *stuff* hits the fan." A voice from the doorway interrupts my lesson. It's Londyn.

The muscles in my shoulder tighten, and my head's on fire. I think I'm allergic to her.

She joins the group, taking a seat on the other side of Mack.

"Hey, Londyn," he says. No one else says hello or even looks at her.

"Um . . ." I can't remember what I was saying. Londyn drums her fingers on the desk like I'm wasting her time.

"What's wrong?" Mack asks.

"Nothing." I shake my head. "Um . . . water is important—"

"We know that," Londyn interrupts. "First graders know that."

I move my water filter from my left to my right hand and back. I can't think with her glaring at me.

"Are you going to demonstrate or what?" she asks.

"I guess." I know how to use my water filter. Grandpa Joe made sure of that. But I'm not supposed to use it for fun. Water filters don't last forever. Each use before TEOTWAWKI is one less time I can use it when it matters.

I stand up and motion for everyone to follow me to the lab sink in the back of the room.

The sub watches us.

"Talking about the water cycle and purification," I explain. "I need to borrow a beaker."

She squishes her eyebrows but then nods once.

I open the cabinet to find a four-hundred-milliliter beaker. Then I take the water purifier from the pouch and turn on the faucet. Before I can begin, Londyn reaches over and shuts off the water.

"No." She stares at me with black-rimmed eyes. "This water is already clean. How do we know the water purification works if you're using clean water?"

"It's a demonstration."

"It's stupid and useless."

I wait for her to call *me* stupid and useless. She doesn't.

"What do you want me to do?" As soon as the question is out of my mouth, I know it's a mistake.

"We need dirty water," she says. "We're preparing for the end of the world, not snack time."

"Yeah." Dominic nods.

"She's right," Spencer says, and I feel like I'm being overthrown. "Let's go outside and find water."

"There's no water near the school. And even with this"—I hold up the purifier—"you can't drink out of puddles. In a real situation, we'd be collecting rainwater—"

"Isn't that what a puddle is?" Londyn interrupts again.

"Rainwater collected in food-grade barrels. Water from a stream or river—moving water—is the best. The rocks act as a natural filter. They reduce a lot of the bigger bad stuff. Then your purifier catches the microscopic crud."

A few of the kids nod.

"So do you want me to demonstrate or not?" I ask.

"What about toilet water?" Londyn asks before anyone can answer my question. "Can you drink toilet water through that thing?" She flicks my water filter with a single finger.

Mack snorts. "Gross. But can you?"

"The water in the tank on the back of the toilet is clean," I explain. "It's the same water as what comes out of the sink."

"What about the bowl?" Londyn asks.

"I don't know. Even if you flush three or four times, does everything go down?" I shrug.

"Wouldn't your fancy water filter catch whatever micro-crap is left? Don't fish pee in the rivers you want us to drink from?"

"Okay, listen. I'm not a urine or toilet expert, but I'm sure there's a difference between toilets and rivers." All I wanted to do was demonstrate how to operate a stupid water filter.

"We could try it out." She smiles.

"No!" I shake my head.

"Let's do it," Spencer says.

Ajay nods in agreement.

"This is wild," Mack says. "Are you really going to filter toilet water?"

"No way!" I say.

"What kind of survivalist are you?" Londyn snatches the water filter out of my hands and heads to the door. "Someone grab the beaker."

"Where are you going?" the sub asks.

"Bathroom break," Mack says.

Everyone follows Londyn. Dominic has the beaker. Mack's cane moves across the floor as he tags along.

What is happening?

Chapter 16

There's no good way for this to end. If Londyn tries to use my water filter, she'll probably break it. If I work it, I'll have a beaker of purified toilet water. My decision doesn't take long. I'm a second behind the group.

"Be right back," I tell the sub. She doesn't try to stop me.

Londyn leads everyone into the girls' bathroom. Spencer and Ajay look around like they're on a new planet.

"Never been in here," Mack says. "Smells nicer than the boys' bathroom."

Londyn pushes open a stall door. The toilet seat is up, and the water is bluish with bubbles.

"Lucky us, it looks like the janitor recently cleaned our drink." She uses her foot to flush. The water swirls and is gone. Then she does it again. We're left with a clear liquid that is still ultimately toilet water.

Londyn shoves the filter into my chest. "Let the demonstration begin, Professor Doomsday."

I take a deep breath. "This is stupid. There's not enough water in the bowl for one person for one day. No one would do this. You need to find a real water source."

"You do it or I will." Londyn takes a step forward. We're the same height. I might even be a half inch taller, but somehow she creates a shadow over me.

"Okay." I hold the water-filtration system. "There are two steps to clean water. Filtration and purification. This gadget does both."

Hopefully.

"This is the intake." I point to a piece sticking out of the side near the bottom. "You attach the hose to this." I slip it on and make sure it's tight. Then I drop the other end into the toilet bowl.

"Ewww," Jade says.

"What's going on?" Mack asks.

"She put it in the toilet," Spencer explains.

"This nozzle is the output." I attach the second clear hose. "As the water runs from the bottom to the top, it's going through a filter that takes out ninety-nine point ninety-nine percent of bacteria and parasites. There's also a charcoal filter that removes chemicals."

"Does it remove cholera and *E. coli*?" Ajay asks. He nervously twists the bottom of his T-shirt.

"I think so."

"Does it remove urine?" Dominic asks.

"Yes." *What other answer can I give?*

Here goes nothing.

"You need to prime the pump," I explain. "You don't want to drink the first few ounces that come out."

I get Spencer to hold the hose over the toilet because I need one hand on the filter and one to pump. As the water drains into the bowl, it sounds like someone peeing.

After five pumps, I tell him to move the output tube to the beaker.

Dominic pulls out his cell phone and takes a picture.

"No pictures." I put my head down. But with my short hair, I can't hide my face.

"What are you doing?" Londyn snaps. I assume she was talking to me, but I look up to see her pull the phone out of Dominic's hands.

"You can't take pictures at a secret club," she says.

When the beaker is half full, I stop.

"There." I point. "Is this enough?"

"I don't know, you tell me. Could you survive for five minutes on that?" Londyn crosses her arms.

"This is a demonstration!" I clench my jaw.

"Right. Now demonstrate by drinking it."

"You drink it." I grab the beaker from Dominic and offer it to Londyn.

"You first," Londyn says. "I'll go second."

"No way, I don't trust you. If I drink it, you'll go around and tell everyone that Eleanor Dross drinks toilet water."

"And I don't trust you. You're the expert. If you're not willing to drink it, then I know your dumb water filter doesn't work."

"It works. It's the best one out there. It was designed for the military." I can't believe I'm bragging about this.

"Then drink it." She leans forward in my face.

"No. Does anyone else want to try?" I offer the toilet water to everyone. No one accepts.

"I'll drink it if you do. I promise." Londyn's voice is fake sweet.

"Me too," Mack says.

He can't see, but my eyes are bugging out of my head.

"This is like our initiation," Mack continues. "If you want to be in Nature Club—aka End of the World Club— you gotta do it."

"But you first," Londyn adds. "It's only fair."

I glance at everyone else. As a group, they look horrified, but they all nod.

My heart races. *What do I do?* I don't want to be known

as the girl who drinks toilet water. But if we all do it, it's like a bond. Everyone will want to keep it secret, like a team of bank robbers. No one can talk.

"Well . . ." Londyn huffs. "We don't have all day. Our rides will be here in *literally* ten minutes."

Without comment, I put the beaker to my lips and take the smallest drink. Maybe a teaspoon. I swallow without tasting. At least I try. Maybe I imagine the iron and dirt flavor.

"Your turn." I lock my jaw and hand the beaker to Londyn.

"Did she do it?" Mack asks.

"Yep," the new kid says.

Londyn laughs. I knew she wouldn't do it. I ball my fist. But before I can take the beaker back and dump it over her head, she takes a sip. Then she shrugs like *no big deal.*

The beaker gets passed to Dominic because he's closest.

"They both drank it," Spencer tells Mack.

Dominic holds his nose while he takes his portion. Everyone tries the toilet water, even Izabell. She fakes taking a sip at first, but Jade calls her out.

"Come on. Do it." Jade elbows her.

Mack is the last to get the beaker. He holds it up and says cheers before finishing it. He definitely drank the most.

"Do you drink toilet water at every meeting?" the new kid asks Spencer.

"Nope. This was special."

"Okay. If anyone gets violently ill tonight, we know the water filter didn't work," I say. "Any vomiting or diarrhea, maybe ask your parents to take you to the hospital. Especially if you see any blood."

"Perhaps you should have mentioned that before we drank it," Wyatt says.

Ajay looks green. "I think I'm going to be sick."

"Not from the water. It wouldn't be that fast. Give it an hour."

After I rinse off the filter, we head back to the classroom. The substitute eyes us suspiciously as we walk in. I'm glad Mrs. Walsh is out. She didn't want us eating dandelions or strange berries. She'd be disappointed to know we drank toilet water.

"Five minutes," the sub warns us. "Start wrapping it up."

As I stuff the water filter back in its pouch, I see the printouts. I almost forgot.

"Here." I hand everyone a sheet. "This is a summary of what's going on, what's new, and the vocab. I wanted to make sure everyone was keeping up. It'll also help the new kid."

"His name is Brent," Mack reminds me.

Londyn snatches her copy from my hand. Probably trying to give me a paper cut, hoping I'll slowly bleed to death.

"And a large-print version for you." I give Mack two sheets.

"So he's not really blind?" Wyatt whispers to me.

I don't get a chance to react before Mack answers. I think it's a rude question, but Mack doesn't get upset.

"Dude, I'm blind and have been since I was born. I can make out stuff up close. Blindness is a spectrum. I prefer Braille or audio for books. My eyes don't get as tired. But large print works too. And Elle doesn't have a brailler."

"Oh," Wyatt says. He turns red from his neck to his forehead. Mack can't see this, but I'm sure he senses it.

Londyn reads her sheet while everyone else shoves them into their bags. I remind them to be careful who they share this information with.

The substitute inspects the room. Once the beaker is put away, we're free to leave. Mack grabs my arm above the elbow. We walk to the pickup line to meet his mom.

"Did we drink toilet water?" he asks.

"Yes." I laugh.

We're almost to the main doors when I hear Londyn running up behind us. I try to pull Mack along faster.

"Hey, hey!" Londyn yells. "Norie."

I keep moving.

"Norie!"

"I think she's calling you," Mack says, and he stops walking.

I groan.

"What?" I turn to her and give my meanest look. I don't

want to talk to her anymore. I'm out of Londyn patience for the whole week.

"You wrote all this?" She holds up the paper I gave out.

"It's mostly from the website." I can't tell what she's after.

"No. I read that. This isn't the same. It's the same information, but it's not the same."

"Yeah, so?" Is she here to criticize my interpretation? Or is she going to make fun of something else?

"I like it."

I stare at her face, looking for a hint of a joke.

"You should write more. I'll help you. And we can hand them out."

"No!"

"That's a good idea," Mack says. "Like a newsletter. We should be warning others. I've been saying that since the beginning."

"And I've been saying no since the beginning. We can't save the world. Email your friends the website or whatever."

"What friends?" Londyn snaps. "I don't have any friends." She clears her throat. "This is bigger than friends anyway. Right?"

"Yes!" Mack says.

"We've gotta go." I yank his arm hard and pull him through the front doors.

His mom's Volvo is two cars back in line. I lead Mack to the car quickly so we don't have to talk to Londyn anymore.

Mack folds up Candy and reaches for the car door.

"I think it's a good idea. We need to do more."

"No, we don't."

Like always, Mrs. Jefferson invites me to dinner. I say no thanks because I need to get home for my brothers. Mrs. Sweeney will drop them off at four, and then they're my responsibility. I'd rather go to Mack's house and eat a nice dinner and play on his Xbox 360.

Not two minutes after I get home, my cell phone rings. It's not Mack, and it's not Dad or Grandpa Joe. But it's a local number, so I answer it.

"Hello?"

"We need to make a newsletter."

"Londyn? How did you get my number?"

"If you used all your brain cells, you could probably figure it out."

"I'm not writing a newsletter." I squeeze the phone. I should hang up before I break it.

"I know you hate me," she says.

"And I know you hate me," I say louder.

Neither of us debates the facts.

"We need to do something," she continues. "This is a big deal."

"I *am* doing something. The Nature Club. Duh?"

"We can do more," she says.

"We?"

"Yes. You and me."

Never would I think of the word *we* to mean me and Londyn Diggs. *We* would more likely be used for me and Sasquatch or me and a unicorn.

"Why?" I ask.

"You're even more annoying on the phone than you are in person. I'm coming over."

"What?"

"Stop asking questions. I'm coming over. I'll be there in twenty. You still live on Oakdale?"

"Yeah." I'm not sure how she knows this.

"Okay." Then she hangs up.

And I've got twenty minutes to move.

Chapter 17

Mrs. Sweeney drops off my brothers before Londyn arrives. They bust through the front door arguing about Pokémon.

"Eat a snack, then do your homework," I yell over their yelling.

They drop their backpacks and coats in the middle of the floor.

"And put away your lunch boxes." I give them the same instructions every day. And Dad will call in an hour and tell them to do all this again. It eventually gets done.

"I don't have any homework," Edward says.

"Liar. You have to read for twenty minutes every night, even if you don't have math or spelling."

The doorbell rings while the boys are pulling off their shoes. Bubbles jumps off the couch, barks a few times, and then hides under the coffee table. She is useless in stopping Londyn from invading my life.

"I got it!" Edward shouts. My brothers run to the door, pushing and shoving each other the entire way.

"It's for me," I say. "And you're not supposed to answer the door if it's a stranger."

Phillip ignores me and yanks it open. Londyn stands with arms crossed like she's annoyed already.

"Who are you?" Edward asks.

"Who are you?" she asks.

"I'm Edward Dross."

"I'm Phillip Dross. Are you Eleanor's friend?"

"Nope," she says.

And I'm glad we got that all cleared up.

"Are you a vampire?" Edward asks.

"Yes," she says without looking surprised. Edward's eyes grow wide, and Phillip laughs. She does resemble a Disney-like vampire. Long black hair with purple streaks, lots of black eye makeup, black nails, and layers of black clothes. All she's missing is fangs. (Which I swear she's just hiding.)

"Go do your homework." I grab them both by the shoulders and pull them away. "Come in," I say to Londyn.

"You invited a vampire into the house," Phillip says, trying to sound serious.

"Phillip! Out!"

The boys finally disappear into the kitchen.

"Let's go upstairs." I don't want Londyn in my room, but it's the only way we can talk without the real monsters bothering us.

"Nice house," she says as we head up, and I can't tell if it's a compliment or an insult. I think it's safe to assume everything she says is meant to be a burn.

"How did you get here?"

"My bike."

"Where do you live?"

"On Meadowlark."

That's only two streets behind me and in the same development. How did I not know we were neighbors?

"My mom and I are living with my aunt," she says, maybe sensing my confusion.

We step into my room. I'm not sure if I should tell her to sit. Maybe if we stand, she'll leave sooner.

"So?" I hold up my empty palms and shrug.

"I like your newsletter, Norie. More people need to see it."

"It's Eleanor."

"I know."

I take a seat on the edge of my unmade bed. She pulls out the desk chair and sits in it backward.

"I can help you," she says. "You write it. I'll put it together, add some art. We'll print it and hand it out in school."

"I don't understand why you want to do this?"

"I don't understand why you don't want to." She wrinkles her upper lip.

"Seriously?" This girl is clueless. "It's not my job to save the kids who've been ignoring me for years." To everyone at that school, I'm either invisible or repulsive. Other than Mack, no one wants to be my partner in class. No one wants to sit with me. No one even talks to me.

"Being ignored isn't so bad." She shrugs.

"When they're not ignoring me, they're laughing at me." I touch my hair and glance at my reflection in the mirror over my dresser. It's still bluish. "So what if they all become *zombies.*"

"Wow." She gives me a funny little smile. "Well, you do have a crappy haircut."

"Shut up."

She ignores me and continues. "I always got the vibe that you want to be alone. You don't hang out with anyone but Mack. It's just you and your boyfriend."

"Ew! Not! My! Boyfriend!" I shiver. That's like calling Edward or Phillip my boyfriend. So totally gross.

"I know he's not your boyfriend." She rolls her eyes dramatically. "But you have to know that's not how everyone sees it. Especially the kids who didn't go to elementary school with us. They watch you holding hands."

"We don't hold hands. He takes my elbow when we walk."

"Whatever. You hold hands when not walking too." She shrugs. "You only do stuff with Mack. I invited you to my birthday party. You didn't come."

"We were eight, and you invited every girl in Mrs. Ball's class." She makes it sound like she reached out to me personally and it mattered that I wasn't there.

"You. Didn't. Come." She repeats it slowly. "And Megan invited you to her fifth-grade graduation party. A pool party. And you didn't come."

"I'm not into parties." I cross my arms. "Why are we even talking about elementary school?"

"You're not a people person, Norie. Everything about you says *stay away.*"

"What about you, vampire girl?" I gesture at her hair and clothes. "This screams, *Stay away, or I'll destroy you.*"

"Mission accomplished."

She doesn't even try to hide how evil she is.

"Then why join our club or make a newsletter? Why help anyone?"

"Who said I want to help?" She tilts her head dramatically. "I want to scare the heck out of them. They need to know the world doesn't revolve around them, and even if it does, it's all going to end."

I swallow hard. That's not the message I want to deliver. No thanks.

"What's wrong?" she asks. "You look like I killed your dog."

If I hadn't just seen Bubbles, I might worry that this was a possibility.

"I'm not really into terrifying people," I finally say. I may not want to save everyone, but I'm not going to cause mass panic—not at school.

"So you don't want to scare them and you don't want to help them. Pick a side already! You can't just avoid everything and everyone, Norie."

"What are you even talking about!" It's not fair to make me choose, but I do anyway. "Helpful is better than terrifying."

She chews on her lower lip and looks at the ceiling like she's deciding. "Okay. I still think terrifying is more fun. You be helpful. I'll be realistically frightening. Our newsletter will have a nice balance."

"What? No."

"Listen. I'm doing this newsletter with or without you. And if I'm in charge, I'm going to terrify every student and teacher at Hamilton. There will be no tips for survival. It'll be all doom." She narrows her eyes.

"You can't force me."

"And you can't stop me. This offer stands for five more seconds. Then I'm publishing the *Doomsday Express* on my own."

"If you're caught, you'll probably get kicked out of school."

"I won't get caught. And does it matter? The world is ending in four, maybe five months. We'll all be out of school."

"Do you swear to be truthful and accurate?" I ask. Even if she says yes, I'm not going to believe her. Though she did drink toilet water, like she promised.

"Unless you're on board, I swear to nothing. If you're my co-editor, we can talk." She taps her wrist like she's wearing a watch. "Two seconds left, Norie. In or out?"

"Fine! I'll do it, but there will be rules. We're not doing this to make everyone panic. We're doing it to share valuable information."

"You *do* want to help people." She laughs. "You're so soft."

I don't know what I want anymore. With the world ending soon, I'm certainly adding to my problems, not eliminating them.

Chapter 18

For the rest of the week, I try to come up with ways to get out of my arrangement with Londyn. Maybe faking amnesia will work. *I promised to what? When did I say that?* But she doesn't bring up the subject of the newsletter either. Not that we've talked. Perhaps we're actually on the same wavelength. A newsletter—and working together—is a bad idea.

Then in social studies class, we're assigned a new project called Civilization in Crisis, and it feels like a sign. We need to write four pages and speak for five minutes on a civilization and its time of crisis. How did the people handle it? Were they successful?

After we're given the rubric, our teacher brings us to the media center to research ancient civilizations.

This project isn't done in groups or pairs, so I'm on my own. I can't even help Mack and avoid my work, because his para-assistant is around to pull books for him. Then she either reads it while he takes notes on his iPad or she sends it to the braillist for him to read later.

I select one of the books that the media specialist, Ms. Richmond, has laid out for us, and then I find a spot alone at a desk against the wall.

I flip through the book. Too bad I can't write about today's humans. We're in crisis, and hardly anyone knows. Maybe in a thousand years, some seventh grader will write a report about me. How I was one of the few surviving humans. How I was prepared, and how I helped my classmates prepare.

Like with a newsletter. It could be a valuable tool. Future seventh graders could use it as a source to understand the 2010PL7 asteroid disaster. Londyn and I need to do a kick-butt job. I want the class reports centuries from now to say, *More people should have listened to Eleanor Dross.*

I shove the book aside. I can research the Aztecs' fear of the eclipse later. Now I want to do what's important.

HAMILTON MIDDLE SCHOOL'S READINESS PAPER

All the information you will need to be prepared for the end of the world as we know it (TEOTWAWKI).

I don't write my name or Londyn's. This might make it harder for students in the future to identify me correctly and give me credit. We can add our names to the last edition. When we have nothing else to lose. Right now, my dad and the teachers don't need to know about our special project. They will shut us down, and we're just getting started.

With only two weeks until Christmas break, we need to get this first newsletter written and printed soon. I sneak my phone out of my backpack and send a message to Londyn.

ME: Wanna work on newsletter after school?

I start to slide my phone back in my bag when it vibrates. I look up to see if anyone else heard the rattling.

LONDYN: Ya. What bus?

ME: My bus?

LONDYN: Duh! We'll work on it at your house

ME: OK. Bus 78

• • •

I usually have a seat to myself on the bus. Sometimes a kid will push onto my bench if something gross happens in the back—like a spilled Yoo-hoo or vomit. They never join me for social reasons.

Today, Londyn sits down next to me. This shouldn't be surprising. She's coming to my house.

"Hi," I say, trying to be friendly.

"Hey." Then she takes out her phone and ignores me. Her thumbs fly across the screen. Maybe she's texting her friends—or whoever. *I'm going to loser Eleanor Dross's house. I'll send you a picture of her dorky room and her dorky underwear.*

My mind goes into overdrive imagining what dorky things she'll want to photograph and share. When I can't take it anymore, I slyly lean over to see what she's writing.

But she's not texting. She's playing a game with a little man on a motorcycle who races through a city.

A feeling of stupidity quickly replaces my feeling of relief. I've got to stop thinking that everyone is out to get me. Only most people.

My house is the fifth stop, and I tap Londyn's shoulder when we have to get up. She follows me without saying anything.

"Want a snack?" I ask when we get inside. "I'll get my computer, and we can work down here."

She looks in our cupboards, opening and closing every one. I run upstairs to get the laptop and some paper. When I get back, Londyn is petting Bubbles.

I glare at my dog, feeling betrayed.

"What's her name?"

"Bubbles."

"She's awesome." That's the nicest thing Londyn's ever

said about anything. Maybe I should have recorded the moment.

"Yeah," I agree. "I've taught her a trick. Wanna see?"

"Sure."

"Bubbles." She looks at me. "Bacon!"

The dog runs to the fridge and plops her butt in front of it.

"That's your trick?" Londyn narrows her eyes.

"Next I'm going to teach her to attack." I try to match Londyn's harsh stare, but she's had too much practice.

After I reward Bubbles with a strip of cooked bacon, I set up my laptop and open the website. It's been a few hours since I checked it on my phone while changing for gym class. There was nothing new at eleven-thirty, but now there is.

"Look at this! Another expert is talking about the asteroid." I read the new post aloud. "'Dr. Gene Yukofski is a former engineer with the European Space Agency. He's worked on the International Space Station and several satellites, including the Pythagoras and the Rebel. He retired twenty years ago and has been following—'"

"Ugh," Londyn interrupts. "I don't need to hear his résumé. What's he got to say?"

I scan down a few paragraphs. "'He's confirmed the orbital path of 2010PL7. It is on a collision course with Earth. His calculations have impact in April.'"

"Does he say where?" She comes up behind me with Bubbles in her arms.

I read the last few sentences. "No."

"Darn. I want a location." She sits down. "We should say something like twenty miles west of Hamilton in our newsletter."

"Twenty miles? If it's within one hundred, we all die."

"Really? That's terrifying. Print it." She smiles and wiggles her eyebrows.

"No."

"Come on." She gives an exaggerated sigh. "We can always change it later."

"No. We're not doing that." I lean back in the chair. "This is really, really real. April. That's not so far away."

I use Google to calculate the days until possible impact. "April first is one hundred thirteen days away."

"I hope it's after spring break," she says.

"Why?"

"Wouldn't you rather have our last days at home rather than in the classroom? You don't seem like a school-loving nerd."

"School is not my best subject. Plus, it's not going to come to that. I bet by the beginning of March the whole world will know. They'll be talking about it on the news and the internet. And everyone will be rushing to the store to buy supplies."

"Guess I should get my bread and milk now," she says. I think she's joking but it's hard to tell.

"Here." I hand her two pages of notes. She sets Bubbles on the floor.

"Norie, we're not writing a novel." She grabs a red pen from her bag and starts circling things on my list. When she's done, she shoves it back to me.

"Write about these. And I'll make some art."

She's picked the scariest parts. Her focus is the impact, the possible destruction, the loss of life, and the aftermath that could last decades. All of it's true. And all of it is the stuff of nightmares.

"And I hate your title. *Hamilton Middle School's Readiness Paper.*" She fake gags.

"This is not going to work!" Five minutes ago, I was proud of what I wrote, and now she's ripping on it. "I warned you. There have got to be tips and real advice. Or I'm not doing it."

"Okay," she says through gritted teeth. "We'll put the truth on the front. An asteroid is speeding toward Earth. It's going to kill billions."

"Probably less."

"In April. There will be floods, famine, droughts, plagues."

"Are you writing a Bible story?" I roll my eyes.

She shakes her head. "The front page is the headlines.

It's got to get everyone's attention. You can give your useless tips and tricks on the back."

"Not tips and tricks. And not useless."

"Chances are, we'll be blown to smithereens." She claps her hands together.

"Not true! The chances are actually slim that we'll be blown to smithereens. Less than five percent." Dr. Cologne wrote about the odds last week. Any one location on Earth has less than a five percent chance of being instantly evaporated. "We can't worry about a direct hit. That's a waste of time. We need to survive after."

"By drinking toilet water," she says.

I shudder.

"That was so gross." Londyn laughs—a sound I've never heard before. "I can't believe you did that."

"I can't believe *you* did that," I say quickly.

"I'm a woman of my word." She holds up her chin. "If you say you're going to do something, you do it. Simple."

Either she takes toilet water very seriously, or she's talking about something else.

"Well . . . um, we have toilet water here. We also have Coke. Which do you prefer?"

Londyn snorts. Her left hand quickly covers her mouth like I'm not supposed to see her natural smile.

"Yeah, I guess Coke is fine." She tries to say it seriously.

I get the sodas and two small bags of potato chips. Londyn selects the barbecue, leaving me with sour cream and chive.

"Hey, I looked through your cabinets," she says as she opens her snack. "I expected a thousand cans of tuna. Your pantry looks like a normal pantry. Aren't you a prepper?"

"No. Well, sort of." I shake my head. "My grandfather is the real prepper. My dad isn't into it. We've got some stuff." I stare at her dark-rimmed eyes, ready to defend my family.

"But not like a whole room full of provisions?"

"Nope." I lead her to the pantry and push aside a box of trash bags on the ground to reveal the four dusty buckets of dehydrated meals that Grandpa Joe gave us for one Christmas. "We got these. They'll last us about a month."

"Hmm." She looks down her nose at me. "I expected you to be more prepared."

"I've got time." I cross my arms.

"You've got nothing. Practically."

Part of me is saying, *Be careful. Don't do this. Do you trust her?* But the other part of me reacts first.

"This way." I wave for Londyn to follow me to the basement.

"You're not going to murder me, are you? Is this where you bury the bodies?" She creeps down the steps until I turn on the light.

"No dead bodies yet. Do you want to see what I've got or not?"

Half the basement is a garage, and the other half is a walled-off area that we call the playroom. It's got shelves of games, baskets of old and broken toys, dusty cases of MREs, too many spiders, and my secret stash of TEOTWAWKI supplies—thanks to Grandpa Joe and his retirement savings.

I move the Barbie house and pull out the big blue bin.

"I always wanted the Dream House." She runs a hand over the pink roof.

"You can have it. I hardly play with it anymore."

She laughs, and I'm relieved she didn't think I was serious.

Dramatically, I pull the blanket off the plastic bin, like a magician revealing his assistant.

"What do we have here?" There's excitement in Londyn's voice. She kneels and starts rummaging through my supplies. She pulls out five bottles of aspirin.

"Medicine will be like gold after SHTF," I explain. "My grandfather has tons of antibiotics. That and insulin will be worth the most."

"What about my chewable vitamins? Will they be worth anything?"

"Pre- or post-chewed?" I ask, and she rolls her eyes but laughs again.

Londyn takes her time going through everything. She looks at each item and then lines it up on the floor. She needs to hurry because I want to put everything back before Edward and Phillip get home.

"I'm impressed, Norie. You seem almost ready."

"Thanks?" I don't sense that she's making fun of me, but I'm only like 90 percent certain. "And this is nothing. You should see my grandfather's basement. He's got more food than some grocery stores and all the survival gear you'd ever need. Machetes, parachutes, life jackets, these pots for melting metal."

"Whoa! Why does he need parachutes?" She looks up at me.

"I think he only has one. He likes to go to these military surplus stores. I guess when you have everything else, you buy a parachute." I shrug.

She starts putting stuff back neatly.

"Seriously, Norie. When the asteroid hits, I'm coming here. Do you think Mack will mind if I'm your BFF just for the apocalypse?"

Chapter 19

The first newsletter is almost done, and it's not bad.
Londyn drew a scary asteroid to go across the top. It looks
like a flaming meatball, but I didn't tell her that. The official
title is *Doomsday Express*. She insisted.

On the front, I write up what we know so far. And the
back has the basic survival information. We use my computer to create the final draft.

"Make the title bigger." Londyn points over my shoulder. We're sitting on my bed. The boys are home, so we can't
work in the kitchen.

"Better?"

"Yes. Print one out."

We read over the hard copy. I'm sure it's filled with spelling mistakes, but we don't care. It's not for teachers, and kids aren't into that stuff. We even have a few emojis—which are definitely not allowed in school reports.

"This is killer," Londyn says.

"I know." We agree for maybe the second time in history. "It's so good. Wish we could put our names on it."

"Right! I want everyone to know it's me telling them their world is ending. I'm behind this." She does her evil cartoon-villain laugh.

"An asteroid is behind this. You're the artist and editor."

She shrugs. "How many should we print? At least three hundred."

"No! That's too many. Twenty-five. Kids can read it and then pass it on to others." Grandpa Joe has promised to take me to the office supply store later to run copies. My printer always jams after four or five sheets.

"You can't go viral with only twenty-five copies." She rolls her eyes.

"Can anything on paper go viral?"

"Two hundred. At least."

"I'll try." I play with a strand of hair behind my ear. "What do you think will happen if we get caught? Remember that kid last year who created a website about Hamilton's worst teacher? He got suspended."

"He deserved to be suspended. It was a crappy website. He had a picture of the eighth-grade math teacher and a lot of unimaginative rumors."

"Didn't he say the teacher was holding kids hostage in his basement?"

"Yep, unimaginative. Boring." She waves the papers in my face. "This is brilliant, A-plus work, ten out of ten, five stars."

"How are we going to distribute them? Shove them in lockers?"

"That's a stupid idea. It'll take too long and there are cameras. I suggest the bathrooms."

"Huh?"

"We'll put some in each bathroom. The school can't record in there. We'll place stacks by the paper towels with a sign that says TAKE ONE."

I nod. "Okay. We can cover the girls' bathrooms. What about the boys'?"

"Mack can help us out."

"There's an obvious flaw with this plan," I say. "He has a big mouth. He's not the best guy for top-secret operations. Maybe we can get Spencer."

"Or we'll sneak into the boys' bathrooms. Meet me before homeroom near the gym."

"Okay."

"Tomorrow, we scare the heck out of Hamilton Middle."

"At least we're clear on your motivations," I say.

"Yep." She gives me a cheesy smile and two thumbs up.

• • •

Grandpa Joe loves our newsletter. "I can't wait to meet your co-conspirator. Londyn's her name? Like the city?"

"Yeah. And she wants to meet you too."

We make one hundred copies. Grandpa Joe keeps a few for himself. (I can imagine him hanging one on his fridge near the "I Love Grandpa" poem I wrote him in first grade.) He even offers one to the cashier as we leave, but I snatch it out of her hands.

"Private Eleanor, I think what you're doing is important and dangerous work," he says as we walk to his truck. "I'm happy to play a small part in your covert operation." He throws his big arm over my shoulder and kisses my forehead.

"Thanks for your help."

The next day, Londyn and I decide to put the newsletters in only the girls' bathrooms because we have a small first batch. We each take half. She assigns me the art and music hallway, and she hits up the ones near the cafeteria and the seventh-grade wing.

Sneaking the stacks into the bathrooms should be no big deal. But my heart still races, and my palms get sweaty like I'm about to give a report. The place is empty. I set my pile on top of the paper towel dispenser. Then I take out a pen and write FREE: TAKE ONE on a sticky note and place it in front. I draw an arrow pointing up, so kids don't think I'm advertising free paper towels.

Later, as we change for gym class, Londyn comes up to me.

"Did you distribute them all?" she whispers.

"I still have a few." I open my backpack and show her. I'm not sure why I kept some.

"Your bag is full of evidence. You'd better get rid of them in case they start questioning us and you get searched."

"Who is *they*?" I twist my paracord bracelet.

"The administration. The police. The FBI." She's trying to be scary, but her mouth twitches into a smile.

"We haven't committed any crimes." I close my bag. "Have we?"

"Wearing a tank top is a crime in this school. It doesn't take much to get in trouble. I'd be careful if I were you."

In the hallway before lunch, kids are reading the *Dooms-day Express*. Seems like everyone has one, even though we only made one hundred. I also spot a teacher with a copy. As I pass, I imagine him grabbing my arm and saying, "You're under arrest."

I've never moved so fast in my life. This probably makes

me an obvious suspect. I'm breathing hard when I get to the cafeteria.

I sit down next to Mack.

"Hey," he says. "Did you make a Braille version of your newsletter?"

"Here." It's not Braille, but I did print a special edition for him with a font size of twenty-four. "And shh. Don't talk about it."

Then something odd happens. Londyn comes to sit with us. She squeezes in between Ajay and Dominic.

"Our newsletter is a bestseller," she says.

"Shh." All I do is shush people. "And it can't be a bestseller. We aren't selling anything."

"Do you think we could sell them?" Her eyes grow big. "How much would you pay for a *Doomsday Express,* Spencer?"

"A dollar?" he says with a mouthful of chicken nuggets.

"Can we not talk about it at school? Please."

But that's all anyone can talk about. My head is spinning as I try to listen to all the conversations around me. I eat my sandwich as fast as I can, then shove the rest of my lunch in my bag and get up. I need some space.

"Where are you going?" Londyn asks.

"Media center. I'm doing extra-credit work."

"She's lying," I hear Mack say as I walk away. "She never does extra-credit work."

In the library, I sit at a round table near the morning-announcements studio. I'm alone for less than five minutes before Mack and Londyn barge in and surround me.

"We're done talking about *you know what,* Norie," Londyn says. "We're sorry." She pinches her lips like she's trying to keep from laughing.

"Sorry to stress you out, Elle. Let's talk about something else." Mack holds out his hand. I don't take it.

"What should we talk about?" Londyn strums her fingers on the table. "End-of-year testing? No, the world will be over by then. The NBA championship game? No. That's after too."

"Can't talk about hockey and the Stanley Cup either," Mack adds. "That's post-apocalyptic. No one is going to be skating when there isn't enough food to eat."

"No Mother's Day, no Father's Day, no graduations, no summer break." Londyn counts off the list on her fingers.

"No new Marvel movie. They always come out in the summer." Mack does a fake cry.

They laugh, and I want to strangle them both.

"And no going to the Conrad School," I blurt out, not sure where that came from.

"No school at all," Londyn says.

I wish Mack would say something like, "No way I'm going to the Conrad School now." Or "I was never going there anyway." He doesn't comment about the stupid school at all.

"You know what we need to do?" Mack says.

"What?" Londyn ask.

"We need a bucket list. A list of all the things we want to do before the world ends."

"You and this dumb bucket list. This isn't the *end* end," I say. "And I'm not getting a tattoo."

"A bucket list is a good idea, Mack," Londyn says. "I want to order one of those kitchen-sink sundaes from Molly's Ice Cream Shop. It has like fifty scoops of ice cream in it."

"That's awesome, dude," Mack says. "Write it down."

Londyn snatches a mint-green sheet of paper from the desk behind her. On one side is last month's lunch menu. On the other, she starts the list.

"The kitchen-sink sundae is gross," I say. "All the flavors melt before you can finish, and it becomes a soupy mess. My family couldn't even finish it."

"Well, I've never had it." She shoots me one of her evil looks. It's been about a day since I've seen one. Good to know she's still got it. "There's not going to be ice cream after April. No electricity. No freezers. No ice cream. This is our last chance."

"The world will rebuild eventually. You will have ice

cream again. Or at least flavored snow. We'll probably experience a mini ice age." I'd hate to think I'd never have another Klondike bar.

"I want to zip-line," Mack says.

"You can zip-line after TEOTWAWKI," I say. "It doesn't require electricity."

"Whatever. I'm putting it on the list," Londyn says.

"I figure we won't have a lot of time for leisure activities with all the hunting and gathering we'll be doing," Mack jokes. They go back and forth coming up with ideas. I ignore them mostly. Sometimes I throw in an occasional groan.

"What's on your bucket list, Norie?" Londyn asks after I sigh at her suggestion of hang gliding.

"The only thing on my bucket list is to have enough food, water, and supplies for me and my family to survive."

"Boring," Londyn says. "And you practically have that."

"Don't you want to do something fun?" Mack asks.

"Nope."

"Or accomplish something incredible?"

"I don't have time to train for a marathon." I cross my arms.

"A marathon?" Londyn raises her eyebrows. "Can you even run a mile?"

"If I wanted to."

"Maybe start with a 5K," Mack laughs. "I'll do it with you."

"Okay," I agree, and they both stare at me like I suggested running through the school naked. "Part of preparing for the end of the world is getting physically ready. We're not going to be sitting at desks all day. After TEOTWAWKI, we'll be hiking, and farming, and carrying heavy stuff, and maybe even fighting off the enemy."

"Fighting off the enemy?" Mack asks. "Who's the enemy? Why are we fighting?"

"People that come to take our supplies. We'll have to punch them and stuff." I air-box to demonstrate.

"And you think running a 5K is going to get you ready for hand-to-hand combat?" Londyn snorts.

"Forget it," I snap. "We're not doing a 5K. And we're not doing a bucket list."

"We're totally doing a bucket list," Londyn says.

"And a 5K," Mack adds.

I give up.

For the rest of the day, I look over my shoulder, waiting for the principal—a gray-haired woman I've never spoken to in my life—to grab me and walk me to her office, where my dad will be waiting. I imagine the office filled with police and lawyers.

But none of that happens. I ride the bus home, and everything is normal. The world is the same as yesterday.

Chapter 20

Mack and his parents go away for Christmas break. They visit family in New Jersey, and then visit other relatives in Florida. He does it every year, so I'm used to it. What I'm not used to is Londyn being around. On the afternoon of Christmas Eve, I get a text.

LONDYN: Can I come over?

ME: sure

I send the message right away, but in my head I'm debating if this is a good idea. We're about to decorate gingerbread houses and do corny family things. What will she think?

LONDYN: is your grandfather there?

ME: he's coming later

LONDYN: Good

Dad is taking care of the meal—mostly just heating up stuff he got from the market. The boys are running around like a litter of rambunctious hyenas. I only have two brothers, but when you put them in a small space, it seems like there are eight of them.

Londyn and Dad haven't met before. She's only been here while he's at work. The minute she arrives, he clearly feels the need to interview her.

"You rode your bike? Where do you live?"

"My mom and I live with my aunt on Meadowlark."

"What's your aunt's name?"

"Susan Caulkins."

"Hmm, I don't believe I've met her." This isn't surprising, because we only talk to one of our neighbors—the Meyers, who live to our right. They're older, and Dad insists on doing stuff for them like bringing in their garbage cans.

"Do you have big plans for Christmas?" Dad asks.

"Nope." Londyn answers all his questions but doesn't give away any more than she has to.

Bubbles greets Londyn with her tail wagging. Londyn picks her up and snuggles *my* dog to her chest.

"I can see you haven't taught her to attack yet," Londyn says to me. Maybe she came over to see Bubbles. That makes sense.

"Well, the boys are decorating gingerbread houses, if you girls want to join in," Dad offers.

"I don't know," I say. "We might work on a school project." Our code for the *Doomsday Express*.

"Over break?" He raises one eyebrow. "I'll be in the kitchen monitoring the building and demolition of edible houses." He leaves Londyn and me in the foyer.

"So what do you want to do?" I ask.

"Let's decorate gingerbread houses."

"Seriously?"

"What? Your dad said we could." She shrugs.

"Okay. It didn't seem like something you'd enjoy. Ya know, a festive activity. You're not the festive type."

She looks down at her clothes like she's noticing them for the first time. She's wearing black jeans and a dark-gray hoodie; both are now covered in white dog hair.

"Sorry. I don't own reindeer clothes." She gestures at my ugly Christmas sweater that has Rudolph on it.

"I've got lots of Christmasy clothes." I point toward my room. "I'd be happy to unload some of them—"

"No! We'll never be the kind of girls who share clothes." She's trying to sound tough, but I laugh. Then she snorts.

She sets Bubbles on the ground, and we walk to the kitchen.

"I've got you all set up." Dad points to the counter separating the kitchen and the family room. The boys have taken over the table, and it's already covered in frosting.

Dad makes us cocoa. We construct our houses, but mine

keeps falling over. Londyn has a steady hand. Her little cottage is up in no time, and she's applying SweeTart roof tiles. I thought she might create a graveyard or haunted insane asylum. But her project is cheery and much better than mine. Despite Dad being an engineer, his constructing skills have not been passed on to his offspring.

We're cleaning up the mess when the front door opens, and we hear a loud "ho, ho, ho!"

Londyn looks at me and smiles. "Is that Grandpa Joe?"

"Yes."

The boys run to the front door, and Londyn is right behind them.

"Merry Christmas Eve, soldiers." Grandpa Joe stands in the doorway wearing a camo jacket and a red Santa hat. Two huge black trash bags filled with gifts are gripped in his hands.

Phillip and Edward pause to salute before trying to relieve him of the packages.

"Put 'em under the tree, boys." He ruffles Edward's hair.

"Hey, Dad," my father says to his father. "I thought we agreed you weren't going to go overboard with the gifts this year."

"These are my only grandkids. I'll do what I want." He shrugs and smiles. I think they've had the same argument for the past few Christmases. "And who is this? Londyn, I presume?" He offers his hand.

"It's so nice to meet you, Mr. Joe. I've heard all about you." She shakes his hand and smiles like she's meeting a celebrity.

"Call me Grandpa Joe. All my favorite people do."

Dad looks at me and raises his eyebrows. He doesn't understand what's going on. Or worse, he does.

"Londyn, I need to show you something in my room." I pull her by the shoulder.

"What?"

"It's a surprise." I gesture to the stairs with my head.

"Fine." She huffs. "But if you got me a present, just know that I didn't get you one. Keeping your expectations in check, Norie."

When we get to my room, I close my door.

"Listen—"

"Are you going to remind me again not to talk about the asteroid or the end of the world or prepping in front of your dad?" She crosses her arms.

"Um . . ."

"Norie, I'm not dense. And you've already warned me."

"But it might be harder with my grandfather here. He was preparing for the end of the world since before we even knew it was going to end." How can I explain this? "He's like a pitcher who's been waiting his whole life for the big game, and now it's time for the Super Bowl."

She clicks her tongue. "Or the World Series."

"Yes." I snap my fingers and point at her. She gets it.

"I'll be good. I promise." She draws an X across her heart with one finger.

We rejoin my family and watch the movie *Elf* in the family room. We eat popcorn and sugar cookies. Bubbles sits on Londyn's feet. Then we play Ticket to Ride. We have to teach Londyn the rules, but it's not hard. She picks them up quickly and comes in second place behind Dad. He never loses.

When it's dark outside, Dad sends me to turn on the Christmas lights in the front yard, and then asks, "Is your friend staying for dinner? You should invite her."

I nod.

Londyn is at the kitchen table playing Jenga with Phillip and Grandpa Joe.

"Are you staying for dinner?" I ask.

Dad comes up behind me. "What she means to say is, you're welcome to stay for dinner."

"Okay," Londyn says.

"But I need you to ask your mom. Make sure it's okay."

Londyn pulls her cell phone from the back pocket of her jeans. She fires off a text. Then looks up.

"Mom says it's okay."

Dad takes a deep breath. I can tell he's not sure if he believes her. I'm no help. I shrug; she could be telling the truth.

"Mom's not feeling good, and my aunt's working. She's a nurse and won't be home until morning."

I never thought about a kid being lonely on Christmas. In commercials and movies, it's always old people who are alone. A gray-haired lady and her cats or the grumpy neighbor who spends most of his time shoveling.

Londyn stays for dinner, and she stays for dessert. We hang out with my family the whole time.

Finally, Dad says, "Londyn, let me drive you home. I don't want you riding your bike in the dark."

"No, no." Grandpa Joe holds up a hand likes he's directing traffic. "We need to open gifts first. Before she goes."

"We'll do gifts in the morning, Dad," my dad says through gritted teeth. I can imagine what he's thinking; we don't have anything for Londyn.

"Just one present. What's the harm?" Grandpa Joe says. "I got something for Londyn and Mack too. You'll have to give it to him when you see him."

"Yes!" Edward cheers. We never open gifts on Christmas Eve. We always have to wait until the actual day. He runs to the tree—Bubbles and Phillip right on his heels—and he starts shaking presents.

"No, sir," Grandpa Joe says. "You don't get to pick. We're opening the ones in the candy-cane paper."

Phillip joins the search for the approved presents. After all their digging, they only find three.

"Where's mine?" Edward asks, pushing out his bottom lip.

"It's a family gift, Ed," Grandpa Joe explains.

Londyn and I move closer. One of the gift tags reads *The Drosses,* one says *London and Family* (her name spelled wrong), and the last is for *Mack and Family.* Phillip hands Londyn her present.

"Thanks," she mumbles, looking uncomfortable.

"Go on!" Grandpa Joe says. Phillip and Edward tear into the Dross gift. Red-and-white paper flies across the family room.

Londyn unwraps hers at the taped seams. I look over her shoulder, wondering what Grandpa Joe got us.

Edward and Phillip get ours open first. Edward holds the box over his head.

"A walkie-talkie," he announces. "Awesome."

"Not just a walkie-talkie. These are dual-band handheld radios capable of both FRS and GMRS. The two-way radio range is up to thirty miles. They operate on batteries, so we won't be dependent on the electric grid. Of course, you need a license for GMRS. And a hand-crank charger isn't a bad idea, but maybe Santa will bring one tomorrow." He winks and adjusts his hat.

"Cool." Phillip works on opening the box.

Dad stares at Grandpa Joe but says nothing. His jaw tightens, and I know from experience that when he does speak, he's going to use his disappointed voice—which is quiet and deep and terrifying.

"Thank you, Grandpa Joe," Londyn says, and then she steps closer and whispers to him. "This is going to be very helpful."

"You're welcome. I want you and Eleanor to help each other out and stay in touch even when you can't text no more. After the asteroid crashes, it's going to be hard—"

"Joe, stop!" Dad snaps. I flinch. I've never heard my dad call his dad by his first name. "You promised no more of this nonsense." Dad moves forward and puts a hand on Grandpa's chest.

Bubbles runs for cover under the coffee table.

"Sorry. Forget I mentioned an asteroid. This is stuff for just-in-case scenarios. Like if we have an earthquake." Grandpa Joe winks at me.

"Joe, let's talk in the other room." Dad speaks to Grandpa Joe like he's talking to one of his own kids. And Grandpa Joe obeys like he's not actually the parent.

They go down the hall to the spare bedroom. We hear the door close, and the voices get loud—including Dad's, and he never yells. But I can't make out exactly what they're saying.

"I hope we don't have to give back the walkie-talkies," Edward whispers.

When the arguing stops, I hear only one set of footsteps in the hall. Dad walks into the family room.

"Londyn, I'd better get you home. It's late."

We put her bike in the trunk of the minivan. I ride in the back seat and let Londyn sit up front. Her gift is in her lap. Neither of us wanted to ask my dad if it was okay to keep it. She gives him directions to a small, pretty house that's completely dark inside and out.

"Thanks for the lift." She opens the door and hops out.

"Help her with the bike, and walk her to the door," Dad says to me as I go to move to the front seat.

"Fine."

"What are you doing?" She struggles to pull her bike out of the back.

"Walking you in." I take the dual-band radio from under her arm.

"What are you? My date?"

"My dad is making me." This must be the right answer because she doesn't complain or say anything else.

She lays the bike on the porch, then takes a key out from around her neck and unlocks the front door. She flicks on the lights in the house and on the porch. I glance inside and see a small tabletop Christmas tree in the living room.

"Are you okay?" I ask, still standing outside.

"My mom's home. I'm fine." The house feels empty and cold.

"Bye." I hand her the present from Grandpa Joe. "Merry Christmas."

And she closes the door without another word.

When Dad and I get home, the boys are already in their pajamas. They're anxious to go to bed. They think it'll make Christmas morning come sooner.

"Where's Grandpa Joe?" I ask.

"He left," Phillip answers.

"What?" I shoot Dad my most serious look.

"I'm sure he'll come back tomorrow." Dad sighs. "But he shouldn't have left the boys here alone. I'll need to talk to him."

I want to say, *Haven't you done enough talking?* Instead, I go to my room. It's been a weird last pre-TEOTWAWKI Christmas Eve.

I text Mack.

ME: what's up?

MACK: Can't talk

MACK: Sorry mom is making us go to mass

I put my phone down. It vibrates a second later; I pick it up, expecting Mack. It's not.

LONDYN: Merry Christmas

Chapter 21

Another newsletter is ready to go by the end of the week. Londyn and I worked on it every day over break. When she couldn't come to my house, we discussed it on the dual-band radio. (We could have a more private conversation on our cell phones, but the radio is fun, and we need to practice using it.) We also saw two movies and went bowling with my dad and brothers. Phillip definitely likes Londyn more than he likes me.

"Why can't *she* be our sister?" he asked when I refused to share my Milk Duds but Londyn gave him M&M's. He had his own box of Skittles that he ate superfast.

Mack gets home from his trip on New Year's Eve and invites me over to watch movies until midnight.

"Can we invite Londyn too?" I ask over the phone.

"Do you think she'll want to?"

"You never know." I'm just saying this; I'm certain she'll say yes.

"Cool. Let's make it a real party. I'll invite the whole Nature Club."

"Please don't. Three is enough of a party for me."

"Fine."

Dad drives Londyn and me to Mack's house around five. I bring Mack's gift from Grandpa Joe. When Dad notices the present, he just sighs.

Grandpa Joe did come back Christmas morning. He got there before we woke up, but instead of playing the role of Santa, he was the Grinch. All the presents he'd brought the night before were gone when we came downstairs. He gave us each one hundred dollars in a plain white envelope. But we were allowed to keep the radio.

Mack's parents have decorated the family room for New Year's. There are balloons and streamers and a table of poppers and noisemakers. They've never gone to this kind of effort for just me. And Mack isn't wearing his usual uniform of jeans and a black T-shirt. He's got on a baby-blue sweater with his jeans. I guess adding Londyn makes it special.

"It's so nice to meet you, Londyn," his mom says. "I've heard a lot about you."

Mr. Jefferson opens bags of chips, and then sets out

crackers and cheese. Mrs. Jefferson brings down a veggie tray. She tells Mack what's on the table and where. He leans close, his face almost in the food, to inspect the buffet.

"Where are the Oreos?" he asks.

"The coconut ones? I'll bring them in later. We've ordered pizza and wings too. Should be delivered around eight."

"Thanks, Mom."

We fill our paper plates with snacks. I even take some vegetables because fresh food will be a luxury during the ice age that will come after the asteroid. I need to get my fill of baby carrots before impact winter. Mack and Londyn sit on the couch. She's in my usual spot. I take the chair next to them.

"Coconut Oreos? Really? That's gross." I shudder. I don't like coconut-flavored anything, including coconuts.

"I'm adding that to our bucket list," he explains. "To try every Oreo flavor."

"Is that even possible?" Londyn asks. "They make new ones like every other day."

"But they have to stop in April," Mack says. "I bet we can try fifty flavors before then."

"*You* can. I don't eat coconut." I gag. Coconut and pineapple are the worst flavors.

"I came up with other ideas for the bucket list too," Mack says. "We should go camping, and ice-skating, and set a world record."

"A world record? In what?" I ask.

"A world record in dumb ideas? We have lots of those," Londyn jokes.

"True," he laughs. "I heard on the TV that Johnson Automotive is going to try to set a record for how many people they can fit in a Fiat. We could do that!"

"That sounds horrible!" Londyn says.

"I agree. I don't want to be squished up against strangers." I imagine what that car might smell like.

"Okay. I'll find a different world record for us to break," Mack says, undeterred.

"So . . ." I try to change the subject. "What movies are we watching?"

"It's an all-apocalyptic evening," he says. "This might be our last New Year's Eve."

"At least the last with streaming," I say.

"We'll start with *World War Z,*" Mack says as he plays with the remote. "Then *The Day After Tomorrow, I Am Legend,* and of course *Armageddon.* It's about a huge asteroid heading toward Earth, and NASA sends up these oil-rig workers—not astronauts—to blow it to smithereens and save our planet!"

"Spoiler alert," I warn.

"Why aren't we doing that?" Londyn asks. "Not us personally, but NASA or the Air Force."

"Maybe they will, but they have to believe Dr. Cologne first."

"Or," Mack says, drawing out the word, "maybe they are getting a team ready to go to space, but it's top secret. They could be building the rocket and megabomb right now."

"Doubt it." I lean back in the chair and throw my feet on the ottoman. My plate of food rests on my lap. "Start the first movie."

"Let's do this. No need to spend the night talking about the end of the world. I want to live it through a big-budget movie." Mack starts the movie, and then pulls his CCTV into his lap. He adjusts his screen so it's only a few inches from his nose.

We watch movies and eat snacks and pizza. They dare me to eat a coconut Oreo, and I do. It's disgusting. Mack opens his present from Grandpa Joe—without his parents around—and we tell him the whole story from Christmas Eve. We have to skip one of the other movies to make sure we have time for *Armageddon.* (Which was a little disappointing because they didn't spend any time preparing for impact.) And at midnight, we high-five and drink sparkling cider.

"So begins our last year on Earth. Cheers!" Londyn raises her plastic champagne glass.

"To our last few months of *life as we know it.*" Why do I

have to keep emphasizing that the world is not ending completely?

"To the bucket list!" Mack shoots off a popper and show-
ers me in confetti.

I know after impact I'll be spending most of my time
with my family. We won't have a choice. But I'm not going
to let these two out of my life. Once the firestorm is over and
the acid rain stops and it's generally safe outside, I'll make
sure we get to hang out.

Chapter **22**

The month of January revolves around Nature Club, the *Doomsday Express,* and our bucket list. (The bucket list is mostly Mack planning out all our Saturday afternoons.) We also have end-of-quarter testing in almost every class, but I don't let that take up too much of my time.

Londyn and I distribute issue number two immediately after Christmas break. We take a little longer on the third one because we don't know what to add—and I don't want to get caught. But then Dr. Cologne puts out an important message.

It's predicted with 90 percent certainty that 2010PL7 will crash into Earth the first or second week of April.

And we have our headline for issue number three.

In Nature Club, I devote one meeting to first aid and the next to bug-out bags. I share my BOB, going over each item, but everyone is obsessed with the MREs. Spencer offers me ten dollars for my chicken pesto pasta. I promise to bring more next time.

"I know a guy," I tell them.

Grandpa Joe hooks me up with a whole case of MREs. And on February 5, approximately two months before the asteroid is expected to crash, I load my backpack with twelve meals and leave my school binder at home.

"Snack time," I announce. They cheer and say thanks, and obviously have no idea what they're in for.

"I'm vegetarian," Ajay says. I throw him the envelope marked *elbow macaroni and tomato sauce*.

"I want pizza," Mack says, holding out his hands. "Is there any pizza? Cheese? Pepperoni? I don't care."

"No," I answer. "Here. Have meatballs in marinara sauce."

Mack dramatically sniffs the unopened pouch and sings, "Yum." It has no smell.

"Each meal has about twelve hundred calories and a third of your daily vitamins and minerals." I hold up the two that are left: beef stew and lemon pepper tuna. "If you were in the army, they'd give you three per day, but you can totally survive on one." The thought of eating more than that makes my stomach hurt.

"Can we eat these?" Spencer asks. "Or should we save them?"

"You can eat these. But you should—"

Spencer tears his open before I finish my sentence.

"M&M's!" he yells.

"Yes. There's also toilet paper and matches. These are military issue. They are meant to be used in the field, not in your house."

"Or in a science classroom," Londyn adds.

"True." I nod. "You should probably have seven of these for each person in your family. They're good in case you need to bug out. Might also be valuable for trade."

"How do you cook them?" Jade turns her package over, looking for instructions.

"You don't have to actually cook them. You could eat them right now. But you can heat them up. Here, I'll show you." I grab Jade's envelope of Mexican-style chicken stew and place it inside the provided heating sleeve. Then I add the flameless ration heater and pour in the pouch of salt water. Steam seeps from the top as I set it upright on the table.

"That's so awesome." Ajay leans closer. "It's cooked by a chemical reaction."

"Yep, no fire needed." I smile like I'm the scientist who invented this. "Now we just have to wait fifteen minutes, and your meal will be done."

"What are the matches for, then?" Brent asks.

"Making a fire, which we're not doing." I collect the matches from everyone and hide them in the bottom of my backpack.

Jade clicks her tongue. "There's a lot of packaging here. This isn't good for the environment. We'll eat these meals in minutes, and this plastic will be around for years."

"Um, I'm just hoping I'm around for years," Londyn says as she dumps the contents of her MRE on the lab table.

"Me too," Brent says.

Everyone unpacks their meals and "cooks" their main course. I assist Mack with his and don't bother making my own. I've sampled enough.

"Again, these are good for when you're on the go. You need other meal options for in your house." I open my backpack and pull out the *Survivalist* magazine. The guy on the cover is wearing a black tank top that shows off his massive biceps, and he's holding a knife that's longer than his arm.

"Oh," Spencer says, "I don't have that issue."

"You can have this one when I'm done." I open to the page I marked and show it to the group. "I'd recommend this. It's a month of food in a waterproof container."

I pass the magazine around.

"After impact, stores will be looted and emptied. You won't be able to buy groceries. And because of the impact on the environment, we won't be able to grow food for a few seasons. You'll need these buckets."

"How many?" Izabell asks.

"My grandfather has a year's worth for every member of our family." But because Dad doesn't approve, we only have four buckets at our house—enough for a month for me, my brothers, and Dad.

Wyatt takes a picture of the ad with his phone.

"Text that to me," Jade says.

"Me too," Dominic says. And Wyatt sets up a group text that includes all of us except Brent, who doesn't have a phone.

"Cell phones will be useless in a few months anyway," Mack says, trying to make him feel better.

The food continues to heat. Spencer touches his and shrieks. The outside gets pretty hot.

"What's going on?" Mrs. Walsh asks from the doorway between the classroom and her office.

"Nothing," I blurt out.

She must suspect *nothing* means *something* and walks over.

"Are those MREs?" She points and smiles.

"Yes." No sense in lying since the letters *M, R,* and *E* are boldly written on the outside of each brown envelope. Actually, it was kind of a stupid question. Mrs. Walsh can read.

"My brother was in the Marines," she says. "He used to bring MREs home, and we'd use them for backpacking trips. I'd mix the peaches with the roll and add one of the coffee creamers and make 'peach cobbler.'" She makes air quotes around the words *peach cobbler.*

"That sounds disgusting," Jade says.

"It was," Mrs. Walsh says. She pulls her lips to the side, and I expect her to ask more questions. Instead, she tells us to be careful. "The packages can get pretty hot." Then she goes back to her desk.

While we wait the last five minutes for the main courses to heat, we arrange the rest of the food from the MREs across the table. Each comes with a side dish like fruit or rice, crackers or a roll, a spread like peanut butter or cheese, a drink mix, seasonings, and the best part, dessert.

"Anyone want to trade?" Brent asks, holding up Tootsie Rolls. "I can't eat them with braces."

"You might want to get your braces taken off before April," I suggest. "Who knows when your orthodontist might be open after impact."

He touches his mouth. "You're right."

"I'll trade," Izabell says. She holds up Skittles. Then Jade offers her crackers and jalapeño spread. She wants pretzels. They start swapping like it's the day after Halloween. Somehow Londyn ends up with two packages of M&M's, but she gives one to me.

When the food is done, they carefully tear open their pouches and grab the provided plastic spork.

"Bon appétit." Mack sloppily scoops out a meatball. We watch him chew and nod. "Not bad."

Spencer doesn't hesitate. He takes a giant mouthful and then another and another. The whole time he makes *yummy* noises.

Wyatt eats a bite of his stew and his face falls. I suggest he add hot pepper flakes. He pours two envelopes on top and mixes it.

"Better," he says when he takes his next bite.

Jade stirs her meal but doesn't eat it. Izabell smells hers and exaggerates a gagging sound.

"Do I need to remind you," Londyn says, "y'all drank toilet water? Just try it."

Jade takes a bite. Izabell follows her lead.

"It's okay." Jade shrugs. "But I'm going to miss real food like French fries."

"Maybe we should plan a last meal," Mack suggests. "I want enchiladas verdes from Taco Casa. Mmm."

"I'd want fried chicken and waffles. Like my mom used to make." Londyn looks at the floor, and then she catches me staring at her. "And the kitchen-sink sundae from Molly's Ice Cream Shop."

"What would you want, Elle?" Mack asks.

I rub my neck and think about the question. "Maybe doughnuts. Baked goods are going to be scarce." The Krispy Kreme HOT NOW sign may never light up again. "And bacon, because, well, bacon is just the best. Goes with everything."

"Wait!" Wyatt looks up from his meal. "Are we not going to have bacon in the apocalypse?"

"At least not often." I shrug. "How are the MREs?"

"Mine isn't so bad," Ajay says. He offers his packet to the group. Spencer takes a scoop. Jade and Izabell share theirs. Dominic gives some of his to Mack and Brent. Wyatt dips his spork in Londyn's pouch. And just like that, it's a communal meal.

Londyn pushes her plastic spork into my hand. "Come on, we're all doing it."

"I've eaten more MREs than I can count." I push away her packet.

"Be part of the team, Norie." She won't stop. "Nor-ie! Nor-ie!" Two months ago, this would have been irritating. I would have gotten upset and yelled and threatened to quit. Now it's still annoying, but not as much. Maybe the asteroid is making me chill. Maybe it's something else.

Chapter 23

The boys are in bed, and I'm finishing my math homework.
I'd rather be working on our fifth newsletter. We distrib-
uted number four today, and students literally ran to the
bathrooms to get a copy. We want to have an edition ready
weekly. But if I don't get my math grade up, Dad's going to
insist on tutoring me and checking my work.

I'm almost done with the second-to-last problem when
Dad comes to my room. Bubbles follows him in.

"Can we talk?" Dad pulls out my desk chair and takes a
seat. It's never good when a parent says this. Either I'm in
trouble or someone's dying.

"Okay." I close my math book, leaving the pencil inside
to mark the spot.

"What is this?" He's holding a copy of our first newsletter.

"Nothing." Stupid answer, but it's what popped into my brain.

"I found it in the bottom of your backpack."

Londyn was right. I should have gotten rid of all the evidence.

"Why were you going through my stuff?" I look around my room for my bag. I must have left it in the kitchen.

"Something smelled awful. I also found a rotten banana." He cringes. "Are you anxious about this asteroid?"

I shrug.

"How often do you visit that website?" he asks.

I shrug again.

"Well, I looked at it. I really looked at it. This Martin Cologne is simply seeking attention. He was fired for his alarmist ideas. His colleagues have all dismissed his theories."

"Other experts believe him now. Like Dr. Yukofski." My hands are balled into fists.

Dad sighs. "I saw that. I think it's part of the hoax."

Hoax? I get that it's hard to believe. I understand that some may have doubts. But hoax?

"What will it take for you to believe them?" I ask.

Dad sighs. "Yukofski has not made a public statement in

a decade. I *believe* someone is pretending to be this reclusive scientist. You have to consider that it might be an impostor."

"I'll consider that it might be an impostor if you consider that it might all be real." My eyes sting and I blink hard to keep from crying.

"Eleanor, give me your computer."

"What?" It sits open next to me on my bed. I put an arm around it like I can protect it.

He holds out his hands.

"You can't take away my computer."

"I'm not taking it away. I'm installing parent-protection software."

"No."

"If you want a computer, these are the rules."

I hand it over. "This is unfair. You're like a Communist dictator. What else are you going to block?"

"I'm blocking the website, and I will be tracking *all* activity. Your internet search history will be emailed to my account daily."

"This is like reading someone's diary."

"You keep a diary? Since when?" He raises an eyebrow.

"I'm not about to now, Stalin." *I think Stalin was a Communist.* "Will you be reading my emails too?"

"I didn't think kids emailed. I thought you only know

how to text." He's trying to joke, but none of this is funny. "Do you remember what we talked about when you first got a computer?"

I look away.

"Everything you do leaves a digital footprint. Never write anything that you wouldn't want your parent or teachers to see. Don't send pictures you wouldn't want to be shared in front of the class. The internet is not a safe place for secrets." He types a few more commands, then hands it back.

"Is your spy machine all ready to go?" I ask.

"And now your phone."

"No! Seriously?"

Every line on his face answers that question. I slap my phone into his palm.

"When can I have it back?"

"As soon as I password-protect the web browser." At least he's not taking it away forever. He plays with it for five minutes before giving it back.

"Done?"

"I'm satisfied." He stands up. "Eleanor, I need you to listen to me. The world is not ending in April. Do you understand?"

"I'm glad Grandpa Joe believes me." I know immediately I shouldn't have said this.

Dad's jaw flexes, and he tilts his head down like a bull ready to charge.

"Your grandfather has taken his *hobby* too far. I don't like it, and I don't want any more of it in this house."

I hold my breath and glance at the prepper book on my desk. Dad follows my gaze.

Please don't take it away. Please, I recite in my head.

"You don't need this stuff." He grabs the book. It's full-on censorship in the Dross house.

"Don't," I mumble, but can't say any more without crying.

He stands, still clutching my book, and then steps closer to me. He holds out an arm like he's going to hug me. I turn away.

"I love you, Eleanor. Good night."

I don't speak. I don't look at him. I hear the door close.

He's cut me off from what I need most.

I shove my math textbook off my bed, no longer in the mood for homework. Bubbles flinches at the noise. When I sniff, she jumps on the bed to check on me.

"We can't let him stop us." I hug my dog. Then I grab my computer and try the website using three different browsers. I can't get through.

I text Londyn.

ME: My dad has blocked me from the website

LONDYN: Why?

ME: He doesn't believe.

And until he does, it's up to me and Grandpa Joe and Londyn. We have to keep this going and not worry about the consequences. Survival is all that matters.

Chapter 24

I'm in serious website withdrawal—it's been over a week. Between classes, I corner Londyn in the girls' bathroom and beg her to invite me to her house. Her family doesn't practice censorship.

"Don't you have to watch your brothers?" she asks.

"They don't get off the bus until three-fifteen. I can still be home in time. I just need twenty minutes on a computer that isn't locked down with parental controls."

"I'm not really allowed to have people over."

"Please. It's important."

"I don't know. I should ask my aunt first." Londyn chews on a fingernail.

"Then call her. Or text her. Now!" We have two minutes until our next class. There's no time to waste.

"She sleeps during the day," Londyn says.

"Do you *not* want me to come over?" I try to get her to look at me, but she's focused on the mirror over my shoulder. "You've been to my house thousands of times."

"Fine! You can come over!"

• • •

Londyn's aunt is getting ready for her night shift when we arrive. She takes two seconds to say hello and then hurries off to make her lunch, which will be more like a late dinner.

"Where's your mom?" I ask Londyn.

"Probably her room. She's always in there."

"Doing what?"

"I don't know. Sleeping. Doing nothing. We leave her alone. That's what she wants."

I want to ask why. *Is she sick? Is she mad?* But it's clear Londyn doesn't want to talk about it. Maybe she doesn't know why.

"Is your dad here?" As soon as I ask the question, I realize she's never mentioned him once.

"What's with all the questions? I thought you came over to use my computer, not write my biography."

Note to self: don't ask Londyn about her family. It makes her more rabid than usual.

I follow Londyn down a hallway and into a bedroom. The walls are a light yellow. The bedspread has a sunflower design and a bunch of round lacy pillows. On the wall are framed landscapes. I spot a school copy of *A Tree Grows in Brooklyn* on the nightstand, a worn basketball near the bed, and the dual-band radio Grandpa Joe gave her in the corner. We've hardly used the radios since Christmas break.

"Is this *your* room? Because it looks like something my aunt Maggie would love. She has lacy towels in her guest bathroom, but you're not supposed to use them. They're for show only."

"Shut up. And stop with the questions. This is not *my* room." She turns away from me to power up her computer—it's a huge old desktop. In the corner, there's a hamper filled with black clothes. This is *definitely* her room. At least for now.

She opens the website and then gestures to the kitchen chair in front of the computer, which is set up on a folding table.

"Thanks." I take a seat and start reading.

RUSSIANS EXPLORING TECHNOLOGY TO BLAST ASTEROID OFF COURSE

Scientists at the Russian Federal Space Agency have created a nuclear-fueled rocket that may be capable of altering the path of an asteroid or a meteoroid. Unfortunately, the range of this technology is not sufficient to clear us from danger. The gravitational pull from Earth and the sun will correct any temporary deflection caused by the Russian craft. Even if the rocket were fitted with missiles (nuclear or other explosive materials), the size of 2010PL7 and the space environment—or lack of environment—would not result in obliteration of the asteroid. A fragmented NEA would still be on a collision course with Earth.

The post went up only three hours ago, but already there are over one hundred comments. I scroll through them quickly. Most are supporting Dr. Cologne and offering to assist by writing emails and making phone calls. A few comments are insults. One stands out.

You're an idiot. This program was announced three years ago and has NOTHING to do with YOUR asteroid. You're a quack who's spreading lies.

Dr. Cologne responded directly to the comment. He doesn't do this often.

The research began years ago. If you took the time to read the article I shared, you'd know that the

Russian government funneled an additional twenty million dollars into the program this week. Perhaps you think this a twenty-million-dollar coincidence.

For the next fifteen minutes, I read as fast as I can, trying not to miss anything important. I need hours (and a faster internet connection), but I've only got minutes to learn the fate of Earth. My heart races like I'm an undercover agent defusing a ticking bomb.

When I click a link about the difficulties of making orbital calculations, the computer freezes, and I bang the mouse against the table in frustration.

"Whoa, take it easy," Londyn says.

"Sorry."

"What's wrong?" She lies on her sunflower-covered bed, tossing the basketball in the air.

"I just don't get how this isn't on the front of every newspaper in the world."

"Is there a location for impact?"

"Not yet." I twist in the chair to face her. "If the asteroid's target is here, there's not much we can do. If it's farther away, a basement can be pretty secure. But it won't make a difference if Hamilton is the bull's-eye. The craters from other strikes are miles wide and thousands of feet deep."

"Are you trying to comfort me?" She stops tossing the ball and stares out the window.

I shrug.

"Well, don't. Because you're bad at it." She hugs the ball to her chest. "And I'm not worried about me."

"Who, then?" I know she only wants to scare the kids at school.

"No one. Never mind."

I narrow my eyes like I can figure it out if I focus hard enough.

"Don't you have to go?" She motions with her chin to the clock on the nightstand.

Londyn is obviously uncomfortable with me in her room. Or maybe she's just uncomfortable with herself in this room. I show myself out.

Chapter 25

I decide to change up things for the next Nature Club meeting. We're heading outdoors and away from the comforts of Mrs. Walsh's classroom. I send a group text message.

ME: bring 2 empty milk jugs to nature club

ME: gallon size

ME: don't ask me why

ME: I'm not telling

And everyone but Londyn (and Brent, who's not on the chat) asks. I ignore them. They'll find out tomorrow.

• • •

"And what will you be doing outside?" Mrs. Walsh asks as the rest of the group files into the room. It's February and about forty degrees out. I don't think she's eager to stand in the cold and babysit us,

"We're going to exercise," I explain.

"And that's part of 'Nature' Club how?" She does air quotes around the word *nature*. My stomach drops. She's onto us.

I shrug. "Humans are part of nature. We'll do a few exercises and then check our pulse. Then drink some water and do it again." I try to make it sound like a legit science experiment.

"That's a very loose interpretation of nature, but okay." She nods. "Stay in the track area so I can see you from here."

"Thanks."

I join the rest of the crew. I didn't warn them to wear sneakers or dress in sweatpants, because running in our regular clothes might be a good lesson.

"Hey, Eleanor," Jade says. "What are we doing?" She's wearing cute black boots that have a little heel and a denim skirt with leggings. This is not going to be her day.

"Why do we need these?" Wyatt holds up his jugs.

I wave everyone over into our usual huddle. They're used to it by now.

"Today we're going to talk about one thing that every prepper should be doing, but most don't."

"Building a bunker," Spencer says. Then he pushes up the sleeves on his sweatshirt like he's literally about to start working.

"No. And every time you talk about bunkers, I think you should give each of us a dollar."

"I like that idea," Jade says.

"We'll be rich," Londyn adds. "Do you have a college savings account? Because we'll be taking it."

Spencer crosses his arms and pretends to be mad.

"What we need is to be physically ready. We need to be in shape. Because AI—after impact—we won't be spending our days staring at teachers and doing worksheets. We'll be on the move." I pump my arms like I'm running.

"Elle," Mack says. "Are you actually suggesting we exercise?"

"Yes." He knows my three least favorite things are sweating, pain, and coconut-flavored snacks, and exercise involves two of those.

"Why did you tell us to bring empty milk jugs?" Ajay asks, holding one in each hand.

"You'll see. Fill 'em up, grab all your stuff, and then meet me on the track." We line up at the sink in the back. I go first, and then Mack. We say goodbye to Mrs. Walsh and head to the school's back door.

Soon as we step outside, my teeth chatter. The sky is

gray, and the clouds are low. Wind blows my hair straight back. I pull on my hood and tie it.

"Wow. When did we move to the North Pole?" Mack asks.

"Get used to it. We could experience years of impact winter."

"I'm beginning to think this asteroid might be bad news."

When everyone gets to the top of the track, I give them the next instructions. "Zip up. Put on your backpacks. Grab your water. One gallon in each hand. And run two miles. Go!"

No one moves. They all stare at me.

"But two miles is eight times around the track," Ajay says, in case I didn't know.

"You can't be serious," Londyn says. "You hate running and almost strangled Mack when he suggested doing a 5K."

"Guys, this is important. It's not going to be like gym class, where you carry nothing, wear the right clothes, and only go outside if the weather is nice. You're going to be running for your lives!"

"Running from what? The asteroid?" Jade puts down her gallons of water and blows into her hands.

"What happened to global warming, Jade?" Dominic asks, pulling his hood so it covers everything but his nose.

"We're not running *from* the asteroid. This is AI. We're running from the aftermath." I jog in place, and no one else moves.

"I'm going inside," Wyatt says. "This club has gotten too weird."

I need to find a way to motivate them. "Wait! Imagine this. It's a week after. You've been in your house the whole time. You can't go out at first because the acid rain would eat through your skin."

Ajay gasps. And Dominic fake gasps.

"But the rain has stopped." I hold up a hand. "This is your chance to go out and get water for your family. You don't know when the acid rain will start again, so you have to move fast. You'll need to run like your life depends on it because it does. Now give me one lap!"

"Yes, ma'am!" Londyn says, and she's the first to take off. Her two water jugs pull her arms down unnaturally.

Jade and Izabell follow, and then the rest except Ajay and Mack.

"I have a question, Eleanor," Ajay says. "If it's been raining acid, where are we going to find clean water? Where are we running to?"

"I don't know. A well. Just run, Ajay."

"Okay."

I offer Mack my arm, and he grabs my puffy coat above the elbow. We jog, each of us carrying only one container.

"I can't believe you're running when you don't have to," he says.

"What do you mean, I don't have to? Of course I have to."
I just shake my head. How does he expect me to be ready if
I don't train?

Mack and I are the last to get back to the starting
point. We've run only one lap, not two miles like I wanted.
My lungs ache from the cold air, but now is not the time to
quit.

"This time . . ." I pause to suck in some more oxygen.
"It's a month after and someone has broken into your supplies and stolen your last box of beef jerky."

"I hate beef jerky," Jade says.

"I don't eat meat," Ajay adds.

"Whatever," Londyn says. "Just go with it." She doesn't
sound out of breath at all.

I put down my water jug and motion for everyone else to
do the same. Except Londyn; I tell her to keep one.

"You need to catch that person or your family won't eat.
They'll starve. They'll die." I pause to look everyone in the
eyes, and to catch my breath. "And that thief who has stolen
from you and who has put your loved ones at risk is Londyn
Diggs."

"What? Me? Why me?"

I lean close to her and whisper, "Start running."

"Oh." And she does.

"Get her!" I yell. "Get the thief. Feed your family."

Spencer yells and sprints after Londyn likes he's storming a castle. Everyone else follows and screams like we're a crazed mob, which I guess we kind of are.

Mack is on my arm again and laughing. We have no chance of catching Londyn. Even with her carrying the water. She's fast and determined.

When she gets back to the top of the track, she doesn't stop. She's got us doing laps, which was what I wanted to begin with. I'd smile, but the cramp in my side is forcing me to clench my teeth.

"Breathe, Elle," Mack reminds me.

"I am!"

We are running at a pace that's barely faster than walking speed. Soon, Londyn is more behind us than in front of us.

"I don't think we're getting our beef jerky back," Mack jokes.

I grunt my agreement. My side hurts. My lungs are frozen. My toes are throbbing. I wish this had been someone else's idea so I could scream at them.

Londyn comes up behind us. "So what torture do you have planned for the next meeting? Maybe we can throw javelins at each other." She seems to be the only one in shape.

"Don't do anything too fun," Mack says. "I won't be there."

"Swimming?" I can only manage a one-word question.

"No. I'm visiting the Conrad School."

It feels like a punch to the gut. He hasn't mentioned that school in forever. It was before Christmas at least.

I stop running and yank him back. "Why?"

Londyn shrugs and keeps moving. She's not going to let anyone catch her.

"I'm going to end up there eventually. If not next year, at least part of high school."

I get in his face. "What are you talking about?"

"What?" He tries to step around me. "Dude, we should be running. We need to set a good example."

"Mack, stop. You aren't going to the Conrad School." My lungs, feet, and side no longer hurt. But my face burns.

"Are you forbidding me?" He forces a laugh. "Will you kidnap me? Lock me up?"

"The asteroid!"

He stops laughing. "I know about the asteroid."

Jade and Spencer pass us. They slow down. I know they're trying to hear what we're fighting about.

"Then why are you looking at that school? It'll be closed down after SHTF. If it is miraculously open, it won't have electricity or clean water. There's no way your parents are sending you."

"But what if it doesn't happen? We should be prepared for that too."

I flinch. Where is this coming from? If he doesn't take it seriously, he'll never survive.

"You don't believe Dr. Cologne?" I ask.

"I totally believe him. Like with ninety-five percent certainty."

"Ninety-five? How is that *totally believing?*" My voice catches in my throat.

"Okay. I'm ninety-nine percent sure he's right."

More kids run past. From the corner of my eye, I can see Londyn at the top of the track.

"Elle, I have to visit the Conrad School. I have to do it for my parents. Doesn't matter what I believe."

"The asteroid is one hundred percent certain," I say. "You're wasting your time."

"Okay, okay," he says. "But you have to convince my parents of that. Do you want to come over tonight and tell them? Think about it, Elle. I don't have a choice."

I can't say anything else. I've always counted on Mack. He's been my friend forever. Without him . . . I don't even want to think about it.

"If I visit the school or not, does it really make a difference?" he asks. "It doesn't change what's happening in April. Right?"

"You'd learn more by coming to Nature Club than visiting that place." I see my angry reflection in his dark glasses.

"You're right. Like today I learned if I run while carrying a gallon of water, I'll end up with a bruised thigh." He rubs his leg.

"I'm serious. You can't leave Hamilton after impact. It won't be safe."

"I promise. I won't. Okay?" He tugs on my arm. "Come on, let's keep running. We have to get these people in shape before April."

Mack might be the most trustworthy kid in all of Hamilton Middle School, but I know he just lied to my face. He doesn't realize what he's risking. Even with all I've done, I may still end up losing my best friend.

Chapter 26

Mack is off wasting his time at the Conrad School, but things aren't as bad as they usually are when he's gone. At lunch, I talk to Londyn, Spencer, Ajay, and Dominic. They all want to know what we're doing at the meeting this afternoon.

"No more exercise, please," Spencer begs with folded hands. "I'm still sore from last time."

"That was two weeks ago," I say.

"I'm a slow healer." He rotates his head and stretches out his neck.

"No working out today. But you should be doing that on your own. That's how you get in shape. Do a little each day." I haven't done any exercise except what's mandatory in gym class, but I don't tell him.

"So what are we doing, Norie?" Londyn asks.

"Fine, I'll tell you. Today is a special two-part meeting. First, I'm going to teach you about the difference between heirloom seeds and genetically engineered seeds."

"That sounds exciting." Londyn fakes a huge yawn.

"And I've agreed to let Ajay give us a space lesson."

"Did you know most 'shooting stars' are actually bits of space rock burning up as they enter our atmosphere?" He does air quotes around the words *shooting stars.* "Technically, they're called meteors. My main astronomy focus has been planets and stars. But I've been brushing up on asteroids, comets, and meteoroids because it seems most important to our future."

I don't see the point in learning about space. The only space object I'm concerned with is 2010PL7, and that'll be pulverized in April.

"If Ajay gets to run a meeting, I want to run a meeting," Spencer whines.

"What would you talk about?" Londyn asks him.

"I could teach y'all how to use a slingshot," he says. "I got one for Christmas, and I've been practicing."

"I want to do something too," Dominic says with a mouthful of sandwich. "I could—"

"Stop! We don't have time," I say. "I have the rest of our

meetings planned out. We've only got a few left. We need to stay focused."

They all start talking and asking questions. I almost miss the good old days when no one spoke to me. Almost.

"I'm going to the bathroom." I shove my uneaten lunch into my bag and get up.

"I'm going too." Londyn stands.

"I actually have to go to the bathroom," I whisper to her.

She shrugs and then follows me into the hall. She's acting weird. I'll admit, we're friends and we hang out a lot. But she's not the clingy kind of friend.

"You okay?" I ask when we're alone.

"I told my parents." She takes a deep breath.

"Oh."

"They're getting a divorce."

"Because of the asteroid?"

"No, you moron." Her insult doesn't have its usual venom. "This divorce has been coming since last summer. At least."

"I'm sorry." I wait for her to say more. She stares at the grimy floor.

But I wasn't kidding. I do have to use the bathroom. I push open a stall door. Once it's closed, she starts talking again.

"My mom and I moved out in the fall. That's why we've been staying with my aunt."

"Okay." I try to stay quiet so she'll keep talking.

"It was supposed to be temporary."

When she pauses, I flush. I leave the stall and go to the sink. Londyn is staring at the same spot on the floor.

"Where's your dad?"

"He's been living with my grandparents in Michigan." Londyn sniffs hard.

I hand her a paper towel.

"Showed my mom the website last night. Told her we all need to be together if we're going to survive this."

"She didn't believe you?"

"Nope." Londyn wipes her eyes with her thumb, leaving a black smudge. "She said I was a brat. Said I was taking my dad's side. Told me to grow up." A few tears run down her cheek. She stops trying to wipe them away.

"My dad doesn't believe it either," I say.

"But at least he's here, and you'll be together." She grabs another paper towel. "And you have Grandpa Joe, your brothers. You're not alone, Norie. Not like me."

"What about your aunt?" I ask.

Londyn shrugs. "She's nice, but . . . I just want . . ."

She doesn't finish, and I don't really know what to say. I try to get her to focus on what we can do now. "We still have time to make your parents believe, and to make my dad. Meanwhile, we need to get ready."

"This asteroid is really happening, right?" She stares at

me, and I can feel a weight on my shoulders and a tightness around my head.

"Yes."

She nods slowly. "It has to happen."

"It will," I whisper.

"And my dad will come home," she says. "And we'll be together."

"Yeah."

. . .

Grandpa Joe picks Londyn and me up after Nature Club. I haven't seen him since Dad put my computer in lockdown weeks ago. I wonder if the two are related.

"Soldiers, how was school?" he asks as we climb into his truck.

"Fine." Honestly, it wasn't our best Nature Club meeting. I think I killed it when I talked about heirloom seeds and gardening. I brought everyone a packet of corn. But Ajay went on and on about space stuff. He even made a PowerPoint presentation. We all got a good nap.

"I've had better," Londyn says.

"How was your—" I try to ask my grandfather about his day, but Londyn cuts me off.

"What's it *really* going to be like? When the asteroid hits?" She turns around in the front seat and faces me.

My eyes open wide. I'm not used to talking about this in front of adults, even if it's Grandpa Joe.

"Depends on the site of impact," I explain.

"If it hits North Carolina?" she asks.

"We're basically vaporized in an instant." I shrug. There's no point giving her false hope.

"What if it hits Montana?" She stares at me.

"I'm not sure where Montana is; if it's farther than a thousand miles, we'll be okay. Anywhere within a hundred miles, we aren't going to make it through the first hour." I shrug like, *What are you going to do.*

"Girls, maybe we shouldn't be talking about this." Grandpa Joe looks at me in the rearview mirror. "I promised your daddy that I wouldn't put any ideas in your head."

"Okay." I don't want them to fight again. I pretend to zip my lips and throw away the key.

Londyn turns back around and faces the road. We drive in silence. Grandpa Joe fiddles with the radio. He seems to get frustrated and turns it off.

"Oh Lord, I can't do it," Grandpa Joe says, and Londyn stares at him because neither of us knows what he's talking about.

"What's wrong?" I ask.

"I can't force you to be quiet. This is too important." He slaps the side of the steering wheel. "Eleanor is right. If the asteroid hits the East Coast, we're goners. But anywhere else, we have a fighting chance. And by God, we're going to fight."

For the rest of the ride home, we talk about all the scenarios and what it'll be like living in the aftermath—lawlessness, disease, filth, and constant fear. Grandpa Joe could specialize in giving kids nightmares. My heart races faster than it did when we ran laps carrying gallons of water.

"But don't worry, soldiers, we'll take care of each other," he says as he pulls into Londyn's driveway.

"Thanks, Grandpa Joe." Londyn jumps out of the truck. Maybe I'm wrong, but I think she looks pale.

She texts me thirty seconds later, before I even get home.

LONDYN: Grandpa Joe gave us our next newsletter

ME: huh?

LONDYN: everything he said about the future

LONDYN: we need to write that

ME: you wanna do fiction?

LONDYN: it won't be fiction in april

Chapter 27

Mack returns a few days later. He does a poor job of hiding his excitement about the Conrad School.

"It was so cool, dude. And you can visit. They allow friends and family to come stay."

"Uh-huh," I say into the phone. I don't encourage him to go on, but I'm still trying to be a good friend and not hang up or scream.

"I wish you could check out the dorms. There are two guys to a room, and on each floor there's a kitchen and a living room. We can cook for ourselves or eat in the cafeteria. The living room has a video game system with . . ." He continues describing every inch of the school.

"Sounds great," I say, as if I'd been listening and not focusing on finding a snack from the pantry.

"Can I be honest?" he says. "I'm really nervous."

"About what?" I open a vanilla pudding cup.

"Duh, the school. I've never been away from home for that long. I'd miss my parents . . . and you. Maybe it's a bad idea to move out when you're thirteen."

"It is a bad idea!" I drop a blob of pudding, and Bubbles licks it up. "Because a giant asteroid is going to crash into Earth before you turn thirteen."

"Do we always have to talk about the asteroid?"

"Do you always have to talk about the Conrad School?"

"Okay, okay. I don't want to fight."

"Me either." I slide to the ground with my back against the pantry door, and we have our first awkward silence in the history of our friendship. With only a month or so left to impact, I don't know how to make him realize what's at stake.

"I thought of something else for our bucket list," he practically yells in my ear.

"What?"

"Rock climbing!"

"No way. Why are you determined to kill us?"

Mack laughs. Then he tells me a story about some senior at the Conrad School who has climbed the highest peaks in the Smokies.

When we hang up, I decide to take a chance. I haven't written to Dr. Cologne since Dad put me under surveillance. I've been worried he'd see it, but maybe he needs to.

Dear Dr. Cologne,

I'm concerned about the asteroid. I know there's nothing we can do to stop it, and I'm doing all that I can to be ready. But not everyone believes. Do you have any more information I can give to my family and my friend? What's the date of impact? You must have a guess where it will hit. You're very smart. I know you're working hard to figure it all out. Anything extra you can tell me will be helpful.

E.J.D.

Seconds after I send it, I get a message. But it's an auto-reply.

Thank you for your email. With the enormous amount of correspondences I receive, I'm not able to personally reply to each. Please see the website for the latest information.

• • •

On Saturday afternoon, I wait outside the climbing gym for Mack and Londyn. Mack won't give up on this new rock-climbing dream, but his parents wouldn't let him scale Everest. A plastic mountain will have to do. I think it's a waste of time. We should be gathering supplies. I've asked Grandpa Joe to get me more heirloom seeds and a wheelbarrow. He promised to put it on his list.

Londyn arrives first. She's wearing only a black hoodie with a hole in the sleeve, and it's freezing out.

"Let's wait inside." I grab the door handle and pull just as a few girls push their way out. I recognize them from school.

"Oh, excuse me," Hannah Carpenter says in a sweet voice. But once she realizes it's me on the other side, her smile turns to a growl. She curls her lip, exposing her braces and her disgust of me.

Three other girls trail behind Hannah. They stop talking when they spot me.

I hold the door as they all pass, keeping my focus on the ground.

"Loser," one of them mumbles, but I don't dare look to see who.

When they're gone, Londyn and I finally go inside, and I release a breath I didn't know I was holding.

"Why are the girls at our school so mean?" I ask.

"Total jerks," Londyn adds.

"But why? I've never done anything to them. Ever!"

Londyn bursts out with a laugh. "They weren't talking to you. I'm the loser." She shakes her head. "You really don't pay much attention to the Hamilton Middle School social scene, do you? You're wrapped up in your own little Eleanor Dross world."

Before I can protest, I start piecing the puzzle together. "Those are your best friends!" I blurt out. "You hung with the popular kids last year."

She groans. "There's so much wrong with everything you said. They *were* my friends. Or that's what I thought."

"What happened?" I ask. "Not that you'll tell me."

She tilts her head down and gives me a sideways glare. "Well, you won't."

"Fine. You wanna know?" She grabs my arm and pulls me to a bench near the windows. She looks over her shoulder like she's making sure no one is spying on us. "I had a back-to-school sleepover at the end of last summer. Hannah, Megan, Arya, and Jesse were hanging in my room when my parents decided it was a perfect time to have an epic fight. Like on a nuclear level. They were throwing stuff and screaming. We heard glass breaking and about a million swear words. I guess my mom had put a tracker or something on my dad's phone and she *caught him*."

"Sorry." I assume she means caught him with another woman, but I don't ask.

"I begged them to shut up," she continues. "They wouldn't stop. Finally, my dad stormed out of the house. When I went back to my room, *my friends"*—she shakes her head—"they were texting everyone about it, making jokes about my parents and me."

"That's awful!"

She nods. "No kidding. I kicked them out."

"Jerks. They deserved it."

"Yeah." Londyn looks off into the climbing gym. I can tell she wants to say something else.

"What is it?"

"Nothing. Let's get ready to climb." Maybe she'll never completely trust me.

We give our permission slips to the guy behind the counter and pay for one hour of climbing. Mack and his dad walk in while we're picking out helmets.

"Who's ready to reach the clouds?" Mack says when he joins us.

"Not me," I say. "But I'm ready to climb thirty feet in a stinky gym."

"Hello, Eleanor. Hello, Londyn." Mr. Jefferson isn't going to leave. We might have been able to convince Mrs. Jefferson. She thinks Mack should be learning to handle stuff on his own. Mr. Jefferson thinks Mack is capable, but he likes to hang close by just in case.

We get our harnesses and another helmet. Mack gives his cane and dark glasses to his dad. Mr. Jefferson finds a seat along the wall. He taps on his phone but also keeps his eyes on us.

"Let's go to the expert wall," Mack says.

"Slow down, Spider-Man," I say.

"We have limited time. Let's make the most of it." Mack holds out his hand, looking for my arm.

"You're very confident. Give it a try." I escort him to the expert wall.

"Who's going first?" he asks.

"You!" Londyn and I say at the same time.

"So much for ladies first." Mack turns, and I adjust him so he's standing in front of the climbing gym employee.

The guy stares hard at Mack. His eyebrows rise up. I don't think Mack can climb this wall. He has no experience. But I get furious when people think he can't do something because he's blind.

"He can do this," I say loudly.

"Okay." The employee holds up his hands in surrender.

We get Mack's harness hooked up to the safety ropes and inspected. The employee works the belay—which keeps Mack from falling if he slips. In seconds, Mack climbs ten feet off the ground by feeling around with his hands.

"Reach up with your left, about two feet over your head," I suggest.

He finds the hold and tries to pull himself up.

"No," the employee says. "Climbing is about using your legs. You have to find your foothold first. Use your leg muscles."

"Okay! Direct me where to go!" Mack shouts.

"Left foot goes up and to the left," the employee says.

Mack lifts his leg and fishes around with his foot.

"Higher. Higher. A little left. There!" The employee is actually helpful.

"Got it."

"Adjust your weight to that foot. Then reach up with your left hand to the green ledge—"

"Can't see."

"Sorry. Reach up over your left ear. There's a two-inch ledge."

Mack grabs hold. The employee continues to give directions, and Mack follows along. He moves foot, hand, foot, hand. In a few minutes, he's halfway up the wall.

"Maybe he *is* Spider-Man," Londyn says to me.

"It is annoying that he thinks anything is possible."
Except the asteroid.

"You two have been friends forever, right?" she asks.

"Since kindergarten. So, basically, yes."

"You're lucky." She flicks the black off one of her nails.

"Well, he makes it easy. He's not a jerk most of the time."

I watch him scamper up the wall like he's invincible.

"More happened with Hannah and them."

"Oh?" I look at Londyn, but she avoids my eyes.

"After they told the world about my parents' epic fight . . .
I mean, they actually recorded parts of it and shared it with
everyone. I sorta got revenge." She clears her throat. "I figured if they shared my secrets, I'd share theirs."

"What did you do?"

"I told Ethan that Megan had a major crush on him. I
told Dominic that Hannah thought he was gross, but she actually liked him. And I told everyone that Jesse only made
the soccer team because her mom was dating the coach."

"Was that true?"

"They went out once. I think." She shrugs. "And I posted
an embarrassing picture of Arya that I'd promised never to
show anyone."

I try to imagine what it could be.

"It wasn't that bad," Londyn says. "It looks like she's
picking her nose."

A bell rings. It's Mack. He's made it to the top. Londyn
and I clap.

"So you got your revenge?" I ask, my voice rising to a
higher pitch. Londyn is a friend, but she's not exactly the
"good guy" of this story.

She turns and gets close to my face. "I know I was a jerk.

I tried to apologize. But it was too late. They said a thousand worse things about me. Every day for the first two months of school, they weren't happy unless they could make me cry."

I remember Londyn in gym class the day she tried to knock my head off with a basketball. Maybe it wasn't about me and my lack of dribbling skills.

"That stinks," I mumble, not sure what to say. "I'm sorry."

"Well . . . in a few weeks, none of this will matter." She steps back.

"I think asteroids have a way of wiping out middle school drama. It's one of the plus sides of the world ending."

"I guess." Londyn smiles slowly. "Asteroids also have a way of scaring the crap out of people. Hopefully."

Mack leans back in his harness, and the employee lowers him to the ground.

His dad comes over and hugs him. "Great job, Mack. I texted your mom and your grandparents a photo."

"Cool. Who's next?" Mack wipes his chalky hands on his pants.

"No thanks," Londyn says.

"I'll try the beginner wall." I look over to where the five-year-olds are climbing.

Mack takes off his helmet. "What! Dudes, you can totally do this. Give it a try."

Londyn looks at me and then at the towering wall Mack

just scaled. It doesn't matter if we make it to the top. An attempt is enough to cross it off our bucket list.

"Okay." I twist my paracord bracelet. "But I'm only doing this because you're not a jerk."

"What?" Mack seems confused.

Londyn flashes me a smile.

"I'll do it too," she says. "Because you're both not jerks."

DOOMSDAY EXPRESS—SIXTH EDITION

April

The asteroid 2010PL7 crashes into Brazil. It's like 100 nuclear bombs going off at once. Millions die, but no one knows the exact number. A cloud of dirt and rock is thrown into the sky. Some rocks even leave the atmosphere and go into orbit. The rest of the debris falls back to the earth, and not just in Brazil. It rains dirt and rock across the hemisphere. The falling sediment burns and causes massive fires and destruction. The smoke blocks out the sun. Some of the homes in your neighborhood are destroyed.

Electricity and phone service is knocked out almost everywhere, including in Hamilton. You don't go to school. People rush to the grocery store to buy food and bottles of water. Shelves are emptied quickly. They think this is temporary, like after a tornado. They are wrong.

The Next Week
At first, neighbors are helpful, and you support each other. You hang out and have big indoor picnics, because you need to eat all the meat and other stuff in the freezer before it goes bad. School is still not open. Your parents don't go to work. Gasoline for cars is scarce because gas stations are emptied. Banks and ATMs are closed and getting cash is almost impossible. Some people get sick because the water in the houses is not safe. They don't know to treat it. It's harder to tell night from day, and the air smells like it's burning. Everything is gray, like you're watching an old black-and-white movie.

A Month Later
You stay in your house with the doors locked and the windows boarded up. Someone keeps a lookout all the time. Your neighbors steal from each other, because everyone is desperate for food and water. You cannot call the police. The cell phones don't work, and cops aren't around. Your family collects rainwater in a large barrel, but it's still full of dust and dirt from impact. The calendar says May, but

it's cold. There's frost almost every night. You cannot plant vegetables. This is the beginning of impact winter.

Six Months After
Sickness is everywhere. A small cut leads to terrible infection. The flu and stomach bugs become deadly. Only a few people are capable of helping. You take a relative to a nurse down the street. She gives you some medicine, but it costs your family a week's worth of food. You work with other people in your community for protection, forming a mutual aid group. You don't let anyone else join unless they have something to offer. It could be skills like hunting or resources like weapons.

A Year Later
You eat once a day, or sometimes once every other day. The streets are filled with garbage and rodents. If you don't have a skill, you are assigned trash collection. The sun peeks through on occasion. Your community will try to plant vegetables this year. The hunters and fishermen have to go farther and farther from your base to find meat, and you worry they won't make it back. You have to believe things will get easier, but you just don't know when.

Five Years Later

Small community schools are open, but only the youngest kids go. Older kids and adults work, doing the farming, trading, security, and medical stuff. You hear on the shortwave radio that a few cities have electricity, water, and even sewage again, but this could be rumors. Your area has solar-generated power for a few hours a week, but it's not reliable. People talk about things getting "back to normal" in a few more years. But you know things will never be exactly like they were. Not after impact.

Chapter 28

"**This is the best thing you've ever written.**" Londyn gives me a small stack of paper. She has printed out our newsletter about the future at her house because Grandpa Joe didn't have time to take me to make copies.

"Thanks." I open my locker. We still have ten minutes before homeroom. Plenty of time to put them in our usual distribution spots.

"I could only make thirty copies. My aunt didn't have much paper."

"Great, our demand is going up, and we have less supply." We learned about supply and demand in social studies, but I can't remember if this is the situation that should be making us rich.

"Relax, Norie. People can share. And I made an email version." She flips her hair over her shoulder and does her best evil smile.

"What?" I glare at her, and her smile falls. "We said nothing goes online. It's too easy to track. Everything online leaves a trail." Now I sound like my dad.

"Don't worry. I created a fake Gmail account. And if they wanted to track us, they would have already. They could have gotten our fingerprints off the first newsletter."

"We're not dealing with the FBI. A middle school principal doesn't know how to run fingerprints. And that only works if you're already in the system. You have to be arrested for something else first."

"Whatever. You don't know what you're talking about."

"Who did you send the email to?" I ask.

"Everyone." She flashes me her evil smile again.

I hold up my hands. "What does that even mean?"

"In the beginning of the school year, the principal accidentally sent out an email that had everyone's email addresses copied on it."

"She did?"

"Yeah, it was like a welcome-back-to-school, you-need-to-buy-a-hundred-notebooks email."

I kind of remember that. Dad printed it out, and we took it with us to Target.

"Wait!" Panic hits my chest first, then my brain. "That email went to parents."

"Really?" She plays with a piece of her hair and avoids looking at me.

"Yes! You sent an email to all the parents in the school!"

"I must have been in my mom's email account. How was I supposed to know that?"

"You weren't supposed to email ANYONE!" I clench my fists.

"Calm down. No one is going to know it's us."

"My dad will."

"Maybe he won't read it," she says.

"He reads anything you put in front of him! Ugh. You've ruined everything!"

"Shut up. I did not!" She pokes me in the chest with one finger.

"What is wrong with you, Londyn!"

"Calm down." She leans forward. Her red face is an inch from mine.

"We agreed to print it." I wave the newsletters. "You did your own thing. You didn't ask me. This is why no one likes you. You can't be trusted." I don't know what I'm saying. I just want to yell.

"No one likes you either. You have a stupid haircut, and you freak out all the time. Like right now! I'm done." She throws her newsletters in the air, then stomps off like the brat she is.

"Good. I'm done too! Don't ever talk to me again. Jerk!" I stand in the hallway, surrounded by the evidence. Tears are threatening to spill out. But I'm not sad. I'm angry—angrier than I've ever been.

"Hey." A kid I don't know stops me. "Is that the *Doomsday* paper?"

"Yeah." I give him my whole stack and slam my locker closed.

When I see Mack in homeroom five minutes later, he already knows about my fight with Londyn.

"I have enhanced hearing," he says when I ask how he knew.

"That's not true."

"Spencer told me he saw you screaming and throwing things."

"*She* was throwing things," I correct him. "Papers."

"What did she do?" he asks.

"She emailed the newsletter to all the parents."

"Why?"

"I don't know. She wants to make everyone's life miserable. Especially mine." I collapse into my chair. "Do your parents read their emails?"

"My mom is the PTA treasurer, and Dad is on the book

fair committee. They know about everything that's happening at school before I do."

"My dad is going to kill me."

"My parents are going to know you're behind this. Your secret is out, Batman." He uses his deepest voice.

"This isn't funny." I turn toward the front of the room, done talking.

I make it through morning announcements and the first two classes without any mention of the newsletter. But in third period, I'm called to the office.

I expect to see my dad or Londyn, but it's only the vice principal, Mr. Young. He's an Asian guy, with a neat black goatee and round glasses. He wears a light-green shirt and a tie with shamrocks on it, even though St. Patrick's Day is a week away.

"I don't think we've met." He introduces himself and motions for me to sit. He has three of our six newsletters lying on his desk.

"Do you know anything about these?" He waves a hand over the papers.

I shrug.

"Did you contribute to these?"

I shrug again.

"Did you hand them out to students? And don't shrug. Answer the questions."

"Do I need a lawyer?" I mean it as a joke. But I'm so nervous it sounds like a kid's terrified request.

"No. We can call your parents if you want."

"What do you want to know? Um . . . I wrote it. I handed them out. I want everyone to be prepared." I don't mention Londyn. I'm not sure why not. I should take her down with me.

"Did you also send an email this morning?"

I give half a nod. "Am I being kicked out of school?"

"No, you're not being suspended. But we need this *Doomsday Express* to stop immediately. It's not appropriate for school. It's not appropriate in general. I believe Ms. Richmond has spoken to all classes about credible sources. Correct?"

"Yes. In the media center."

"This site you reference is not a credible source. The author is not reliable, and his motivations are questionable."

I keep my mouth closed. If Mr. Young doesn't think a Harvard astrophysicist is credible, he's not going to care at all about what a seventh grader with a C-plus average has to say. And I can't think of any better motivation than saving humankind.

"I don't want to see another one of these at school. Is that understood?"

"Yes, sir."

"You will also refrain from using that email list for any purpose. That was not supposed to be available, and you've taken advantage of someone else's mistake. That's not appropriate Hamilton Hawk behavior."

"It won't happen again." Now I'm making promises for Londyn. Who knows what she'll do next? And who cares as long as she leaves me out of it?

"Thank you, Eleanor. I wish we'd met under better circumstances." He scribbles something on a pink form. Then he hands it to me.

Across the top it reads *Disciplinary Record Sheet.*

"You'll need to have a parent sign this and return it to me in the morning." He smiles like he's given me an award, not a prison sentence.

"Why do you need this?"

"Because if it happens again—and I'm certain it won't— we'll have a record that you were warned and understood the consequences."

He really makes it sound like I need a lawyer.

"Okay. Can I go?" The room feels hot, and his smiling is too weird.

"Not quite."

Chapter 29

Mr. Young leaves his office, and a second later, Mrs. Walsh walks in.

"Hello, Eleanor." She takes a seat next to me and turns so our knees are practically touching.

"You wrote the *Doomsday Express*?" her voice is barely above a whisper.

I nod and don't look at her.

"I thought so." She takes a loud breath. "And the Nature Club? Is that part of this doomsday plan too?"

"Yes," I whisper, twisting my paracord bracelet around and around.

"I see. Did Mack help with the newsletter?"

I shake my head.

"What's wrong, Eleanor? What makes you think the world is ending?" she asks.

"The website." I look up quickly and see her shrug.

"I haven't read it."

So I tell her everything about finding the website, learning about prepping from my grandfather, and starting the club to help others get ready.

"Oh, Eleanor." She touches my shoulder and I cover my face. I shouldn't cry, not in front of a teacher.

"And I'm not going to ask you if you believe me. My dad doesn't. If you . . . I just don't want to think about it."

She doesn't say anything until my eyes meet hers. "Thank you for telling me. That was brave of you. I know you care about me and the kids in your club. You're a good person."

I wait for a *but*—like how most adults talk to me. It doesn't come.

"I'm scared," I whisper. Months ago, I didn't care about anyone but Mack and my family, but now I feel responsible. "What if we're not ready? I don't want anyone to be hurt or worse."

"That's understandable." She nods. "These are big questions for anyone. Scientists know of at least five major extinctions."

I nod. "I read the book you gave me."

"That's right." She snaps her fingers, remembering. "So you know it has happened before, and it may happen again. I've read arguments that say we're experiencing a sixth extinction now. Our climate is warming, and our oceans are becoming increasingly acidic."

"Jade talks about this a lot," I say.

"I like that kids are concerned for our planet. Gives me hope. There may be time to turn things around."

"I don't think we can turn the asteroid around." I grab a tissue off the desk and blow my nose.

She gives me a sad grin.

"What do you need me to do, Eleanor?" I don't think an adult has ever asked me this question before. They're always telling me what they need *me* to do. Not the other way around.

"If you tell everyone about the asteroid, they'll believe you. At least the kids in your classes. Then they'll tell their parents. And maybe we can save people. They won't become zombies!"

"Zombies?" She raises her eyebrows.

"Sorry. Not zombies like brain-eating monsters. Those aren't real. *Zombies* is a term for people who aren't prepared for the end of the world. They'll be forced to walk around aimlessly and to scavenge for food and water."

"I've learned something new." She folds her hands

across her lap. "But I cannot tell my classes about the asteroid. Students may believe me, but the parents certainly won't. They don't appreciate it when we stray from the curriculum. I once got an angry email because I mentioned that one college was superior to another, in my opinion. A teacher's influence is restricted in many ways."

I nod. But I feel like she's making excuses.

"What about you?" I ask. "Are you going to be a zombie?"

"I don't want to be a zombie at all." She smiles again. "I think a certain amount of preparation is a good idea for all households. Last year when we had that ice storm and the power was out for three days, my husband and I ate potato chips and marshmallows for dinner."

"This is more than an ice storm, Mrs. Walsh." Every muscle in my body feels tired.

"I know, Eleanor. Thank you for sharing this. You've done your part. But once you give a person the information and the tools, you have to let them choose what to do next. Don't you think?"

I shrug.

"I give students the lessons, the textbooks, the worksheets. I can warn them about bad grades and possible failure. But I cannot force them to do homework. It's their choice."

She's made her choice. I can tell.

"I'm late for math." I stand up.

"Wait." She holds up a hand. "I hate to do this, Eleanor, but we have to shut down the Nature Club. I'm sorry."

I don't say anything, just nod because I'm not surprised.

• • •

When I get off the bus, our minivan is in the driveway. I've never thought about running away before, but this would be a good time. Too bad my BOB is in my closet. If I could sneak in and grab it, I could survive on my own for at least a week.

I find Dad in the kitchen talking on his phone. He holds up a finger, which I assume means "give me a minute."

I nod and head upstairs. Bubbles follows. My room is a mess, but I notice right away that something is missing. My laptop. Running away is looking like a better and better option.

Dad knocks on my door a minute later.

"Where's my computer?"

"You and your computer . . . you and the internet need a break."

"Why?" I can feel the phone in my pocket. *Please don't take that away too.*

"I got an anonymous email today that sounded like it could have been written by you. I also got a call from Mrs. Walsh."

I cross my arms and fall back on my bed. Everyone has betrayed me. Bubbles jumps up and tries to lick my cheek, but I push her away.

"I looked through your computer," Dad continues. "You didn't send the email. So I have to assume you have a co-conspirator or two. Mack? Londyn?"

"When can I get my computer back?" I ask.

Dad ignores the question. "This has to stop, Eleanor. The asteroid isn't a threat. This guy is deranged. He's not a scientist or an expert."

"Yes, he is. He's from Harvard."

"That doesn't matter. He's a disturbed man. And you've emailed him directly. This goes against my rules. I've warned you about—"

"I had questions. It's not like I invited him over or made plans to meet him somewhere."

Dad turns white. "Thankfully. But you cannot contact strange men on the computer. You're putting yourself at risk. The thoughts of what could have happened . . ."

"He's a good guy. He's trying to save the world. Think about that, Dad."

"I can't believe he's had such an influence on you." Dad steps closer and reaches out for my shoulder, but I duck away. "I'm your father. I love you. I'm telling you he's wrong. You need to—"

"Get out!" I yell.

Dad's face looks like I've slapped him. "Excuse me?"

"I want to be alone. Get out." I spit as I yell.

"Eleanor . . ."

"Go away!" I scream so loud my throat hurts.

He shakes his head. "We'll talk again when you calm down." He leaves my room.

We'll talk when you're ready to listen to me. Which is probably never.

Chapter 30

For over a week, Londyn has been missing from lunch. Not just from our table; she doesn't even show up in the cafeteria. Maybe she's been eating in the bathroom or the media center or in prison. I don't care. Because of her, I don't have my computer or Nature Club, and Dad and I barely talk. He says stuff like "good morning," "I love you," and "fold the laundry." That's it.

But today, she's back in the cafeteria, sitting alone at her booth in the section usually reserved for adults.

"Hey, look," Ajay says. "It's Londyn."

"So." I've already noticed but don't want everyone else to know I've noticed.

"Where is she?" Mack asks.

"She's sitting by herself again," Spencer explains.

"Oh gee, I wonder why," Mack says sarcastically. Then he gets up.

"Mack, where are you going?" I ask through clenched teeth.

"I'm going to invite her to sit with us." He opens Candy. "I know she messed up, and I was mad too. But life is short, Elle. You may have heard: there's an asteroid heading our way."

I grab Mack's arm. "She's the reason Nature Club got shut down."

"She made a mistake." He pats my hand. "And she didn't write those newsletters alone."

"You're blaming me for this?"

"No," he says. "No blame. And just because the *school* says we can't have a Nature Club doesn't mean *we* can't have a club. We'll meet somewhere else."

"Like in Eleanor's bunker," Spencer suggests.

"I don't have a bunker!" I say for the thousandth time. "And you owe us each a dollar for mentioning it!"

Mack pushes my hand away. "BRB." His cane moves back and forth as he walks toward the booths along the wall.

I shove half my peanut butter sandwich in my mouth and almost choke when I try to swallow. If she comes over here, I'm leaving. *I'll* sit by myself.

But Londyn doesn't return with Mack.

251

"She won't join us," he says.

"Good."

"Dude, not good." He sits down. "She says you're mad at her."

"I am."

"And she's mad at you. But she used a harsher word. One that's not appropriate in school."

"So what?"

"Why are you so mad?" Spencer asks with a mouthful of Cheetos.

"You know why!" As I struggle to open my bag of chips, I crush half of them. "Why is she mad at me? I didn't do anything."

"I'll find out," Mack offers. He gets up again and makes his way to her table. He cuts off a line of sixth graders coming in for lunch.

"Girls." Spencer shakes his head. "So much drama. You're friends. You're not friends."

Dominic and Ajay nod like Spencer has said something wise.

"Shut up, Spencer. Londyn and I were never real friends. We had a common goal. That's all." I pack up what's left of my lunch in my bag. I don't feel like eating anymore.

Ajay holds up his hands. "We should all calm down. Don't yell. No good comes from yelling."

"And boys are as dramatic as girls," I say. "Spencer, you refused to be partners with that kid in gym class because he called you a woodchuck."

"That was different. That was bullying!" Spencer points a finger in my face.

I hear Candy's tapping as Mack comes back to our table. He's still alone.

"She's mad at you for screaming at her and calling her names." Mack sits.

"See? Yelling doesn't do any good. Ever." Ajay shakes his head.

"Yeah, because I was mad at her. She can't be mad at me for being mad at her. That is dramatic. And stupid." Maybe Spencer is right.

"She's also mad about the newsletter," Mack continues. "She thinks you don't want to do it anymore."

"We can't!"

"Maybe you can't hand it out at school, but you can still write it. The newsletter was good, Elle."

"The newsletter was useless. We are less than a month away from the end of the world, and I bet not a single person at this school is ready."

"I am," Spencer says. "I got a water filter *and* a first-aid kit."

"Awesome. You'll survive a day or two."

"Elle, calm down. So the club is over, and the newsletter is over. It's not like the world is ending." Mack slaps the table. "Oh wait, it is. Admit that you liked Nature Club and you liked writing the *Doomsday Express.*"

"I did," I say without hesitation. "And she ruined it all." It's like Mack isn't even listening to me.

"She was part of all the good stuff too. And with an asteroid heading our way, is this the time to hold a grudge?"

"She's good at holding grudges," Spencer says. "All girls are."

"Stop!" I shoot Spencer a look and then turn toward Mack. "I don't care what she does. None of it matters. Tell her she can sit here if you want."

"You tell her."

"No."

"Fine!" Mack says. "You're the most stubborn person I know. At least I thought so. Until I met Londyn. Now it's a tie." He slides out of his seat and turns toward Londyn's table.

I almost shout, "No, I'm more stubborn!" But I realize he doesn't mean it as a compliment.

Of course, Londyn doesn't return with Mack. The lights dim. There are only five minutes left of lunch anyway.

"She wants you to go talk to her." Mack sits, and he groans like it takes real effort or he's got arthritis.

"I'm not going—"

"And she's not coming. So figure it out, Elle. Just figure it out. I bet I've walked a mile already."

"Whatever." I get up. But I don't head to Londyn's table. I purposely go the long way to the trash cans.

Out of the corner of my eye, I see her get up. She stretches and takes her time. But eventually, she walks toward the trash cans too.

We meet standing next to giant yellow bins filled with uneaten cafeteria food that probably didn't smell any better before it was dumped in.

"Mack says you're done being mad." She studies the ends of her hair like we aren't talking about anything important.

"Is that what he said?" I roll my eyes.

"I'm done too."

"Okay."

"I think we should make another newsletter." She stops playing with her hair and looks at me.

"No."

"I won't email it. I won't put it on the internet. I promise."

"The newsletter isn't helping. Not that you wanted to help anyone. You want to scare your enemies. I get it."

"Not anymore."

I tilt my head. I don't believe her.

"I mean . . . this is getting real. I read the website every night, and I'm . . . I'm scared." She pulls a folded piece of paper from her pocket.

"What's this?"

"Read it. It's from the site."

I unfold the paper.

IMPACT—APRIL 7

For those living in the United States, I've calculated impact to be April 7. The impact velocity will be a minimum twenty-one miles per second. If the strike occurs on land, the transient crater will be fifty-two miles wide and the final crater closer to ninety miles across. The thermal radiation impact will be four seconds after physical impact, with the duration of irradiation lasting thirty-three minutes. Effects of the thermal radiation will include third-degree burns, wood and paper fires, and asphalt melt. A seismic aftershock will measure a ten on the Richter scale and begin twenty seconds after impact.

I read it twice but can only focus on—and understand—the date.

"How many days until the seventh?" I ask.

"Three weeks from yesterday."

Some kid tosses his lunch into the garbage and chocolate milk splatters on my arm. I start walking toward the cafeteria doors. Londyn follows.

"I need to get online. Can I come over to your house?" I ask.

"No."

My heart falls. I guess we aren't over our fight.

"I'll get a computer. I'll bring it to your place," Londyn says.

I almost smile. Almost.

"What do you mean by 'get a computer'?" I ask. "Are you going to steal one or something?"

"I'll borrow one. Tomorrow." She doesn't say who she's borrowing from. And I don't ask.

The bell rings, and lunch is over. Londyn and I are surrounded by kids, most of whom will soon be zombies.

"Are we good?" I ask. "Do we need to apologize or hug or something?"

"We're good. Let's save the hugging until after we survive this asteroid."

Chapter 31

On Thursday, every class lasts an eternity because Londyn is coming over after school and bringing a computer. I can finally get online again and read the website. It's been weeks since I snuck on. Mack and Londyn promised they're monitoring it and updating me, but I need to check it out for myself.

Mack rides the bus home with me. The school's swim season is finally over, and he has more free time to focus on what's important. He's wearing his paracord bracelet today. He doesn't always. But I do. I wonder if this means something.

Londyn arrives about twenty minutes after the bus

drops us off. She rides her bike and has a small laptop in her backpack.

We set up in my room.

"Do you know the Wi-Fi password?" she asks.

"I think so." I type, and pray that Dad hasn't changed it. The website pops up on the screen.

"Oh my gosh, there are dozens, maybe hundreds of new posts." I turn to Mack, who is sitting on the floor with his iPad in his face and Bubbles at his side. "Have you read these?"

"Some," he says. "It's a mess."

"Yeah," Londyn agrees. "Dr. C. is letting anyone post now. It's like if the school let students teach classes. People are saying whatever they want."

I scroll. "There's got to be a way to sort this."

Londyn leans over and moves the cursor with the touch pad. The screen is now only Dr. Cologne's posts.

"Thanks." I read the newest one.

It goes without saying, tracking asteroids and other objects through space requires constant calculations and adjustments. Space bodies are affected by not only the gravity of the sun, planets, and neighboring moons, but also other bodies in space. An impact from a meteoroid or asteroid could alter 2010OPL7's trajectory. It could save Earth. So far, this has not happened. With each passing day, I'm more confident of impact. The date is undoubtedly April 7. The location, however, will not be known until hours before, if at all.

Two years ago, the Chinese government lost contact with one of its retired, smaller space stations. They could no longer control it or even find it for a period of time. They knew it would not orbit our planet indefinitely. Earth's gravity would drag it to the surface. Until the space station entered into the atmosphere or was spotted on military radar, no one knew where it would crash. It landed in the Pacific Ocean without incident. We didn't learn any lessons from that mistake. We need better surveillance and ways to defend against space debris, both natural and human-made. Unfortunately, these technological advances will not happen before April. We must prepare for an impact.

"I'd never heard about that Chinese space station," I say. "Seems like they should be more careful."

"I looked it up," Londyn says. "It was a real thing. It weighed like eight tons, but most of it burned up in the atmosphere. They said it was probably only two tons when it finally crashed into the ocean. The scariest part was that it was running on nuclear energy. It wasn't quite like a bomb, but close enough."

"This asteroid is three or four miles wide. It's not going to burn up in the atmosphere." I blow my hair out of my eyes and keep scanning the website.

"I know." She sits down on my bed. "I wish we knew where it was heading. There's got to be some scientist with a supercomputer who can figure it out."

"When it gets closer, we'll know." I rest my chin in my palm and study the screen.

"We'll be fine," Mack says. "It'll probably crash in the ocean too. Earth is seventy percent water. Those are good odds."

"Yep." Because Londyn seems nervous, I don't tell her an impact in water could be as bad as one on land. The average depth of the ocean is two and a half miles, while 2010PL7 is at least three miles wide. It'll send water vapor *and* debris into the atmosphere. Impact winter would come sooner and be worse.

"It could be like other natural disasters," Mack continues. "Like a tsunami or earthquake. The Red Cross will visit victims and hand out water. There will be a telethon with celebrities."

"That guy who wrote the *Hamilton* musical will make a new song to raise money." I force a laugh that lasts too long.

"But people die in tsunamis and earthquakes," Londyn says.

"Sorry, I shouldn't joke about that." Mack puts down his iPad and adjusts his dark glasses.

"I just wish my dad would come home. Then I don't care what happens. If he was here . . ." Londyn hugs her knees to her chest and hides her face.

I close the laptop and sit next to her on the bed. I don't know what to do or how to make her feel better. There's nothing in my bug-out bag or in the blue bins in the basement meant for comforting someone who is hurting on the inside.

I touch her leg. She reaches up and squeezes my hand. The room is quiet and still until Bubbles farts—filling the space with sound and smell.

"That wasn't me!" Mack says.

Londyn laughs and lifts her head. "Can we take a break from talking about the asteroid?"

"Yeah," I say, and she lets go of my hand.

"Let's do something on the bucket list," Mack suggests. "We've only done a few things. I want to bungee jump."

"No!" I snap. "No bungee jumping. I hate heights. Indoor rock climbing taught me that."

"One of the advantages of being blind. No fear of heights!"

"Where's the list?" Londyn asks.

"Elle has it. I think she planned to destroy it."

I get up and shuffle papers on my desk. "It's right here." I hold up the mint-green sheet.

"Give it." Londyn reaches for it. I know she's still worried about her family, but at least this gives her something to focus on.

Her finger slides down the ideas and comes to a stop. "This one."

I look at what she's pointing to. "Who put karaoke on here?"

"Mack made me," Londyn admits.

"Yes, yes, yes. Let's do it. Jade told me about a coffeehouse that does karaoke on Fridays." Mack is on his feet like we should leave right now.

"I hate singing. No way I'm doing it in public." I cross my arms.

"You're probably bad at it too," Londyn says.

"We can sing apocalyptic songs," Mack suggests. "Like 'It's the End of the World as We Know It.'"

"That's a real song?" I ask.

"Dude, how do you not know that one? It's your theme song."

Londyn looks at me and shrugs.

"I'm not singing in public," I repeat.

"We'll do it right here. Right now." Mack tells his iPad to play the song. We listen to it three times at top volume. Then he finds the karaoke version.

"I love it!" Londyn screams over the music. She pulls us up to stand on my bed like it's a stage. I hold the iPad with the lyrics, but we jump around too much for me to read them.

We sing the words. We get them mostly wrong. We don't care because *it's the end of the world as we know it and we feel fine.*

Chapter 32

I make ziti for dinner. Italian food is my favorite, and it's easy to cook. Noodles, sauce, and cheeses. Bake. Voilà! And it's special tonight, because in just over two weeks, I won't be able to *voilà* anymore.

Edward is complaining that the sauce is too spicy when my cell phone buzzes. I assume it's a text and ignore it. But then it vibrates again and again. Someone is calling.

"Can I answer it?" I ask Dad.

He nods.

I grab the phone off the counter. Londyn's name is on the screen.

"Hello?" She doesn't call very often.

"Turn on the TV. Channel twelve. Now."

"Why?"

"Turn it on. Just turn it on!"

"Okay." I rush into the family room, almost tripping on Bubbles, and grab the remote.

On the television, a news anchor is thanking some reporter for a story on a wildfire. Then he looks into the camera to introduce the next segment.

"This is it!" Londyn yells.

"A former Harvard professor is getting a lot of attention online with his dire prediction." Dr. Cologne's picture flashes across the screen.

"Oh my gosh!" I scream.

"What is it?" Edward screams.

Phillip and Edward jump out of their chairs and join me in the family room. Dad gets up more slowly.

"Dr. Martin Cologne claims a three-mile-wide asteroid will collide with Earth on April seventh. He's amassed a large following of believers, including some prominent individuals. Celebrities like Josh Cannon and Martha Freeman, religious leaders around the world, and the mayor of the town of Clevelandville, Wisconsin."

"I'm calling Mack too. Hold on!" Londyn yells in my ear.

I look back and forth between the TV and Dad. This is on the news. He has to believe it now. This is the NEWS. This is what we've been waiting for!

On TV, a bald white man talks to a reporter. "Cleveland-ville will be ready, because we aren't taking any chances. We aren't gambling with people's lives." The camera shows a basement full of food and bottled water. Rows and rows of it.

The report comes back on. "Reading through the website, we realized that the residents of Clevelandville aren't the only ones preparing. We met Bill and Rosemary Keene. Bill has quit his job as a manager at a 911 call center. And Rosemary has left nursing school. They've cashed in their savings to build this bunker. They've asked that we not give their exact location."

On-screen, Rosemary walks us through their bunker. Pointing to an air purifier, she says, "We can stay down here for six months. Minimum."

I wish we had a real bunker. Though I hate the thought of being stuck in a small space with Phillip and Edward for more than six minutes.

My phone beeps. I hear Mack and Londyn both on the line.

"Dude, it's your scientist!" Mack says.

"I know. Shh." I pull the phone away from my ear to hear the TV better.

"According to the website," the reporter continues, "thousands of people have made major life changes."

Dad shakes his head.

"It's not too late," I whisper to him, then focus back on the TV.

"But is Dr. Cologne right?" the reporter asks. "We've contacted NASA's Jet Propulsion Laboratory in California."

"There is absolutely no threat posed by this asteroid," a black woman in a gray suit says. "While 2010PL7 was originally classified as a near-Earth asteroid when it was discovered in August of 2010, it was quickly removed after several agencies verified it would not approach the twenty-lunar-distance threshold. It has a zero percent chance of entering Earth's atmosphere. Zero."

"Dr. Cologne says he's calculated an inevitable impact," the reporter says. "Is he wrong?"

"Yes. There are millions of meteoroids and asteroids. Hundreds pass by Earth every year. Our Sentry system monitors these situations and makes predictions one hundred years out."

"Sounds like that technology could have helped the dinosaurs."

The woman grins. "Definitely."

The reporter comes back on alone. "Dr. Cologne spoke to us via Skype." The scientist appears on-screen. "Dr. Cologne, we cannot find an astronomer to corroborate your findings that an asteroid will strike Earth in the next few weeks."

"No, you cannot find an astronomer brave enough to

admit that I'm right. They are worried about backlash from the community. They've seen what's happened to me. I was dragged from my office. Fired!"

"If the world is ending, what do they have to lose?" the reporter asks.

"What do they have to gain? These scientists are preparing. They aren't concerned about you and me. They know this is happening and they are taking care of their own."

"Dr. Cologne, are you suggesting they're keeping these findings secret?"

"What I'm saying is that an asteroid will strike Earth on April seventh. You can choose to be ready, or you can choose to put your family at risk. I will be ready."

The reporter turns to the camera. "One way or another, we will find out on April seventh."

As the anchor and the reporter joke about how they would like to spend their last week, Dad picks up the remote and flicks off the TV.

"Can you believe Dr. Cologne was on the news?" Londyn shouts in my ear. "He looks older on TV than he does on the computer. And he's a little scary."

"This is great." I feel a pressure lift off me. "Mack, did your parents watch too?" I wonder if Grandpa Joe saw.

"Yeah," he says. "I guess everyone knows now."

Dad stares at me. His eyes narrow. The muscles in his jaw twitch.

"I have to go, guys. I'll call you later." The ziti in my stomach churns.

"Is that true? Is this really going to happen?" Phillip asks. "Are we going to be hit by an asteroid?" His face turns red like he's having an asthma attack. He doesn't have asthma, but I saw a kid named John have an asthma attack during field day in fourth grade.

"No. It's not happening." Dad massages the bridge of his nose. "They were illustrating the lunacy of this doctor. They were poking holes in his theories."

"No." I shake my head. "He had answers for everything. He answered every question. Weren't you listening?"

"Weren't you?" Dad snaps.

I flinch.

"I'm sorry." He walks back to the kitchen. "Please go to your rooms. I need a minute to think. I'll be up soon."

"But, Dad, the world is—" Phillip is close to tears. I grab his arm.

"Come on." I squeeze, and for once, he trusts me. I walk him and Edward to their room. Bubbles is right behind us.

"Is it true?" Phillip asks, grabbing the stuffed T. rex from his bed and hugging it to his chest.

"Yes." I lift his chin so he's looking at me. "But you don't need to worry. Okay? Grandpa Joe and I will take care of you. And Dad too."

"An asteroid killed all the dinosaurs," he says. "They're extinct."

"I know. But we're smarter than dinosaurs."

"Stegosaurus had a walnut-sized brain," Edward adds as he jumps on his bed.

"Good to know." I turn back to Phillip since Edward doesn't need any reassuring. "I've known about this asteroid for months. The basement is full of supplies, and I've even emailed Dr. Cologne—the guy on the TV. He told me that the asteroid won't strike in North Carolina. It'll probably hit Antarctica."

He nods at my lie.

"We will survive impact and we have everything we need for the weeks and months after. I promise, we will be okay. You believe me, right?"

"Yeah."

I'm tempted to give him a hug but instead mess his hair. He slaps my hand away and practically growls at me. And I know he'll be fine.

In my room, I text Londyn.

ME: That was awesome. The news! The REAL news!

LONDYN: Totally awesome

ME: My dad saw. He's not happy.

LONDYN: What happened?

ME: Nothing yet. He's thinking.

LONDYN: crap! thinking adults are never good

ME: I know

LONDYN: I hope my dad saw it!

LONDYN: I'm going to look for a link. I'll email it to him.

ME: OK. TTYL

Waiting for Dad is like waiting for a flu shot. It takes forever, I'm dreading it, but there is no avoiding it either. I keep my door open. I can hear him slowly walking up the stairs. My heart speeds up with every step.

I hold my breath, thinking he might go to the boys' room first. He doesn't.

"Eleanor," he says, making my name sound ten syllables long. "I've tried to tell you that this prediction is not real."

I twist my paracord bracelet.

"For some reason, you won't believe me. You won't believe any other scientists. You'll only listen to this discredited crazy man with a website. I've been asking myself why that is."

When he looks at me for an answer, I look away.

"I thought maybe it was your grandfather's fault. For years he's taken you kids survival camping and fed you MREs like they're an actual dinner. Maybe all the practice has made this inevitable to you."

I shrug.

"I don't think that's it. You haven't been enthusiastic

about Grandpa Joe's prepping in years. Not since elementary school."

"I don't—"

"Listen for a minute." He pulls out my desk chair and sits. "Are you hoping this is real? Do you want the world to end? Do you believe this possible catastrophe is a good thing?"

"No." I sniff hard. Londyn wants the world to end so her parents will get back together. That's her, not me.

"I don't know what you're feeling exactly. I've never been a twelve-year-old girl, and without your mother here . . ." He takes a deep breath that makes his body shake. "Maybe I'm not asking the right questions. I don't always know what you need."

"I don't need anything." *Except for you to believe me.*

"Is something happening at school? It's not always easy for you, and that's okay. You don't have to do it alone."

"School's fine."

"Then what's going on, Eleanor? Please talk to me."

"Nothing. I don't want the world to end. That would be stupid." I play with a loose thread from my blanket.

"Wanting to change a situation is not stupid. It's normal. When adults don't like something, we try to change it. Or we complain a lot. Kids your age don't have the same options." Dad rubs the back of his neck. "I think we should have you talk to someone."

"To who?" I ask.

"A doctor."

"Dad, I'm fine. I don't want the world to end. I don't want Dr. Cologne to be right. I don't. I promise." I pull a blanket up to my chin, and Bubbles jumps up and tries to wiggle her way into my fortress.

"But you think he's right." Dad speaks softly.

"He is!" Bubbles jumps away from me. "How can I make you believe me?"

"You can't." Dad moves from the chair to my bed.

I turn over and bury my head in my pillow. He rubs my back.

"Eleanor, I love you." He takes another deep breath. "I'm here when you're ready to talk. Whatever is bothering you, I hope you'll let me help."

I try to nod with my head buried. He waits for me to say more. It feels like an hour. My eyes fill with tears and every muscle hurts.

"I need to go check on your brothers," he whispers. "I'll be back."

I lie still. I want to melt into my bed. Just stay here forever and not worry about anything. Bubbles nudges me until I pet her head.

When Dad does return, I pretend to be asleep, and Bubbles does too. I can hear him move stuff on my desk. Then he kisses the top of my head.

"Love you," he whispers.

When he leaves, he shuts the door. My room is dark. The only light comes from the small power light of my laptop. Dad's given it back.

I'm so confused right now.

Chapter 33

Mack's parents don't believe Dr. Cologne either. They refuse to cancel their spring break trip to Aruba, and an island is the worst place to be. If the asteroid is early and it hits in the Atlantic, they have no chance of survival.

"You shouldn't be leaving," I say to Mack.

"I know, Elle. I don't want to."

We sit in the Jeffersons' living room. Mrs. Jefferson walks through every few minutes, spying. She's not happy with Londyn and me because she thinks we've got Mack believing the world is about to end. (She's already had a long discussion with my dad about the whole thing.) And I'm not happy because, in my gut, I know Mack doesn't believe—not even 99 percent like he claimed two months ago. He's only playing along. I thought that might be enough to get him through, but now I'm worried.

"Are you even a little prepared?" Londyn asks. She's probably angrier than me.

"I've got a water filter and a dual-band radio," he says. "And a cool bracelet." He touches the gray paracord on his wrist.

"That's only because Grandpa Joe bought you that stuff," I remind him.

"I read the website this morning. The date is definitely April seventh. I'm back on the fourth. We'll survive impact together. I promise." He smiles, like always.

Ten minutes later, Mrs. Jefferson tells us she needs to take Londyn and me home. They have a plane to catch. Mack walks us to the door. I grab his hand before I leave.

"Be safe," I whisper.

"Bring me home a seashell or something," Londyn adds.

I turn to walk out, and for some reason, I notice a pile of mail on the table next to the door. On top is a large opened envelope from the Conrad School. If Mrs. Jefferson wasn't right behind me, I'd grab it and read it. But that's not really necessary. I'm 100 percent certain of what's inside.

• • •

Three things I would do over a *normal* spring break: sleep in, binge-watch Netflix, and eat raw cookie dough as I wait for the first batch to bake. This is not a normal spring break. Now I wake early and log on to Dr. Cologne's website first thing and monitor the situation all day. Dad and I don't talk about my recently returned computer (which no longer has parental controls) or the website. We both pretend like I'm not on it all the time. He does ask me "How are you feeling?" about a thousand times a day.

Since Dr. Cologne was on the news, the site crashes a lot. A little robot pops up on the screen with a sign that reads: *We're temporarily unavailable. Sorry for the inconvenience.* The problem is caused by too many visitors, and it's hard to tell if they're friends or enemies. Dr. Cologne has now turned off all the comment options. Only he's allowed to post anything—as it should be.

Grandpa Joe comes over for dinner during the week. Dad hovers and doesn't allow me to talk to Grandpa Joe alone. It's like we're prisoners and Dad is the guard. When I can't take it anymore, I just blurt out my question over pizza.

"Did you see Dr. Cologne on the news?"

"Nope, I missed that." Grandpa Joe takes a bite of pepperoni and doesn't say another word about the subject.

Dad sighs.

Saturday, I invite Londyn to sleep over. Something we've

never done. She rolls out a sleeping bag on my floor and we fight over who gets to cuddle with Bubbles. I let her win.

I click off the light and climb into my bed.

"Good night," I say. The moon lights the room enough that I can see half of Londyn's face.

"T-minus three more days," she says. "I don't feel ready."

"You're ready," I say. "You have supplies, and you will come here. We'll be fine."

"Why won't people believe us? It's like a horror movie where we tell everyone not to go into the basement, and they still do."

"Have you heard from your dad?" I ask.

"He promises that he's taking it seriously. But he won't come home. Maybe after impact, he'll finally change his mind. I just hope it's not too late."

"I'm sorry." I turn toward the window. The moon is nearly full, and the sky is clear. The night sky a week from now will be completely different. We'll be covered in real darkness.

"Do you think Mack will be okay?" she asks.

"Yeah," I answer quickly, because that's what I want to be true.

"He jokes about it and plays along." She props herself up on her elbow. "I don't think he's being serious."

"I know."

"And he's blind. He's capable of anything in *this* world, but after, will things be different? It's going to be hard. It won't be the hallways of school. It'll be the woods or city streets with abandoned cars and *zombies.*"

"We'll watch out for him," I say. And I want that to be true too. It's impossible to know where people will end up. Families will be sticking together. Groups of friends from middle school aren't going to matter.

"I'm glad I got to know you, Norie." She calls me the name I once hated but now don't mind.

"Yeah."

"You've been nice to me, and I didn't always make it easy."

"I haven't always been nice to you," I say.

"I know," she laughs. "I was trying to take the high road. You were mean for a while. Like really mean."

"Okay. I get it. You weren't very nice either. You threw a basketball at my nose."

"I did? When?"

I can't believe she doesn't remember. "And you forced me to drink toilet water."

"And you forced *me* to drink toilet water."

"Okay, let's agree we were both awful people."

"Yeah, we're not the type meant to save the world."

"I look forward to suffering in the apocalypse with you."

I laugh, but I'm completely serious.

Chapter 34

The website headline on the night of April 5 is clear.

IMPACT APRIL 7, 10 A.M. EST

I read the post. The time is plus or minus three hours. So it could be as early as 7 a.m. or as late as 1 p.m. We're less than forty-eight hours from the next mass extinction. Suddenly my skin is cold, but my insides feel hot. My heart races, and I can hear it in my ears.

The post says nothing about location but promises an update tomorrow. An initial prediction should be possible. I imagine Dr. Cologne tracking the asteroid's course the way a meteorologist forecasts a hurricane's path.

I send a text to the Nature Club group. They reply with emojis and GIFs.

I call Londyn. She listens and then hangs up because she needs to reach her dad.

I call Mack. He assures me we will be all right.

I call Grandpa Joe. He doesn't answer, and I leave a message.

I tell Dad. He shakes his head and says for the millionth time, "It's not real."

None of it feels like I'm doing enough. Desperate, I email Dr. Cologne, knowing Dad will be angry.

Dear Dr. Cologne,

I'm afraid. No one will listen to me. What can I do?

Sincerely,
E.J.D.

I watch my email all night waiting for a reply. I fall asleep before midnight. For some reason, I wake up at 3 a.m., and there's a response.

E.J.D.,

Extraordinary times call for extraordinary measures. Don't waste a moment. Next week, you don't want to be saying "I should have . . ."

Best of luck. Stay safe.

Marty

My heart races again. He's right. I text Mack and Londyn. They don't reply, and I assume they're sleeping. It's up to me. I need to make every kid at school aware.

There's only one way to reach the whole school at once. I know I'll get in trouble. Big trouble. But none of that will matter after Tuesday. Nothing will matter after Tuesday.

This is going to involve public speaking and an accomplice or two. I send another text to both Mack and Londyn.

ME: I need you!!!

ME: We're taking this to the next level.

• • •

I stay up the rest of the night preparing and writing notes on index cards with everything I need to say. I end up with thirty-two of them. It's not likely I'll get through all of them.

Londyn calls me around six, and I give her the plan. She's in. I never had any doubts. Mack is the one I'm worried about. He doesn't call me until two minutes before I need to leave for school.

"Dude, what's up?"

"I need your help." I explain the plan.

"That's not going to work, and even if it—"

"Stop! Are you going to help me or not?" There isn't time to debate. This needs to happen today.

"No," he says. "It's a bad idea, Elle. Just give it up."

I knew this might happen, but I'm still shocked. Mack always says yes to everything. He's all in all the time.

"Anyway, it's not like I'd make a very good lookout. I'm blind."

"Stop joking. This is not a joke!"

"You need to stop. You've done everything you can. You started a club. You wrote a newsletter. You've shared that . . . that website." Mack is definitely not joking anymore.

"You don't believe it."

"Don't you think it's weird that there's not another scientist in the entire world who will back him up? I mean . . . come on."

"You don't believe it," I say again.

"I'd believe it if NASA or any other space agency said it was even remotely possible. No one agrees with Cologne."

"That's not true. The website is full of physicists and astronomers who say he's right."

"Those posts could be from anyone."

"I can't believe we're having this conversation now. A day before the world is going to end. You've been with me since the beginning, Mack. You're my best friend. Why would you—"

"It was fun. We were having fun. The club. The bucket list. Even the drinking-the-toilet-water part."

Dad calls me from downstairs. It's time to go to school.

But the room is spinning, and everything is happening at once. The world's ending. Mack won't help me. He won't be around. This is it. This is the start of the end.

"Elle? You there?"

"No." I hang up and head to my last day of school ever.

Chapter 35

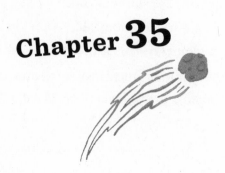

So, we're going to storm the newsroom, hijack the camera, and warn the whole school that we may die tomorrow." Londyn reviews my plan.

"Pretty much."

The studio for the morning announcements is a room in the back of the media center. There are windows with blinds between the two spaces, allowing us to peek through.

The morning-news crew has had the same eight kids all year. They rotate jobs. Each day, there are two anchors, at least one cameraperson, and a producer who makes sure that everything goes smoothly.

"What about Ms. Richmond?" Londyn points at the

media specialist. She's the only teacher around. "Do you think she'll have a key?"

Ms. Richmond sits at the checkout desk.

"We'll barricade the door. Move a desk in front of it. She won't be able to push it open. She'll have to go for help."

"What about them?" Londyn bites her lip and nods toward the four kids preparing for the announcements. "We need them out."

"I know. What do you think? Maybe a distraction of some kind."

"I could faint," Londyn suggests. "Or pretend I'm choking."

"Do you think they'll come running to your aid?" I ask.

"They might not offer to help, but they'll come to watch. Maybe even take a video of my final moments—hoping I pee my pants. And then they'd post it online."

"I think we should lie. We'll tell them that they're wanted in the office or something."

"It's worth a try."

I didn't eat breakfast, and my stomach should feel empty. Instead, it feels full of cement. This has to work.

But before we go into the studio, I hear a familiar voice. It's Mack.

"Hey, Ms. Richmond." He's talking to the media specialist. "Can you assist me, please? I can't find a book."

"Sure, Mack." She stands up. Everyone knows and loves Mack, which is annoying most of the time. But now he's using his powers to help me. At least, that's what I think he's doing.

"I want the Braille version of *Counting by 7s.*"

"Let's search." She walks out from behind the desk. The Braille library is in a separate room down a small hallway.

"I thought you said Mack wasn't part of the plan," Londyn whispers.

"I don't know what he's doing. But this is our chance. Come on."

I watch Mack and Ms. Richmond disappear down the hallway. I take a breath. I hope the kids in the studio believe my lie about being needed in the office. *Keep it simple. Don't overexplain.*

But Londyn speaks first.

"Oh my God!" She pushes open the door. "There's a raccoon loose in the hall."

"Really?" the girl asks.

"It's freaking out. Hissing and running all over. Probably has rabies. We were told to stay here. They're going to do a lockdown drill any minute."

"I wanna see," one of the boys says.

"No, stay here," Londyn says.

I can only nod.

But the news crew takes off. Luckily, they leave all the

camera equipment behind. This isn't exactly Channel 12 Action News.

"Let's roll!" Londyn says as soon as the room is clear. She quietly shuts the door, twists the lock, and slides a desk in front of it. "Do you know how to turn on the camera?"

"I think so." And even though morning announcements aren't supposed to start for five more minutes, I press the button, and I'm live.

I skip the Pledge of Allegiance and take a seat at the news desk.

"Good morning." My voice shakes. "My name is Eleanor Dross. I'm the author—or co-author—of the *Doomsday Express*. You probably already know that. Um . . . and I have a special announcement." I pull the note cards from the back pocket of my jeans. Londyn gives me two thumbs up.

"Tomorrow, Earth will be hit by an asteroid over three miles wide. The damage from the impact will be massive. The crater could be a hundred miles across. But the devastation will span the globe. No electricity. No clean water. Food will be scarce."

A sudden loud knock on the door makes me jump. It's the student news crew.

"People have chosen not to believe. But this will not be the first time a space rock has hit Earth. The dinosaurs went extinct after a massive asteroid hit the Yucatán Peninsula in Mexico sixty-five million years ago. Most didn't die instantly. The world experienced an ice age and the large animals starved."

The kids bang and kick at the door. Behind them, I see Ms. Richmond jogging across the media center.

"Keep going," Londyn says.

"A small meteor, about a tenth the size of 2010PL7, exploded over Tunguska in 1908. It destroyed almost eight hundred square miles of forest."

A muffled voice vibrates through the door. "Unlock this door now."

Londyn sits on the desk. Her legs swing freely. She smiles and doesn't turn around.

"We're running out of time. You need to be ready. Stay home tomorrow. Stock up on all the food, water, and medicine that you can. This event could change the world for months or more likely years."

Ms. Richmond is playing with keys. Mr. Young, the vice principal, has joined her. They get the door unlocked and try to shove their way in.

"It's all online!" I share Dr. Cologne's website address. I repeat it three times. "Please trust me. Take care of yourselves. You can survive this. Good luck, Hawks."

The door knocks against the desk and Londyn laughs. "Better hurry."

"And to my Nature Club allies, you know what to do. This is what we've been preparing for." I give the peace sign and then turn off the camera. I've never given anyone the peace sign, but this feels like the right time.

"Nicely done, Norie." Londyn hops off the desk. It falls forward as the vice principal and two teachers push open the door.

"Careful," Londyn warns. "This equipment is expensive."

Chapter 36

Getting suspended requires a lot of conversations and paperwork—Dad and I arrive home only about thirty minutes earlier than if I'd taken the bus. I'm not allowed to return for four days. That's after impact, so I guess my public school days are over. Mr. Young suggested in-school suspension, but I flipped out.

Dad was polite and calm at school. And in the van, he kept quiet. Now that we're home, I want *him* to flip out.

He goes to the kitchen and turns on the coffee maker. I follow, still hoping for some yelling or at least a serious lecture.

"I looked at the website today," he says as he scoops grounds into the back of the coffee maker.

I'm not sure if this is good news or not, so I say nothing.

"Cologne still predicts the impact is tomorrow. Correct?" He's looking at the coffee maker, not me.

"Yes."

"So after tomorrow, things will go back to normal?" He finally turns to me.

"There's no normal after tomorrow. We should—"

"Eleanor!" he interrupts. "If there's no asteroid, then what? Will you be able to go back to school without trying to start a riot? Will you do your work? What's going to happen?"

I blink a few times. The questions are ridiculous, and I don't have real answers. I try to guess what he wants to hear. "Yeah, everything will go back to normal."

The smell of coffee fills the kitchen. He takes a deep breath. "I hope so."

In my room, I need to do two things—check on my friends and on the website. I open my computer first. Dr. Cologne posted that he's in an underground bunker, but he doesn't say where. The impact is still predicted for 10 a.m. tomorrow, and the location remains unknown.

Next, I call Londyn. She received the same fate I did— four-day suspension. A woman answers Londyn's phone. Could be her mom, but it's probably her aunt.

"Um, hello," I mumble.

"Eleanor, Londyn is not allowed on her phone while she is suspended. Do not call or text. She is unavailable."

"Okay. I'm sorry."

"You should be! That was a stupid prank. I'm disappointed in both of you."

It feels like she slapped me through the phone. My mouth hangs open and my eyes blur.

"Not a prank," I finally say. But she's hung up.

Next, I call Mack. He doesn't answer, so I send a text.

ME: What's up?

It took me several tries to come up with that message. *Sorry* and *Thank you* and *Are you okay?* all felt wrong.

When the boys get home, they're excited to see Dad. It's a beautiful spring Carolina day with clear blue skies and warm weather. They take Bubbles for a walk. I seem to be the only one who senses the looming doom.

A half hour later, Mack finally replies.

MACK: Just got home

ME: did you get in trouble?

MACK: I was questioned I charmed my way out of it

ME: of course you did

MACK: All they had was circumstantial evidence

ME: what does that mean?

MACK: Means they have no proof

MACK: And I didn't do anything wrong

I pace around my room. It's true. He didn't technically do anything wrong, but he knew I was planning to overthrow the school-run media and kinda-sorta assisted.

ME: glad you're not in trouble

MACK: I gotta go TTYL

ME: WAIT!!!!!!!!

ME: where are you going to go tomorrow?

ME: do you have a place

ME: you can always come here

MACK: I'll be fine I promise

MACK: We'll talk soon

Yes, we will. I call him immediately, but he doesn't answer. It rolls over to voice mail. I try again and again. It doesn't even ring. He's turned off his phone.

•   •   •

I can't eat dinner. I can barely breathe. *End of the world* is trending across all the social media. I've checked and rechecked the website. Dr. Cologne has promised that we are at least ten hours away. I searched the internet for more information, but it all points back to his site.

"Eleanor, are you okay?" Dad asks as I stare at my untouched chicken.

I shrug.

"What's wrong with Eleanor?" Phillip looks at me and then at Dad.

"Is she sick?" Edward asks.

"She's not sick," Dad says.

"We need to go to Grandpa Joe's!" I suddenly blurt out, though the thought isn't sudden.

"No," Dad says.

Edward's eyes grow huge. "Can we? Please?"

Dad stares at me. "No. We are not going anywhere."

"It's the safest place for us."

Dad lets out a long breath and then gets up from the table. I think for a moment he might agree. As he walks into the hallway, he pulls out his phone.

"What's going on?" Phillip asks.

"I don't know."

"You said we'd be safe." He looks up at me with wide eyes.

"We are safe. Now be quiet."

I strain to hear what Dad is saying. He's yelling, but the words are muffled. I can make out very little except a swear word and the name Joe."

"Dad's very mad," Phillip says.

"Thanks for that observation."

The yelling stops and Dad walks back into the kitchen. He holds out his cell phone for me.

"It's your grandfather," he says. "He needs to talk to you."

I take the phone and stand up. I want to talk away from the table, but Dad puts a hand on my shoulder and I sink back into my chair.

"Hello?"

"Eleanor, the asteroid is not coming."

I don't reply.

"Do you hear me? There's no asteroid." It sounds like he's talking through gritted teeth.

"He's making you say this stuff." I glare up at Dad. My throat is dry and aches.

"It's the truth, Eleanor," Grandpa Joe says. "There's no asteroid heading to Earth."

"Why are you doing this?" I yell into the phone. I don't want to fight my family. I just want to keep everyone safe. Why can't he understand?

"I'm sorry, sweetheart. I should have said this a long time ago." He sniffs.

"Stop! You know it's real."

"It's not."

"It is!" I scream.

"I have to go," he whispers. "Be good. Give your brothers a hug for me."

"No. Come tell me to my face!" My yelling is met by silence.

I grab my napkin and wipe my nose. I take deep breaths and force myself not to drop any tears. Dad gently takes his phone and rubs my back with his other hand.

"Why don't you get ready for bed," he says. "It's been a long day."

"We'll sleep in the basement." I manage to say this without crying or begging. It's an order. I'm in charge.

"I want to sleep in the basement," Edward says.

"It's the safest place in the house. I've been getting it ready," I say.

"Eleanor, I don't—"

"Please, Dad. Please. I can't stay in my room." My brief moment of self-control is over. My eyes, my nose, and my heart betray me. I sob. "Please. Please."

"Oh, Eleanor." Dad wipes his own eyes. "You can sleep in the basement if you want. If it'll make you feel better. But you are just as safe in your room. There is no danger. I promise."

"Can I?" Edward asks.

"We all are," I answer for Dad. "We have to stay together."

Dad takes a breath. I don't care if he believes me. In less than twenty-four hours, he'll know the truth. For now, I need to keep my family safe. It's up to me.

"Awesome," Edward says.

Phillip isn't as excited. He grabs my hand and says, "Thank you."

While Dad cleans up dinner, I move my computer, phone, dual-band radio, and sleeping bag into the basement. Phillip and Edward bring down their sleeping bags, stuffed animals, books, and games like it's a sleepover. I pull out the supplies Grandpa Joe has helped me collect.

"Wow!" Edward says, impressed by my assortment of meals, tools, and other equipment. I give them both bedrolls so they don't have to sleep on the floor.

I set up my computer and the radio on an old coffee table. Dr. Cologne tracks the asteroid like NORAD tracks Santa Claus's movement on Christmas Eve. He's certain it will be tomorrow. I'm certain too.

I send more texts to Mack.

ME: check out the site

ME: be alert

ME: be safe

It's like launching them into a void. I call again, knowing he won't answer, and leave a voice mail, hoping he might listen.

"Hey, I know you don't think the asteroid is real. I'm not sure when you stopped believing or why. That's not important now. I get that you don't trust Dr. Cologne because you don't know him. But you know me, and I need you to trust *me,* Mack. Every part of me knows that this is real—my heart, my brain, every cell in my body. Please. You're in danger. If something happened to you, I couldn't handle it." I pause. This shouldn't be a message; it should be a conversation. "Call me. Okay? Please." I disconnect and wonder if I'll ever hear from him again.

Bubbles joins us. She sniffs each of our sleeping bags, searching for the right spot.

At bedtime, Dad reads Phillip and Edward a chapter from *Harry Potter* and then tells us good night.

"Where are you going?" I ask as he turns to go upstairs.

"I'm going to watch a little TV. I'll be down later."

"Promise?"

"Yes."

It's dark except for a small night-light. Dad tells me no phone or computer because the boys won't fall asleep. So they get to rest, and I don't.

My brain will not shut down. I didn't do enough. I couldn't make Mrs. Walsh believe me. Or Mr. and Mrs. Jefferson. I couldn't even make Mack believe me. And I don't know if Grandpa Joe believes or not. If something happens to any of them, it's my fault. My chest aches. I feel like I've been running the mile in gym class and actually trying, hard.

I stare at the wall. I stare at the ceiling. I put a pillow over my head. Nothing works. I'm still awake when Dad comes down. He gives us each a kiss and then lies on the old couch in his work clothes.

"Try to sleep," he whispers. "Staying awake and worrying won't help anything."

Next thing I know, I wake to a BOOM!

Chapter 37

"Oh my God!" I scream. A dull light comes through the open door at the top of the stairs. The boys are still asleep. Bubbles shakes beneath the end table.

And Dad is gone.

I spring out of my sleeping bag and run to the bottom of the stairs. I don't know if I should search for Dad or stay with Phillip and Edward. If they don't have Dad or me, what will happen to them?

A flash of light brightens the small basement windows on the other side of the room. It's darker than daytime but not night.

"Dad," I call out.

No answer.

I scramble up the stairs, closing the door behind me. Dad isn't in the family room or kitchen. Rain pounds the sides of the house. The tree in the front yard is bending over from the wind.

"Dad!" I scream. "Dad!"

He runs out of his bedroom in a towel, with a half-shaven face.

"What's wrong?"

"It's happening!"

"Eleanor, it's a thunderstorm. It's just bad weather."

"No!" I shake my head again and again.

"Relax, honey."

"Please, come downstairs, come back." I take a breath. "Come back." It feels like I'm choking. "Come back. Come . . . come back. Come back." I gulp air and repeat myself over and over.

"Okay. Okay. Hold on."

He disappears. I'm crying. Choking. Shaking.

There's another clap of thunder.

Dad is back, dressed. He wraps his arm around me.

"Let's go downstairs."

My throat is raw.

Dad follows me back into the safety of the basement. He checks on the boys, who are still asleep, while I lure a terrified Bubbles from beneath the table. She hates storms, but this is definitely something more. Animals can sense things. I hug her close as I open my laptop.

The Wi-Fi is weak. The website takes time to load. When it finally refreshes, a giant clock fills the screen. It's a countdown.

"Oh God."

2:08:41
2:08:40
2:08:39

I click every link on the website, looking for information on the location of impact as precious seconds tick away.

"Come on! Come on!" I yell at the computer. "Tell me."

"What are you doing?" Dad asks.

"The website doesn't say where! How can he not know where?"

"Because it's not real, Eleanor." He gives me his pity look, but I don't have time to feel ashamed about it.

"What's happening?" Phillip sits up in his sleeping bag.

"Nothing," Dad says quickly.

"Is the world ending?" Phillip asks.

"No," Dad answers again, and he squats down next to him for extra reassurance.

I grab my cell phone and text Mack, because this *is* the end, whether people choose to believe it or not.

ME: Come over

ME: Come over now!

ME: The asteroid hits in less than two hours

The dual-band radio sits on the table, charged and ready. I call Londyn, hoping her aunt hasn't taken it away.

"Londyn?" I try the channel we used months ago. "Londyn? Come in. Londyn? Please." I flick the knob, going channel to channel, searching for my friend.

"Answer me!" I yell. Bubbles runs away and hides under the table again.

"El-ea-nor," Dad says, drawing out my name. "I need you to calm down."

Edward is awake now too. My brothers crawl out of their sleeping bags, staring at me with wide eyes. I turn off the radio.

"I gotta go to the bathroom," Edward whispers.

"It's not safe." I stand and block the stairs.

Dad steps in front of me. He places his hands lightly on my shoulders but doesn't force me to move.

"I'm taking the boys up. We won't leave the house. We can be back down here in five seconds."

"You promise not to leave?" I glance at my computer.

1:55:10

"We won't go anywhere."

"No school?" Edward asks, bouncing up and down.

"We're staying home." Dad's eyes are locked on mine, and I believe him.

"But I have a math test," Phillip says.

"It'll be all right, buddy." Dad rubs his half-shaved face.

I abandon my spot protecting the exit. Edward runs by me. Phillip follows more slowly.

Dad pauses. "Come upstairs, please. We can turn on the twenty-four-hour news channel. Bring the computer." He lets out a breath. "We'll monitor the countdown. We can be—"

The doorbell interrupts him, and my heart jumps in my chest. *Mack!* That's my first thought as I fly up the stairs. My whole body vibrates with each step.

Phillip yanks open the front door as I come down the hall. But it's not Mack on the porch. Londyn stands there, soaked and pale.

Suddenly, I'm not alone. I crush her in a hug. She squeezes me back, and my T-shirt gets damp. Her hair, her jacket, and her bag are drenched. I suck in deep breaths through my nose so I won't cry. A few tears escape.

"Does your mom or your aunt know that you're here?" Dad asks behind me.

She nods her head once slowly, and we all know she's lying.

"I'm calling them," he says. "They need to know you're safe."

I pull Londyn inside. Before closing the door, I stare into the rain and look for Mack. But I know he's not coming.

Londyn follows me to the basement. I point to my PC and the countdown.

1:52:08

"Did you see this?"

"Yeah," she answers. "Where's Mack? He should be here."

"I know. I've sent texts begging him to come over. I warned him not to go to school. No replies."

I get Londyn a towel. We sit crisscross on my sleeping bag. Bubbles crawls out from under the table and joins us. She's not shaking as much as before.

Londyn sets her wet duffel bag next to us. "I brought us a last meal." She unzips the bag and pulls out a box of store-bought cake doughnuts, a can of chocolate frosting, and a bag of bacon bits.

"Someone told me baked goods will be hard to come by." She forces a weak smile.

We set out a little picnic on my sleeping bag. We spread frosting on the doughnuts with our fingers and sprinkle them with bacon bits. We give Bubbles her own small helping of bits.

The minutes tick by. Time moves slowly but also too fast.

The storm is letting up. It's still lightly raining, but the thunder and lightning have stopped. Londyn stands and brushes doughnut crumbs from her lap. She walks to the window that faces the backyard.

"It's quieter, and the sun's trying to come out," she says. "Maybe it'll be a nice day."

1:32:20

"The weather has nothing to do with the asteroid," I tell her, and she shrugs. "This waiting is the worst."

"I know. I can't wait for this day to end." She sits on the bottom step. Bubbles runs over and pushes her way into Londyn's lap.

"There's got to be more online." I open another browser window and type in a news site. The third story down on the right side of the screen has a picture of Dr. Cologne.

"Here!"

Londyn doesn't move. She just strokes Bubbles' head. "I'm ready for this to be over. Ready to move on."

I start reading. " 'Dr. Martin Cologne, the disgraced Harvard astrophysicist' "—I pause to swallow—" 'is still declaring today to be the end of the line for humanity. For months, he's prophesized the asteroid named 2010PL7 will strike

Earth on the morning of April seventh. But according to NASA, the asteroid is safely thirty million miles away from our planet and poses no threat, not today or in the next century.' "

I shake my head. "This doesn't make sense."

"Maybe it does," Londyn mumbles.

"Why are you saying that?"

I try different news sources—dozens of them. They all make fun of Dr. Cologne. No one's taking him seriously, even on the final day. I do a Google search on 2010PL7. Most of the hits bring me back to Dr. Cologne's website, but I also find someone's social media account from Singapore. He's posted a picture of the asteroid that he took with his telescope. The potato-shaped mass glows in the dark sky and looks bigger than the moon. The post has ten thousand "likes" and it only went up a half hour ago.

"This is it! Londyn, come here."

She slowly puts Bubbles down and walks over to me. Her shoulders are slumped and her hands are in her pockets.

"Look!" I hold up my laptop.

She studies the screen and nods. "Did you read any of the comments?" She places a finger on the touch pad to scroll.

"No." I set the computer on the floor.

"You should. People think it's Photoshopped." She sits down next to me on my sleeping bag.

I don't read the comments, because I can see the evidence

with my own eyes. It's real. It's 2010PL7. It's what we've been waiting for.

I return to the countdown.

1:03:30

We both stare at it, but for the first time, I'm not sure we're seeing the same thing.

"I guess we'll know soon enough." She plays with the shoelace of her boot. And there's nothing else to say. We just wait.

The door at the top of the stairs opens and Dad quietly walks down. Bubbles waits for him at the bottom.

"Do you need to go outside, Bubbles?" He bends down and scratches her head.

"I don't want her to go out," I say. "I'll clean up any mess."

Dad clenches his jaw. His eyes flash to the computer.

0:49:10

"Londyn, your aunt said I need to take you home. You're grounded and should not have left the house." Dad speaks softly.

"No!" I grab her arm. "Dad, you can't."

He doesn't look at me. "You have five minutes."

Londyn nods.

"No!" I shriek. "You're not taking her."

Dad goes upstairs without saying another word. My eyes fill with fresh tears.

"No. Don't go. He's not going to drag you out of here. Just sit down." I tug on her jeans, but she steps back.

"Norie, it's not happening." I can't tell if she's disappointed or relieved.

"Just . . . just a little longer. It's coming. Less than an hour."

"This is really messed up, ya know." Her voice cracks. "You *want* the world to end. You're practically begging for it."

"That's not true."

"Don't lie. I know it's true because I wanted the same thing. This was supposed to fix things. How messed up is that?"

"No," I protest weakly.

"This was going to get my parents back together. And get revenge on all the girls who have been jerks at school. I thought the apocalypse would make things better. And so did you."

"Not better. I never said better."

"You wanted something—anything—to keep Mack from leaving."

What I *want* is to cover my ears and to scream, so I don't have to listen to this. "I don't want it to happen," I tell her. "But we can't avoid it."

"Stop!" She shakes her head and bites her lower lip. She

won't look at me. I follow her eyes to the computer screen. The countdown is gone.

SITE NOT FOUND

"It's over," she whispers.

"The website just crashed because so many people are on it. It's happened before." I don't admit that it's not the same error message. There's no cute little robot holding a maintenance sign: *We're temporarily unavailable. Sorry for the inconvenience.*

"It's not happening, Eleanor." She looks sad and determined at the same time. "Deal with it. We're stuck in the world *as we know it.*"

"No." I shake my head.

She offers me her hands and pulls me up. We stand eye to eye.

"It's going to suck going back to school." She wipes her cheek and laughs. "But then, a lot of things suck."

"Please don't go."

But she turns and leaves. When she gets to the top of the stairs, she yells back, "See ya Monday, Norie."

And I'm all alone. Maybe forever.

For the rest of the day, I stare at the computer screen and wait for the world to explode. It doesn't. At midnight, I finally get a call from Mack.

"Dude, are you okay?"

I'm tempted not to speak. He went silent for over twenty-four hours. He didn't believe Dr. Cologne. He didn't believe me.

"I'm fine."

"Liar."

"I don't know what happened." I mean this on every level. I don't know why I trusted Dr. Cologne. I don't know how things got so out of control. I don't understand why people thought that I knew anything. I know nothing.

"You sure made an impact. Pun intended. Half the school was absent today."

"But you went." I sniff hard.

"My parents made me," he replies quickly.

"I'm tired, Mack. I don't want to talk right now." I close my eyes. "But I need to ask you one question, and for you to be honest with me. Are you going to the Conrad School next year?"

Seconds tick by before he answers.

"Yes."

I don't hang up on him, but I get off as quickly as I can and turn off my phone.

Then I lie back on my sleeping bag and try not to cry.

I fail.

Chapter 38

"I want to stay home again," Edward says on the morning of April 8. "Why doesn't Eleanor have to go to school?" He takes a spoonful of cereal, and milk dribbles down his chin.

"Because she got suspended," Phillip answers.

"What does that mean?"

"She broke the rules, and they won't let her come back."

I roll my eyes and push my eggs around my plate.

"Enough. Brush your teeth, boys. We're leaving in five minutes." Dad shoos them out of the kitchen.

"Not fair!" Edward shouts from the hallway.

Dad leans on the table and tries to get me to meet his

eyes. "I have a meeting this morning, but I'll be home by lunchtime."

"I'm fine," I say. Neither of us believes me.

"I'll be home by lunch," he says again.

Dad and the boys leave like it's a typical Wednesday. And it is for them. I'm home alone with Bubbles and my cell and a world that will never end.

I turned my phone back on when I woke up, and it blew up with messages. None of them nice. Kids calling me *loser* and *liar* and worse. Dominic says he's going to fail seventh grade because of me. Jade claims I ruined her reputation. Brent wants to know if I got the date wrong.

In my room, I open my computer again and try to reload Dr. Cologne's site.

SITE NOT FOUND

I send an email.

Dr. Cologne,

I'm confused. Why did you do this?

E.J.D.

I don't expect a reply. Ever!

As promised, Dad comes home at lunchtime. He's carrying three sandwiches because Grandpa Joe joins us. We sit around the kitchen table. I mostly nod as they tell me every-thing will be okay.

"You'll be fine," Grandpa Joe says. "You're a Dross. You're a survivor." He puts a gentle hand on my arm, and I shrug it off.

"Did you ever actually believe?" I stare at my sandwich.

"Sure," he says. "I thought it was possible."

"Anything is *possible*. I want to know if you ever really believed Dr. Cologne." I meet his eyes for just a second.

"At my age, you tend to be a bit skeptical about every-thing. You'll see."

"I wasn't skeptical, and I didn't know you were skeptical. Not until two days ago. You bought me the supplies. You gave me the book. I thought you believed it all." I rub my eyes with the back of my thumb.

Dad lets out a loud breath.

"I got carried away," Grandpa Joe says. "I liked that you were interested in prepping and survival again, and in your old grandpa. I didn't think it hurt any to play along."

"Play along?" My voice breaks. "I wasn't playing."

"I know that now." His eyes look glassy, and I turn away. "Eleanor, I'm sorry. I wish I handled things differently. I should have listened to your daddy. Maybe we could have put a stop to all this before . . ." His voice trails off.

Before what? Before I went crazy. Before I drove away my friends. Before I became the joke of Hamilton Middle.

"I'm just really sorry, sweetheart." Grandpa Joe gets up from the table. He places a hand on my back and leans down to kiss the top of my head.

I don't move. I don't talk.

He sniffs loudly. "I'm going to head home now."

"I'll walk you out," Dad says. The moment they step foot into the hallway, I hear my dad reassure his dad that everything will be okay. And Grandpa Joe mumbles that he's sorry again. Then the front door opens and closes, and I'm cut off from their conversation. I wish I could still hear, because I need to know how everything could possibly ever be okay again.

I toss Bubbles what is left of my sandwich. Then I curl up on the couch and basically stay there until the next week.

• • •

On Monday, Dad drives me to school. He wants to follow me in, but I won't let him.

Walking through the halls today is worse than on the first day of sixth grade. Everyone stares at me. Some whisper. Some make sure I hear what they're saying.

"That's the girl who said the world was ending."

A few eighth-grade boys throw balled-up pieces of paper.

"Watch out for impact!"

Jade and Izabell surprise me at my locker. I force a

smile. For a second, I feel like I can breathe. But Jade's eyes narrow.

"I can't believe I listened to you," Jade says.

"I'm sorry."

"I stood up for you after you were on the morning announcements." Izabell squeezes a notebook to her chest. "I swore on my life that you were telling the truth."

"Sorry. I thought I *was* telling the truth." I sniff.

"I'm so embarrassed," Jade says.

"Me too. I'm sorry." I don't know what else to say. I'm about to walk away when Londyn appears.

"Hey, girls." She flashes a quick smile. "Give Norie a break. Okay? We've had a tough week. Suspension. Huge disappointments. Like asteroid-sized disappointments."

"Come on, Iz. We have to get to homeroom." Jade pulls her friend down the hall.

Londyn lets out a loud puff of air. "Well gee, isn't today going to be fun?" She smirks. "I'll see you at lunch. If we survive that long."

When Mrs. Walsh calls my name in the hall, I pretend not to hear her, keeping my eyes focused on the floor. But in her class, I'm cornered. I tell her everything is fine and force a wide smile to prove my lie. Then I give her back the book she lent me.

"Eleanor, I'm sorry," she says. "I feel like science let you down."

I shrug. "Well, one scientist did."

At lunch, a backpack sits in my usual spot and Londyn is missing. I silently stand next to the table, and Ajay, Dominic, and Spencer have a loud conversation about a video game and purposely avoid looking in my direction. The message is clear. I'm not welcome.

Mack is busy setting out his organic food and probably doesn't realize I'm here. He'll be gone—for real—soon enough.

I turn to leave, and Spencer calls out with disgust, "Farewell, Madame President."

"Elle?" Mack's head snaps up. "Elle?"

I say nothing and walk toward the cafeteria exit.

A second later, Candy's tapping the floor.

"Elle? Where you going?" he asks.

"I don't know."

"Wait for me," he says.

"Why?" I stop, and Candy knocks into the back of my foot.

"I can't go into the girls' bathroom, but if you're going to the media center I can—"

"No!" I cut him off. "You're leaving anyway. Do it now. Why wait?"

"Me going to a new school isn't about leaving you." He holds out his hand, wanting me to take it. I don't. "Saying goodbye to you will be the worst part. You're the main reason I think about not going."

I suck in a breath. "You said you *are* going."

"I am," he says softly. "But I think about staying too. Staying here with you. Dude, this is a hard choice."

But it is a choice.

"Come eat lunch with us." He turns like he's about to head back, but he waits on me.

"They don't want me there."

"Elle, I'll talk to them, and if they don't listen, I'll rough 'em up." He lifts Candy as if he's going to swing it like a weapon.

"No thanks."

"Then we'll sit somewhere else or go somewhere else. I don't want you to be alone, Elle. Not now or ever."

"Just stop! Stop being nice, okay? It would be easier for me if we had a big fight and hated each other." I take a step back and look at the exit.

"I guess we could, if that's what you want." He tries to keep his face serious, but the corners of his mouth twitch into a smile. "Do you want me to insult you? Throw some shade?"

"Yes. Do it."

"Um." He twists Candy. "You're stubborn and bad at Xbox."

I groan.

"You never offer me your pudding cup at lunch. That's selfish."

"You don't like pudding," I say.

"I like pudding sometimes." He pauses and then sighs. "That's a lie. I don't like pudding. Ever."

"I know."

"Oh, I got it." He stands up straighter. "I hear you have a really bad haircut."

I cover my mouth to stop a laugh. "It's growing out. And it's not blue anymore. So . . ."

"Dang. This is hard. Do you want to insult me instead?" he asks.

"No. I guess we're not meant to have a big fight. What do we do now?"

A class of sixth graders walk into the cafeteria and pass between Mack and me. We wait for them to move away.

"I guess we'll just have to stay friends." He holds out his hand again, and this time I take it. He squeezes my fingers. I still hate that he's leaving, but I have some time to get used to it.

"We should go find Londyn," I say.

"Good idea."

Since students aren't allowed to wander the school, she can only be in a few places. We catch up with her in the girls' locker room. Mack sneaks in once I assure him the coast is clear. Her face is red and blotchy, but she smiles when she sees us.

"Mondays are the worst," she says.

I take a seat next to her on the bench. "Do you think Tuesdays will be any better?"

She throws an arm over my shoulder and gives me a quick squeeze. "Maybe in the year 2080."

Chapter 39

Dad brings home Chinese food for dinner on Friday.
Phillip and Edward eat mountains of fried rice and heaps of
sweet-and-sour chicken. I pick at an egg roll.

Edward gives us endless details about recess, and Phillip
talks about some reading contest his media specialist has
set up. Dad listens and asks questions, but he keeps glanc-
ing at me.

I say nothing.

When we're done, the boys clear their spots. I give my
egg roll to Bubbles—she gets a lot of table food since the
non-impact started messing with my appetite. Dad waits
until Phillip and Edward are out of the kitchen before he
says anything.

"How was your day?"

"Fine." I put my plate in the dishwasher and walk toward the stairs, knowing he's going to stop me.

"Eleanor, you've been saying you're fine all week. But you don't act fine and you don't look fine," he says. "I have to assume it's been one of the worst weeks."

I nod because I can't speak.

Dad walks over and wraps me in a tight hug. I squeeze my eyes shut and tears roll out.

"I should have listened to you," I mumble into his shirt. "I'm sorry. You were right. I was stupid."

"Shh." He kisses the top of my head.

"I'm so stupid."

He releases me and steps backs. "Don't say that."

"But I—"

"You were wrong." He waits until I look up. "That's all. You were wrong about something. And unfortunately, all your friends and classmates were witnesses to your mistake. The question is, did you learn anything from this?"

"Yeah. Dr. Cologne is a quack. He deserved to be fired from Harvard." I wipe my nose with my sleeve.

Dad chuckles. "Yes. But there's always going to be Dr. Colognes."

"I guess." I'm never going to trust anyone on the internet again.

"Eleanor, I know you're not going to believe me, but

things will get better. This week was a lousy week. Now it's behind you. Next week will be a fraction better."

I nod to make him happy, but I don't buy it.

"If things don't improve, you need to tell me. I don't want every day to be the worst. You are not alone in this. Okay?"

I nod again.

"Promise me," he says.

My brain is telling my mouth to say *I promise,* but different words slip out instead. "Mack's leaving me!"

Dad cocks his head like he doesn't understand.

"He's going to a different school next year." I try to explain. "I don't want him to leave. He can't. It's not fair."

Dad doesn't say anything because there's no way to fix this. He's not about to let me drop out of school.

It takes me a few minutes to stop crying. Dad gives me another hug.

"Can I go upstairs now?" I ask.

"Sure. But I'm here if you need me."

My computer sits on my nightstand. I hit refresh on Dr. Cologne's website. It's still down. I wonder if he's in his bunker somewhere without Wi-Fi. Or is he hanging out with friends, laughing at those who believed him?

Ten days ago, I thought time was running out. Now it looks to go on forever, and I have nothing to fill that space.

I'm tired of being alone with my thoughts. I'm tired of sitting on my bed and scrolling through the internet. There do not appear to be any other looming disasters—I've checked. After watching two hours of YouTube preppers, I just want to scream at them, "You don't know what's going to happen!"

I want to be done with it. All of it! Then I realize I can be.

With the stroke of a single key, I start deleting the emails. Next, I erase the website from my internet history. I throw out my notebook with the dinosaurs on the cover. I find a few printed newsletters in my backpack, take them downstairs, and shred them. Now that I've started, it's like I can't get rid of things fast enough. I'm ready to throw out my bug-out bag and clear out the basement, but I need permission.

I find Dad reading in his room.

"Can you help me?" I hold out my BOB.

His face falls.

"Don't worry. I'm not getting ready for the end of the world." I scratch the back of my head. "I want this all behind me."

"Happy to help," he says.

Bubbles follows us to the basement, where Dad and I pack up most of the supplies Grandpa Joe gave me. We keep one water filter, some freeze-dried food, and the flashlights. Just the normal stuff that's recommended for a hurricane-preparedness kit. The rest we carry out to the minivan.

I write a note and stick it to the top of a box.

Grandpa Joe,

I don't need this stuff anymore. It's not for me. I don't want to be a prepper. But I wouldn't mind going camping. What do you say? Just no MREs. We'll eat hot dogs and s'mores.

Love,
Eleanor

"I'll bring this to your grandfather tomorrow," Dad says.

I nod. "Thanks. But be nice about it, okay? This wasn't his fault."

Dad raises his eyebrows. "I know. But he still had an influence."

"He just wanted to be helpful." I shrug. "And he wanted to keep the people he loves safe."

"I could say the same thing about you." Dad squeezes my shoulder.

Back upstairs, I unclasp my paracord bracelet and place it in the jewelry box on my dresser. Then I let out a big breath.

"Feels different, huh?" I ask Bubbles, who doesn't bother to answer. "Feels good."

For the first time in months, my room—my life—is prepper-free and without reminders of the apocalypse. The world didn't end. And that's something I have to live with. We all do.

There's just one more thing I need to take care of.

Chapter 40

It's been over two weeks since the world didn't end. Some people still glare as they pass me in the halls, but the evil comments are less common. Every day, Mack, Londyn, and I eat lunch alone, but not in the locker room. We sit in the booth that Londyn once claimed as her own. Maybe this is just how it's meant to be. That doesn't mean I can't try to make things better.

Before homeroom, I pull Mack and Londyn into a huddle.

"We need one more Nature Club meeting," I tell them.

"Dude, no way Mrs. Walsh is going to allow that. I don't think teachers trust you anymore." He twists Candy in his hands.

"Not at school."

"Where?" Londyn asks.

"Molly's Ice Cream Shop. Saturday."

Londyn's eyes grow big, and a slow smile spreads across her face.

"We have a few things left on our bucket list," I continue. "Mack, can you spread the word? For some reason, people still like and trust you."

"Yeah," Londyn agrees. "Norie and I are like the plague."

"I got this." Mack holds out his right hand, and both Londyn and I place ours on top.

• • •

On the last Saturday of April, Dad drives Londyn and me to Molly's Ice Cream Shop. We're ten minutes early on purpose. I want to put in our order before everyone arrives. This is my treat, even if it will cost almost all the money I have left from Christmas.

Mack arrives next. His mom holds open the door, and when she sees me, she nods before leaving. I guess she's not mad anymore.

"Over here!" I yell.

Candy taps across the tiled floor. I love that sound. I'm going to miss that sound. Londyn guides him to a seat at the table.

Jade and Izabell walk in together. They aren't smiling

and happy like Mack. But they came, and that's something.

Londyn pats me on the back and whispers in my ear, "Even if this is a disaster, remember, we're getting ice cream."

I laugh.

Spencer, Ajay, and Dominic arrive next. They're joking around and trying to yank each other's hoods up. But when Dominic sees me, his expression hardens.

"Thanks to you, I might have to repeat seventh grade!" He slumps down in a seat. "I'm behind in everything because you said there would be no grades and no end-of-the-year testing."

I stare at my shoes.

Once Wyatt and Brent show up, the ten of us crowd around a table made for six. I don't take a seat. They want to order ice cream, but I tell them to wait.

"What is this 'meeting' about?" Spencer asks, doing air quotes around the word *meeting*. "Are you going to tell us about another catastrophe? Maybe an alien invasion."

"Maybe the sun is about to burn out," Dominic says. "The world will fall into darkness."

"Stop." I hold out my hands.

"If the sun dies," Ajay explains, "darkness will not be the problem. The sun's expanding mass will first engulf Mercury and then—"

"I don't care," Jade cuts him off. Suddenly, Ajay is on the receiving end of Jade's disgusted looks.

"I forgot." Ajay slaps himself in the forehead. "You are obsessed with global warming. That is how you want the world to go."

"Please stop." I set my hands on the sticky table and lean forward.

"Nuclear war. That's what's going to do us in," Dominic says.

"Ebola!" Spencer yells.

"A robot revolution," Brent adds.

"Thanks for coming!" I shout to get their attention. The whole restaurant goes quiet for a second and looks our way. My face burns.

Londyn stares at me. When I meet her eyes, she nods and smiles.

I clear my throat. "I know April seventh didn't turn out like we thought it would."

"Like *you* thought!" Spencer snaps.

"Come on, dude," Mack says, rocking in his chair. "You all bought it. You all thought the world was going to go *boooooom!* None of you came to school on the seventh."

Spencer grunts.

I say, "It's okay. I get it. I started this, um . . ." *Lie? Conspiracy?* "I brought it up. And I kept bringing it up."

Everyone's glaring at me. Only Londyn, Mack, and Wyatt look like they don't want to strangle me.

"I believed Dr. Cologne. Even after my dad said it wasn't true and Mrs. Walsh said it wasn't true. I believed it all." I ball my hands into fists. I've never publicly declared that I acted like an idiot before.

"I wanted it to be true," I continue. "I don't always like school. I'd be happy for it to end."

Dominic sighs. "Me too."

I swallow hard. "And the thought of facing each day without . . . my best friend, well . . . living off canned foods for a few years seemed like a better deal than going to school without Mack."

I focus on the ceiling because I don't want to know if they're giving me hateful stares.

"But then we started Nature Club and things got better. I looked forward to our meetings. It was my favorite part of school."

I risk a glance. Izabell gives me a half smile.

"And you guys seemed to like the club too. Right?"

"I did," Mack says.

"But you like everything," Londyn jokes.

"Doesn't matter if I liked it," Dominic cuts in. "I'm failing."

"You wanted TEOTWAWKI to be true too," Londyn says.

"You'd rather the world end than do more math homework. Admit it." She picks at her nails. "We all had a reason for believing."

"I just thought it would be cool," Spencer says with a shrug.

Londyn rolls her eyes. "None of you were forced to go to Nature Club. That's all I'm saying."

"If we could just focus on me. This is about me." No one laughs at my joke. "I can admit that I wanted this asteroid to hit. Not anywhere close to Hamilton. Siberia would have been good. I didn't think I could handle school alone."

"Aw, Elle . . ." Mack's voice trails off.

"But once we had the club, I hated school a little bit less." I hold my thumb and finger about an inch apart. "I liked showing you guys stuff about prepping, and getting ready for the end."

"So you were doing it to have us follow you around?" Spencer asks.

"No. I believed it. One thousand percent believed it," I say. "I guess I'm trying to say I'm sorry. Sorry for getting you mixed up in this doomsday scenario. Especially you, Londyn. You got suspended because of me."

She shrugs like it was no big deal.

"It was fun! We drank toilet water," Mack reminds us all, just as a waiter arrives carrying a huge bowl.

"One kitchen-sink sundae." He sets it down. Fifty scoops of ice cream, with fifty little whipped-cream hats, jiggle.

"Are you trying to bribe us into forgiving you?" Brent asks. "If so, you're forgiven."

"No, I'm done saying I'm sorry. This is the thank-you part. Thanks for being part of Nature Club."

"Well, you're welcome." Mack leans in to inspect the bowl, his nose practically on a maraschino cherry.

"Be right back with the individual bowls," the waiter says.

"Don't bother," Londyn says. "We only need spoons." She hands out the silverware.

"I've been part of every club at Hamilton," Wyatt says. "This is the only one that ever got shut down. Makes it special." Then he digs in.

"I can't eat dairy," Ajay tells me. "But I appreciate the gesture."

"I'll eat your share," Dominic offers. He looks up and smiles at me.

"Not if I do it first." Spencer plunges in.

"Thanks," Izabell says as she gets her spoon.

"You're welcome. Enjoy."

"I mean, thanks for everything," she says. "I liked Nature Club. It was fun."

"It was," Jade admits. "You've inspired me."

"I have?"

"I'm starting a Save-the-World Club in the fall. You're welcome to join."

"I'll think about it."

• • •

Everyone—except Ajay—eats until their stomach hurts. All that remains in the "kitchen sink" is a grayish sludge with flecks of sprinkles and nuts. Londyn, Mack, and I are the only ones left at the table. We still have twenty minutes before Mrs. Jefferson picks us up. We're going to a Japanese zombie movie. "Foreign film" is one of the few doable things left on our bucket list that doesn't require running.

"We should start a new bucket list," I say as I drag my spoon through the melty mess. "Now that we have endless time, except for, well . . ." I pat Mack's hand. "Except this dude is leaving us." Walking into Hamilton Middle next school year without Mack on my elbow isn't going to be easy.

"I'll be around plenty," Mack says. "And I've got the first thing for our new bucket list. Never eat a kitchen-sink sundae again. I might throw up."

"Me too." Londyn clutches her stomach. "But we're still getting popcorn, right?"

I pretend to gag.

"Listen, Elle, Londyn. Maybe I won't go to Conrad next

year," Mack says without a hint of joking. "I could wait until high school."

"Nope. No way," I snap. "You're going. You'll play an instrument. You'll join the swim team. You'll miss me terribly. You're going." I cross my arms.

"Dang," he says. "Look at Elle laying down the law." And he laughs, which almost makes me want to take back what I said.

"So, what else for our list?" I pull a small notebook and a pen out of my back pocket. I'm prepared for this.

"Paris!" Mack says. "Remember? You want to go to Paris."

"Oh good," I say sarcastically, "we're being realistic."

"The world isn't ending in six months, Elle. We've got all the time we need. We'll go to France when we're sixteen."

"Write down *marathon*." Londyn taps the notebook with one finger.

I shake my head. "I don't want to do a marathon."

"We'll do it when we're sixteen," she says. "Write it down."

And I do. But I also add "Run a 5K," which seems much more realistic and is something we can do before we're teenagers.

"I think we should all go to prom together," Mack says. "And in college, we should go on a beach trip over spring break."

"I want to see a volcano," Londyn says. "An active one that's spewing lava." She claps her hands together once like an explosion.

The ideas come faster than I can write. Some are things we can do now, like snowboarding and midnight bowling. Others are things we'll do when we're in high school, like dating (not each other!) and nose piercing. And the rest are just someday suggestions. Those are my favorite. I like the idea that sometime in the future, Londyn, Mack, and I will be standing on the Great Wall of China or swimming with sharks (in a very strong cage, of course).

The waiter comes and takes the bowl away; it's almost time for zombies. Londyn offers her elbow to Mack, and I hang back to leave the last of my money for a tip. I watch them making their way to the door.

I don't have a clue when the world is going to end. Or *end as we know it.* I'm glad 2010PL7 didn't destroy it all, but I'm no longer sorry I believed it was going to. If I hadn't become friends with Londyn or the other kids in Nature Club. I wouldn't have created a bucket list—or be creating a new one now. I wouldn't have a mark on my permanent record.

I guess it really was TEOTWAWKI after all; I'm not the same Eleanor I was last year. One world has ended, and I admit—even though Mack is leaving—I like the new one we've created.

Dear Reader,

By nature, I'm a worrier. I worry about little things like oversleeping, running out of ice cream, and spelling mistakes. And I worry about big things like global warming, the safety and health of my family, and the lack of empathy in the world. One thing I do *not* worry about is asteroids. After researching near-Earth objects (NEOs) for this novel, I'm confident there is no imminent risk of global destruction due to a rock from space.

Earth is continuously battered by tiny particles of space dust—about 100 tons per day. Thankfully, Earth has an atmosphere, which shields us from most of these mini-impacts, unlike the moon, which takes constant hits. Very large objects are tracked by NASA and other space agencies. Scientists can say with certainty that no known asteroid (or other NEO) is predicted to hit Earth in the next one hundred years.

Still, on occasion, small previously undetected asteroids do crash into Earth, as the Chelyabinsk asteroid did. (See page 341 for more information.) The damage from such an event is localized and does not cause a global threat or risk of mass extinction. According to NASA, in the period from 1994 to 2013, approximately 550 small asteroids entered Earth's atmosphere, and most harmlessly burned up before reaching the surface (again, Chelyabinsk being the exception). On the other hand, in 2013 alone, there were 1,595 earthquakes of magnitude 5 or greater worldwide, resulting in over 1,500 deaths. There's never been a confirmed human fatality due to a meteoroid or asteroid strike.

So instead of worrying about asteroids, meteroids, or comets, I encourage you to take a scientific approach to astronomy and physics—visit planetariums, read books, check out legitimate websites. If you'd still like a little something to worry about, perhaps stress about a grizzly bear attack? Or an upcoming school project? Or maybe you should just go have a nice bowl of ice cream (kitchen sink-sized, of course).

Thank you for reading my book,

Stacy Mc.

IMPACT

Thanks to its atmosphere, Earth has a natural shield against most impacts. Asteroids, comets, and meteoroids usually burn up on entry. However, throughout Earth's history, there have been a few large and notable impact events.

Chicxulub (66 million years ago)

This is the impact that led to the dinosaur extinction, also known as the K-T extinction, also known as the Cretaceous-Tertiary extinction. This asteroid (or possibly a comet), which was at least 9 kilometers (5.6 miles) wide, crashed into modern-day Mexico, creating a crater 180 to 200 kilometers (112 to 125 miles) wide. The impact triggered earthquakes, tsunamis, and volcanoes. The shock wave created winds of over 1,000 kilometers (600 miles) per hour. Fiery debris flew into the air, and when it fell back to the ground, it ignited fires around the world. The resulting smoke and dust blocked out the sun, and Earth experienced a global winter. Much of Earth became a harsh and barren landscape, and approximately 75 percent of animals and plants went extinct.

Chesapeake Bay (35 million years ago)

A sizable asteroid (or possibly a comet) crashed near modern-day Washington, DC, creating the largest impact crater in the United States. The impact location was a shallow sea. The crash sent billions of tons of debris and water into the atmosphere and created a fifteen-story wave that washed across the land. The asteroid completely vaporized upon impact. Left behind is a crater 90 kilometers (56 miles) wide and 1.9 kilometers (1.2 miles) deep. This impact did not result in a mass extinction event.

Tunguska (June 30, 1908)

A little more than 100 years ago, over 700 people witnessed a fireball explode over the Tunguska River in a remote area of Siberia in northern Russia. Scientists think the meteoroid exploded roughly 5 to 10 kilometers (3 to 6 miles) above Earth. Because of war and difficult terrain, it was almost twenty years before researchers were able to travel to the center of the event. While there was no impact crater, 200 square kilometers (500,000 acres) of forest were flattened from the force of the explosion, and 80 million trees destroyed. The dead pines were found lying in a circle, projecting outward from the center of the blast site. The explosion is thought to have been a thousand times greater than the one created by the atomic bomb that was dropped on Hiroshima, Japan. The meteoroid's size has been estimated at 50 to 100 meters (150 to 300 feet) wide, but without fragments or an impact crater, it's difficult to determine.

Chelyabinsk (February 15, 2013)

Traveling at over 65,000 kilometers (40,000 miles) per hour when it entered Earth's atmosphere, this asteroid was captured on video as it streaked over Chelyabinsk, Russia. The space rock, weighing 11,000 tons and measuring 17 to 20 meters (56 to 66 feet) wide, exploded 22.5 kilometers (14 miles) above Earth's surface. Fragments were discovered 80 kilometers (50 miles) north, at the bottom of frozen Lake Chebarkul, including a 650-kilogram (1,400-pound) chunk. While the asteroid did not create an impact crater, the shock wave damaged roofs, shook buildings, and shattered glass across an area of 518 square kilometers (200 square miles). Over 1,600 people were injured, mostly from broken glass. (Since light travels faster than sound, people witnessed a flash outside and ran to their windows to get a better look. The sound wave came next and shattered the windowpanes.) Scientists say the meteorites from this event are approximately 4.5 billion years old—nearly as old as our solar system.

DEFINITIONS

 **asteroid:** a rocky object (metallic and nonmetallic) that orbits the sun and can range in size from 530 kilometers (329 miles) to less than 10 meters (33 feet) across

comet: an ice-and-rock object orbiting the sun, often with a coma (which is an atmosphere) and tail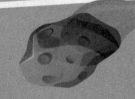

meteor: the bright streak created by a meteoroid, an asteroid, or a comet (or a chunk of a comet) entering Earth's atmosphere (sometimes called a shooting star)

 meteorite: a meteoroid that lands on Earth's surface

 **meteoroid:** a small piece—smaller than 1 kilometer (0.62 miles), and often only a few millimeters (fractions of an inch), in size— from an asteroid or comet that orbits the sun

ACCORDING TO NASA

ASTEROID FACTS

From nasa.gov/mission_pages/asteroids/overview/fastfacts.html

Every day, Earth is bombarded with more than 100 tons of dust and sand-sized particles.

About once a year, an automobile-sized asteroid hits Earth's atmosphere, creates an impressive fireball, and burns up before reaching the surface.

Every 2,000 years or so, a meteoroid the size of a football field hits Earth and causes significant damage to the area.

Only once every few million years, an object large enough to threaten Earth's civilization comes along. Impact craters on Earth, the moon, and other planetary bodies are evidence of these occurrences.

Space rocks smaller than about 25 meters (about 82 feet) will most likely burn up as they enter the Earth's atmosphere and cause little or no damage.

If a rocky meteoroid larger than 25 meters but smaller than one kilometer (a little more than a half mile) were to hit Earth, it would likely cause local damage to the impact area.

We believe anything larger than one to two kilometers (one kilometer is a little more than one-half mile) could have worldwide effects. At 5.4 kilometers in diameter, the largest known potentially hazardous asteroid is Toutatis.

By comparison, asteroids that populate the main asteroid belt between Mars and Jupiter, and pose no threat to Earth, can be as big as 940 kilometers (about 583 miles) across.

READINESS KIT

We don't need to be ready for an asteroid strike, a zombie apocalypse, or the rise of machines, but natural disasters—like snowstorms, hurricanes, tornadoes, earthquakes—can occur in many parts of the world. A basic emergency prep kit can be useful in these situations and beyond. The U.S. government recommends the following items.

BUILD A KIT

Adapted from ready.gov/build-a-kit

Make sure your emergency kit is stocked with the items on the checklist below. Most of the items are inexpensive and easy to find, and any one of them could save your life. Headed to the store? Once you take a look at the basic items, consider what special needs your family might have, such as supplies for babies, grandparents, or pets.

After an emergency, you may need to survive on your own for several days. Being prepared means having your own food, water, and other supplies to last for at least seventy-two hours. A disaster supplies kit is a collection of basic items your family may need in the event of an emergency.

Basic Disaster Supplies Kit

To assemble your kit, store items in airtight plastic bags and put your entire disaster supplies kit in one or two easy-to-carry containers such as plastic bins or a duffel bag.

A basic emergency supply kit could include the following recommended items:

- water—one gallon of water per person per day for at least three days, for drinking and cleaning
- food—at least a three-day supply of nonperishable food
- battery-powered or hand-crank radio and a NOAA Weather Radio with tone alert
- flashlight
- extra batteries
- first-aid kit
- whistle to signal for help
- dust mask to help filter contaminated air, and plastic sheeting and duct tape to make a shelter if needed
- moist towelettes, garbage bags, and plastic ties to help keep clean
- wrench or pliers to turn off electricity and water
- manual can opener for food
- local maps
- cell phone with chargers and a backup battery

Additional Emergency Supplies

Consider adding the following items to your emergency supply kit based on your individual needs:

- prescription medications
- nonprescription medications such as pain relievers or anti-diarrhea medication
- glasses, contact lens solution
- infant formula, bottles, diapers, wipes, and diaper rash cream
- pet food and extra water for your pet
- cash or traveler's checks
- important family documents such as copies of insurance policies, identification, and bank account records saved electronically or in a portable waterproof container
- sleeping bag or warm blanket for each person
- complete change of clothing (appropriate for your climate) and sturdy shoes
- household chlorine bleach and medicine dropper to disinfect water
- fire extinguisher
- matches in a waterproof container
- feminine supplies and personal hygiene items
- mess kits, cups, plates, paper towels, and plastic utensils

- paper and pencils
- books, games, puzzles, or other activities for children

Maintaining Your Kit

After assembling your kit, remember to maintain it so it's ready when needed:

- Keep canned food in a cool, dry place.
- Store boxed food in tightly closed plastic or metal containers.
- Replace expired items as needed.
- Rethink your needs every year and update your kit as your family's needs change.

Kit Storage Locations

Since you do not know where you will be when an emergency occurs, prepare supplies for home and vehicles.

- Home: Keep this kit in a designated place and have it ready in case you have to leave your home quickly. Make sure all family members know where the kit is kept.
- Vehicle: In case you are stranded, keep a kit of emergency supplies in your car.

LEGITIMATE SOURCES

The abundance of information available on the internet makes our lives easier and richer with knowledge. With a few clicks, we can find out who won the big game, how many steps to the top of the Statue of Liberty, and the chemical composition of a sugar molecule. However, mixed in with this useful and correct information are mistakes, hoaxes, and outdated materials. These false websites and posts can be hard to spot, and no agency polices them.

There is no surefire way to check whether a website is legitimate, but these ten signs should make you pause:

1. A sloppy website with multiple misspellings, poor grammar, broken links, and obviously altered photographs. Also, beware of the overuse of caps (the site seems to be SCREAMING to get your attention).

2. A stolen domain name. Fake sites may add a ".co" to a legitimate source. For example: nytimes.com might be nytimes.com.co.

3. An old publication date or a site that has not been updated recently. Science, technology, and

current events are changing all the time, so check the date, especially when using a source for research.

4. Information that cannot be verified on another site. If it's true news or factual information, you will find multiple sources reporting on it.

5. No "About" page or section. A legitimate source will list authors and/or organizations as contributors to the website.

6. No "Contact" page or section. There should be an email or a form to contact the authors or website sponsors.

7. A website that feels emotional. An illegitimate site may try to make the reader angry or scared.

8. Too many ads. Since most websites are free to visit, we're likely to see ads on legitimate sites. However, if there seems to be an abundance of ads, especially pop-up advertisements, the intention could be to sell products or services, not to share information.

9. Random statistics with no links to the reported data. When a site says "75 percent . . ." or "three out of five . . . ," the source of this information should be clearly referenced.

10. Vague wording instead of specific information. Instead of numbers, you may read *a lot, most, many, a few,* or *hardly any.* Instead of a specific person's name, you may read *scientist.* Instead of an exact location, you may read *in the Midwest.*

These signs are not a guaranteed way to determine if a site is legitimate. This is a complicated issue. For additional help, talk with your librarian or media specialist and discuss internet safety with a trusted adult.

FTLOA—FOR THE LOVE OF ACRONYMS

AI: after impact

aka: also known as

BOB: bug-out bag

BOL: bug-out location

MAG: mutual aid group

MRE: meals, ready-to-eat

NEA: near-Earth asteroid

NEO: near-Earth object

SHTF: stuff hits the fan

TEOTWAWKI: the end of the world as we know it

WROL: without rule of law

SOURCES

Websites

"Asteroid or Meteor: What's the Difference?" NASA Space Place. Last updated September 24, 2018. spaceplace.nasa.gov/asteroid-or-meteor/en.

Boslough, Mark, and David Kring. "Chelyabinsk: Portrait of an Asteroid Airburst." *Physics Today.* September 1, 2014. physicstoday.scitation .org/doi/10.1063/PT.3.2515?journalCode=pto.

Brusatte, Stephen L., et al. "The Extinction of the Dinosaurs." *Biological Reviews.* Wiley-Blackwell. July 28, 2014. onlinelibrary.wiley.com/doi/full /10.1111/brv.12128%20.

"Chicxulub Impact Event: Regional Effects." Lunar and Planetary Institute. Accessed January 4, 2019. lpi.usra.edu/science/kring /Chicxulub/regional-effects.

Culler, Jessica. "NASA and International Researchers Obtain Crucial Data from Meteoroid Impact." NASA. Last updated November 6, 2013. nasa.gov/content/nasa-and-international-researchers-obtain-crucial -data-from-meteoroid-impact.

Dunbar, Brian. "Asteroid Fast Facts." NASA. Last updated August 7, 2017. nasa.gov/mission_pages/asteroids/overview/fastfacts.html.

The Editors of Encyclopaedia Britannica. "What Is Known (and Not Known) About the Tunguska Event." *Encyclopaedia Britannica Online.* Accessed January 4, 2019. britannica.com/story/what-is-known-(and -not-known)-about-the-tunguska-event.

"Frequently Asked Questions (FAQs)." NASA/JPL Center for Near-Earth Object Studies. Accessed January 4, 2019. cneos.jpl.nasa.gov/faq.

Hadhazy, Adam. "Tunguska—100 Years Later." *Scientific American.* June 30, 2008. scientificamerican.com/article/what-happened-at-tunguska.

Hauser, Christine. "That Wasn't a Meteorite That Killed a Man in India, NASA Says." *The New York Times.* February 6, 2016. nytimes.com/2016 /02/10/world/asia/that-wasnt-a-meteorite-that-killed-a-man-in-india -nasa-says.html.

"ISTE Standards for Students." ISTE, International Society for Technology in Education. Accessed January 4, 2019. iste.org/standards /for-students.

Kaiho, Kunio, and Naga Oshima. "Site of Asteroid Impact Changed the History of Life on Earth: The Low Probability of Mass Extinction." *Scientific Reports.* Last updated November 9, 2017. nature.com/articles /s41598-017-14199-x.

Lineberry, Denise. "Near-Earth Objects Impact Our Lives." NASA. Last updated August 29, 2013. nasa.gov/larc/astronomical-impact-in-the -chesapeake-bay.

Phillips, Tony. "The Tunguska Impact—100 Years Later." NASA. Last updated June 30, 2008. science.nasa.gov/science-news/science-at-nasa /2008/30jun_tunguska.

Popova, O.P., et al. "First Study Results of Russian Chelyabinsk Meteor Published." Phys.org. Last updated November 6, 2013. phys.org/news /2013-11-results-russian-chelyabinsk-meteor-published.html.

"The Probability of Collisions with Earth." NASA/JPL. Accessed January 4, 2019. jpl.nasa.gov/sl9/back2.html.

Schulten, Katherine, and Amanda Christy Brown. "Evaluating Sources in a 'Post-Truth' World: Ideas for Teaching and Learning About Fake News." *The New York Times.* January 19, 2017. nytimes.com/2017/01/19 /learning/lesson-plans/evaluating-sources-in-a-post-truth-world-ideas -for-teaching-and-learning-about-fake-news.html.

Shekhtman, Lonnie, and Jay Thompson. "Asteroids." NASA Science, Solar System Exploration. Last updated December 19, 2017. solarsystem.nasa.gov/asteroids-comets-and-meteors/asteroids/in-depth.

Talbert, Tricia. "Five Years after the Chelyabinsk Meteor: NASA Leads Planetary Defense." NASA. Last updated February 28, 2018. nasa.gov /feature/five-years-after-the-chelyabinsk-meteor-nasa-leads-efforts-in -planetary-defense.

Talbert, Tricia. "Planetary Defense Frequently Asked Questions." NASA. Last updated August 29, 2017. nasa.gov/planetarydefense/faq.

Tedesco, Edward F. "Tunguska Event." *Encyclopaedia Britannica Online.* Last updated September 10, 2018. britannica.com/event/Tunguska -event.

"What Is the Difference between a Meteor, a Meteoroid, a Meteorite, an Asteroid, and a Comet?" HubbleSite. Accessed January 4, 2019. hubblesite.org/reference_desk/faq/answer.php.id=22&cat=solarsystem.

Books

Brusatte, Steve. *The Rise and Fall of the Dinosaurs.* New York: William Morrow, 2018.

Rusch, Elizabeth. *Impact!: Asteroids and the Science of Saving the World.* New York: Houghton Mifflin Harcourt, 2017.

Acknowledgments

I write alone (unless you count the sleeping dogs that hang out in my office), but I do not create books alone. So many people have helped make this novel a reality. I couldn't do any of this without them.

Caroline Abbey, my amazing editor, who has been there from initial idea to draft number seventy-seven. (Maybe we didn't have quite that many.) It's been a fun and epic journey. Her patience and thoughtfulness cannot be topped.

Lori Kilkelly is everything a great agent should be: honest, funny, tough as nails, encouraging. And she always knows the right thing to say to keep an author sane. She's my fairy *godsister*.

My first reader is Carolyn Coman. There's not a smarter teacher and mentor in the world. Without her I'd have either a thousand-page mess or a ten-page mess. And I'd definitely be curled up on the floor weeping.

High fives to the wonderful team at Random House Children's Books. I appreciate all the hard work it takes to create and promote a beautiful book. Kathy Dunn, Michelle Nagler, Michelle Cunningham, Barbara Bakowski, Kristin Schulz, Polo Orozco, and everyone else on the Random House team.

The character Mack Jefferson originally did not belong to this story. He was from another, unfinished manuscript. But after meeting the staff and students at Tracy's Little Red School House in Winston-Salem, I knew Mack had to stay. Thanks to Chris Flynt and Kim Flanagan and the rest of the TLRSH family. I also received feedback on Mack from my friend and fellow author Lisa Rose. She's a kind and amazing person, and the mother of a kind and an amazing daughter, Victoria. (While inspired by these people, Mack is an entirely fictional character.)

The fictitious Bill and Rosemary Keene mentioned in this book are named after Bill and Rosemary Keene of North Carolina. They won a spot in this novel through a contest sponsored by the Independent Booksellers of Piedmont, North Carolina. (Beyond their names, any other similarities to Mr. and Mrs. Keene are purely coincidental.)

Thanks to my running-with-gallon-water-jugs guinea pigs: Spencer Postle, Ryan Engle, Graham Davis, and my children. They showed it can be done, and I have the video footage to prove it.

Chris Hays and Heidi Burns graciously offered assistance and resources for identifying legitimate sources. It's a complicated issue, and their insight as educators is appreciated.

The kidlit community is both small and vast, and it's almost always kind. Alan Gratz, Barbara O'Connor, Sherri

Duskey Rinker, Aaron Reynolds, Salina Yoon, John Claude Bemis, Lisa Yee, and Kate Beasley have all selflessly shared their expertise and knowledge with me.

No one understands a writer the way other writers do. I'm forever grateful to my writing buddies, Laura Gehl, Camille Andros, Lori Richmond, Peter McCleery, Jason Gallaher, Anthony Piraino, Deb Beauchamp, Megan Bryant, and Tara Luebbe. Thanks for joining me on this wild ride and holding my hand through most of it.

Thanks to my friends at Bookmarks—one of my favorite places. I'm often greeted with hugs and congratulations (and book recommendations).

Much love and thanks to my mom for the enthusiasm for each new title.

And a big thank-you to my dad, who every week asks, "What are you working on?" and listens as I give him a lengthy, rambling answer.

To all my friends and family who support me on good and bad days: Glen, Suzanne, Bob and Fran, Frank and Stacey, Kristen and Andy, Jess and Brian, Gram, Abby, Alaina, Kara, Paige, Ellerie, Gavin, my aunts and uncles, my LK Literary family, my Electric Eighteens friends, Mabel, Julie, Jen, and Penny (and a shout-out to Sarah C.).

I can't write an acknowledgment without mentioning the dogs. Jack, Munchkin, and Reykja: I could get so much more done if you didn't insist on playing several times a day.

And finally, all my love and thanks to *the fam*. Cora, Lily, Henry, and Brett: you are the reason it's all possible, and without y'all, nothing matters. Love ya!

Also, a quick hi and thanks to Lin-Manuel Miranda. (I plan to keep acknowledging him until he acknowledges my acknowledgment.)